MUSIC
TELLS ALL

MUSIC
TELLS ALL

E. R. Punshon

With an Afterword by

Gavin L. O'Keefe

RAMBLE HOUSE

2013

ISBN 13: 978-1-60543-734-7

Preparation: Gavin L. O'Keefe & Fender Tucker

Cover Art & Afterword © 2013 Gavin L. O'Keefe

"That two and two make four, and never
   five nor three,
The heart of man has long been sure, and
   Long is like to be."

A E. Houseman

CHAPTER I

HOUSE TO LET

"IF," SAID OLIVE moodily, "we wanted a house with twenty bedrooms and ten bathrooms, we could pick and choose."

"But," remarked Bobby, a trifle nervously, for he was never quite sure to what lengths Olive might not be driven in her desperation, "we don't, do we?"

Olive thought the remark superfluous and unhelpful. She said so. Then she said:

"What's the good of being a what-d'you-call-it at Scotland Yard if you haven't a roof to your head?"

"I am not," said Bobby at his most dignified, "a what-d'you-call-it at Scotland Yard. I am temporary-acting-junior-under-deputy-assistant-commissioner—unattached."

"Don't use so many long words," said Olive.

"Well, head cook and bottle washer might convey the same idea," Bobby conceded, "but still we have got a roof to our heads, haven't we?"

"An hotel roof," Olive said. "What's the good of that except to keep out the rain? Especially when all they want is to get you out so they can get in someone else who'll pay more. Especially us, because they daren't overcharge a—a cop," said Olive, who knew wives should never allow their husbands to get above themselves. She added: "Old Mrs. Hague is being pushed off."

"No loss," grunted Bobby.

"She was rude to one of the chamber-maids," said Olive, slightly awe-struck, "and the maid complained so Mrs. Hague has to go. The manager said he could have as many guests as he wanted but maids mattered."

"Mrs. Hague was rude to us," observed Bobby, and Olive pointed out that the manager didn't mind that. Guests, he considered, could settle their own affairs, but he had to look after the staff, and to-day the staff is always right. Bobby said he supposed he must be going. He had a dull day before him, he said. Nothing but a lot of dry routine work. Any intelligent typist could do it just as well. Olive, who had been looking at the paper, gave a sudden startled exclamation and grabbed him by the arm.

"Bobby," she gasped, all trembling excitement, "listen to this. 'To Let. On a three-year term. Attractive country cottage. Four bed, two rec., garage. All services. Large garden. Twenty miles from town. Rail and 'bus convenient. References required. Apply: Box 3752.' Oh, do you think. . .?"

"No," said Bobby, "I don't. Too good to be true. Practical joke, very likely."

But Olive refused to think so basely of human nature.

"I am going to answer it," she said firmly.

"What is one more twopence ha'penny stamp among so many?" Bobby asked and departed.

Bobby thought of it no more. Olive tried not to. No good indulging in wishful thinking. But two days later she found a letter waiting for her on the breakfast table. She opened it without expectation. She read it again to make sure. Then she gasped: "Bobby. Look," but could get no further.

"What's the matter?" asked Bobby, who had just arrived, fresh from shaving in cold water because there was no hot, as the hotel's stock of coal had run out. He said: "The coffee can't be any worse than usual and this isn't the morning for bacon—or anything else much," he added, surveying the bleak prospect on the breakfast table.

"It's an order to view," said Olive faintly.

"View what?" asked Bobby.

"That cottage. You remember? The advertisement I answered. There's an order to view. It says how to get there. Look."

Bobby looked. Doubtfully. He said:

"You can bet your life there's a snag somewhere. Most likely it's been bombed and repaired by the village carpenter. Or burnt down. Or the previous tenants all died of small-pox."

"Bobby, be quiet," ordered Olive.

"Or it's haunted," Bobby continued relentlessly. "A poltergeist very likely," and Olive looked troubled, for recently they had both listened to a broadcast about poltergeists and Olive's general faith in the stability of furniture in general and lumps of coal in particular was not yet fully restored.

But she rallied bravely.

"I don't care if there is," she said, untruthfully. "Better a poltergeist and a house than no poltergeist and no house. Ring up the Yard and tell them you can't come to-day. 'Urgent private affairs' is what you say, isn't it?"

"Just like that?" asked Bobby.

"Just like that," said Olive firmly. "And do be quick. I expect there'll be dozens and hundreds of people there and a queue miles long. Don't let's bother about breakfast."

"My girl," said Bobby, and now it was his turn to be firm, "you sit down and eat what there is to eat—if any."

Olive sighed but obeyed. After all, even a husband must be humoured at times, and Bobby's appetite was one thing that remained constant in a kaleidoscopic world.

"Only do be quick," she urged.

"No good breaking our necks for nothing," Bobby told her. "There's sure to be a snag in it somewhere. No need to advertise if there wasn't. Besides, I may not be able to get away."

But he knew, and so did Olive, that there was not likely to be any difficulty. For at present his position at the Yard was undefined, his duties and responsibilities not yet clearly laid down. In a week or two there was to be a conference at which the work of the department would be re-organized. Bobby had an idea that his job would be largely advising, helping and directing both the new men joining a C.I.D. sadly depleted during the war, and those returning after six years in the forces. All would need instruction in the new

methods available for fighting the new methods always being evolved in the underworld. It was a recent case he had
managed to bring to a successful conclusion, so saving the
Government of the day from the possibility of a few unpleasant moments at question time in the House, and even
from the risk of the loss of votes in the country, that had
earned him his present appointment. He had a feeling that
perhaps it was really intended to keep him in reserve for
emergencies. But emergencies are rare, even in these sadly
troubled days, and no doubt he would find his time fully occupied with instructing and advising till the Yard could adapt
itself to new peacetime conditions. So far, however, he had
had little to do except routine work. Not that he minded. A
period of comparative leisure was welcome enough while he
himself settled down in new surroundings and while Olive
wrestled with her housekeeping problems—or rather, tried to
find a house to keep.

"I suppose," she said now, as impatiently she watched
Bobby chewing his way through what the hotel management
called 'omelette aux choux' because they thought it sounded
better in French, "it wouldn't be any good sending a tele-
gram or something to say we're taking it?"

"It would not," said Bobby. "For one thing there's no
'phone number and no address, except the cottage itself and
most likely that's empty. For another, there's sure to be a
snag in it somewhere and probably a pretty big one. Something fishy somewhere."

"I don't know how you can be so horrid," Olive protested. "If there is," she added ominously, "I don't suppose I
shall ever forgive you. For goodness gracious sake, hurry up
and tell the Yard and get the car out. There isn't a moment to
lose," and in her mind's eye she saw an ever-lengthening
queue outside that attractive cottage, with themselves always
at the far end. "It's no good looking for the marmalade," she
added, "we finished the preserve ration the day before yesterday, and besides, you can't possibly want to eat any
more."

"More?" asked Bobby, surprised. "Did you say 'more'? Oh, well, I suppose 'more' is a relative term."

However, he went off then to get the car and make sure there was enough of the petrol ration left for the needs of their trip. Fortunately, when they arrived at their destination, it was to find all Olive's gloomy anticipations of mile-long queues totally unfounded. A quiet and peaceful scene, with no sign anywhere of the eager, clamouring crowd they had both expected. The house itself really had, just as the advertisement said, an attractive appearance. It stood well back from the road in a large well-tended garden and the design was simple and pleasant. There was a tiled verandah on which on warm days it would be possible to sit out. There were convenient-looking outhouses, a garage large enough for two cars, which meant ample room for all the impedimenta cars collect by some deep-seated law of attraction. In front were flowering trees and shrubs, at the back were fruit trees, and Olive said:

"If we come here, we shall have fruit—fruit," she said again, her voice lingering lovingly on a word of which she had almost forgotten the significance.

"We aren't here yet," said Bobby.

"Wet blanket," said Olive.

They fell silent then, sitting there and looking round, absorbing the quiet beauty of the surrounding scene. At a little distance was visible, above tree tops, a church tower, and they heard the clock slowly chime the hour, the sound gentle and muffled in the distance. Nearer, showed the chimneys of a large house, the building itself hidden by a row of tall poplar trees. No other habitation was in sight, except for a smaller cottage they had passed two or three hundred yards further down the road.

"I suppose," Olive said, drawing a deep breath, "it is real, isn't it?"

"It looks a jolly little place," Bobby admitted, and quite forgot to add that there was sure to be a snag in it somewhere.

Olive said:

"You might pinch me, will you? so I can be sure I'm awake . . . ai—ee, you beast, I didn't mean a hard pinch, I meant a teeny-weeny one."

"I wanted you to be quite sure," Bobby explained.

"I wonder," said Olive, letting, in spite of herself, doubt creep into her mind, "I wonder what the kitchen's like? I don't suppose there would be any hope of a resident maid. They want cinemas and things. I might be able to get someone from the village to help."

"We aren't here yet," Bobby reminded her. "Time enough to worry about maids and help when we are. What do we do now? No one about. No 'To Let' board, nothing to show where you get the key. And the garden gate padlocked."

He sounded his horn in the hope of attracting attention. The only result was that Olive gave him a reproachful glance.

"Oh, don't," she said, "not with everything so quiet and lovely. Couldn't you go and look for someone to ask? They would know in the village most likely or there's a house over there. You can see the chimneys behind that row of poplars. Or that cottage we passed down the road. They might know there."

"I suppose we have come to the right place," Bobby said doubtfully.

"If we haven't," Olive told him, "I shall probably die of heart failure on the spot. Serve you right, too."

Bobby was studying the directions given on the order to view they had received.

"Seems all right," he said. "It says, 'Fern Cottage, Steep Lane.' This is Steep Lane and there's the name on the garden gate. It's empty, too."

"Oh, look, someone's coming," Olive said.

Walking up the road towards them was a tall woman, dressed entirely in black, a sombre spot in the bright sunshine, her shadow dark before her on the white and dusty road. She came slowly, not looking at them, her gaze directed straight down the road, far into the distance, but not as though there were anything there it watched; a strange abstracted gaze, as of one who lived only either in the past or in the future, or indeed it might be in some other world. A handsome, stately figure she presented in her slow progress towards them, and yet one that seemed, as it were, alien to and apart from all that lay around.

It seemed at first as if she meant to pass them by unheeded, almost indeed as if she failed to distinguish them from their surroundings. Bobby, overcoming an odd reluctance to question one who seemed so much apart from common things, began to alight from the car, with the intention of speaking to her as she passed. But it was she who spoke first, and her voice was deep and strange in its suggestion of unheard, undetected undertones as she said:

"Is it Mr. and Mrs. Owen? Mr. Fielding asked me to say he was sorry he had been obliged to go to town. He asked me to look out for you and give you the keys. When you have finished, will you please lock everything up just as it was and return me the keys. I live at the cottage down the road."

When she had spoken she turned without waiting for a reply and went back as she had come with the same slow, measured step, with the same strange manner of being somehow apart and aloof and separate, In a way nothing could have been more commonplace and ordinary than this production by a neighbour of the keys of the house they had come to look at. None the less, both Bobby and Olive felt they had been through an experience beyond the ordinary, an experience fraught with meanings, implications, inferences that were beyond their apprehension.

CHAPTER II

MUSIC OF DOUBT

FOR A MOMENT or two they stayed, watching that tall and upright figure as it receded down the road, a little black blob of shadow dark behind. Bobby turned to the garden gate and unfastened the padlock. As they were walking up the path he said:

"I hope that woman isn't going to be the snag in it."

"Well, how can she?" Olive asked. Then she said: "It was a tragic face."

Bobby opened the front door—each key on the bunch was neatly labelled. They entered the hall or rather the lounge, for so it was clearly meant to be. Everything seemed bright, airy, clean. The whole place had apparently been newly decorated. Olive felt that the lounge wall-paper was one she might almost have chosen herself, a shade too dark perhaps, but that could be relieved by a judicious choice of curtains and cushions. She said:

"Let's find the kitchen. If that's nice, too . . . but I don't suppose it can be. Nothing can be perfect."

"Wet blanket," said Bobby.

But the kitchen was perfect or at least so it seemed. Olive could only stand and gaze. There was even one of the new heat preservation stoves. She said slowly:

"If you hadn't been so mean about it, I should ask you to pinch me so I could wake up. This can't possibly be real."

"I know now what the snag is," Bobby said.

"What?"

"The rent. Most likely it's a thousand a year."

"Then we'll pay it," said Olive with decision, "and I'll take in washing or lodgers or something." She went to the window. "Fruit trees," she said with a kind of dreamy ecstasy, "one—two—eight—ten. Bushes, too. I shouldn't wonder if those aren't gooseberry bushes. I never saw a gooseberry last year. If they are and it's a good crop, perhaps I'll let people I'm very fond of have one or two each. But that's not a promise."

They proceeded to explore the rest of the house. There may have been defects—dark corners, awkward turnings, inconveniences of one kind or another, but if so they passed unheeded and unnoticed. There was only one room where the decoration aroused Olive's criticism. She thought the paper gaudy and that the colours in the frieze and the paper swore at each other, as the French say. A little awkward and inconvenient in shape, too. It was one of the smaller of the four bedrooms, and, after careful consideration, Olive made up her mind that it would do nicely for Bobby who wanted a separate room to work in and for his papers, reference books and so on.

They made a tour of the garden over which Olive uttered little cries of breathless delight, though Bobby was less enthusiastic. His back was already beginning to ache in anticipation. When Olive wondered wistfully if it would be possible to get anyone for occasional help from the adjacent village of Much Middles, Bobby wondered equally wistfully if there was any hope of finding a jobbing gardener there.

Finally they tore themselves away. They locked up and went to return the keys. Olive was feeling a trifle depressed now. Reaction probably. She felt it was too good to be true and she even omitted to rebuke Bobby when he observed that he never feared the Fates so much as when they proffered gifts. Also he murmured something about lunch, but Olive shook her head firmly.

"We've got to wait to see Mr. Fielding," she declared, "even if we don't have anything to eat all the rest of the day."

It was now Bobby's turn to feel depressed.

"What about having a try in the village?" he suggested timidly. "There should be a pub or something there."

"Mr. Fielding might come and bring someone with him and let it behind our backs," give pointed out, though she didn't care to think anyone could really do a thing like that. "We mustn't run unnecessary risks," she said.

They had reached the other cottage now. This was a real cottage in the workaday sense of the word, built for a labourer for whom anything would do, though apparently there had been one or two improvements. When they knocked, the woman they had seen before came to the door. They could see her more plainly now. A ravaged face, Olive thought, yet striking and distinguished, that of one who had seen much, felt much, suffered much and not with resignation. Rebellion rather. The features were large, the nose prominent and defiant, the dark and distant eyes like two overshadowed pools to which the sun never came. Nowhere did she show any concession to current feminine fashion. Her complexion was all her own; her hair black, thick, abundant, was caught up at the back of her neck; and her figure was tall and straight and graceful as a mountain pine. When she saw them she did not speak but stood aside as if to make room for them to enter. Olive held out the keys, saying they had come to return them. The other made no attempt to take them. She said in that deep voice of hers in which it seemed there always sounded such far-off mysterious undertones:

"Mr. Fielding will be back soon. You had better wait here to see him. That is, if you wish to take the cottage."

"Oh, we do," Olive exclaimed. "It's lovely. But we mustn't trouble you. We can wait in the car."

The woman did not answer in words nor did she move from where she stood at one side, or make the least gesture of invitation. Nevertheless it was somehow as though she impelled them to enter and it was almost involuntarily that they obeyed. They found themselves immediately in a fairly large room that had evidently once been the cottage kitchen. Now the cooking stove had been removed and replaced by a sitting-room grate. One end of the room was occupied by a magnificent grand piano. The other furniture consisted only of a few wooden chairs and a table—but a table laid for four people. The walls were perfectly bare. There was not an ornament to be seen, not a photograph or anything of the kind, not even a vase of flowers. There were not even shelves to hold the piles of music heaped up on the floor. But before the fireplace lay a superb Persian carpet that must have been extremely valuable, though Olive's housewifely eye perceived at once that it badly needed brushing. The rest of the floor was bare boarding and equally in need of a sweep and a scrub. But the grand piano shone like the dawn and Olive decided that it was dusted and polished every morning. Their hostess said:

"Lunch is not quite ready yet."

"Oh, but," Olive protested, "we couldn't think of troubling you. It's awfully good of you—" she glanced at the other's hand and saw no wedding ring, "Miss—"

"Bellamy," said the other.

"Miss Bellamy. It is awfully kind of you, but really—"

Somehow her voice trailed away into silence. She had the feeling that Miss Bellamy was not listening, that she had sunk again into some distant world of her own. Olive's silence seemed to recall Miss Bellamy to her surroundings, as if only silence reminded her of the presence of others. She said:

"Mr. Fielding asked me to say would you please wait for him, if you liked the cottage. He wants to get it settled. I expected him back before this. If he doesn't come soon we will have our lunch without him."

"It's most awfully good of you," Olive repeated, "and we do want to wait to see Mr. Fielding. The cottage is just lovely. Only it's a shame to bother you and food's so difficult."

"There is plenty," Miss Bellamy said in her indifferent tones. "That is, for a light lunch. An omelette." Perhaps, though it did not seem that her eyes ever rested on either of them but only on some far-off thing visible to her alone, she saw that Bobby winced slightly at the word omelette, for the memory was still with him of that other omelette—'omelette aux choux'—with which he had wrestled that morning. It was almost in explanation that she added: "Not dried egg—with eggs my hens laid this morning. There'll be some fruit from the garden I bottled last year. I can't offer you a fruit tart. I haven't enough fat left."

"It sounds," said Olive, slightly overwhelmed, "simply most tremendously delicious and wonderful."

"I've managed to get some cream," Miss Bellamy added.

"Cream?" repeated Olive incredulously. "Cream?" she repeated once more, and very nearly said: "What is cream?" so long was it since she had even heard the word.

"There was some milk left over at the farm," Miss Bellamy explained, "and they let me have it. So I set it and skimmed it this morning." Then she added in the manner of one stating a simple fact, such as 'it's a fine morning' or 'it's a quarter to one': "I am probably one of the best cooks in England."

With that she went away and Olive turned helplessly to Bobby.

"Well!" she said simply and then again: "Well!"

"Let's hope she is," Bobby said.

Miss Bellamy came back into the room. She was carrying a bowl of strawberries—no less—and another of cream, rather thin cream perhaps, for the skimming had been on the comprehensive side, but cream all the same.

"I'll give Mr. Fielding five minutes more," she said, "and then, if he isn't here, I'll put the omelette on." She put the strawberries and the cream on the table and said: "Strawberries are difficult to bottle, but I'm good at that, too."

"It's . . . it's wonderful," Olive said, quite at a loss for words. "You can't think how greedy I feel. I'm sure we both of us—"

Again she left her sentence unfinished with that same odd feeling that Miss Bellamy was not listening, that she might as well have not been there for all she heard or heeded. And again Olive's abrupt silence seemed to recall Miss Bellamy to her surroundings.

"If you will come upstairs," she said, "I will show you where you can wash your hands. Your husband must use the scullery. There is no bathroom here. The W.C. is outside."

"Please don't bother about me," Bobby said, slightly embarrassed.

Olive obediently followed Miss Bellamy upstairs. Bobby went to look at the grand piano. It was not the sort of instrument one expected to find in a small country cottage. Then he went to look at the Persian rug lying before the fireplace. A lovely thing. He could not even begin to estimate its value. Yet everything else in the room was cheap and simple in the extreme. Olive came back. She said in a low voice:

"Such a bare little room upstairs. A tiny iron bed with a mattress like a board. The dressing-table is an old packing case. There's only one chair and that's broken. There isn't a single ornament or picture or anything, except a small oil portrait, of an oldish man with a grey beard, over the head of the bed. But there's another Persian rug like this and just as lovely, and the toilet set on the packing-case table is tortoiseshell and silver and must have cost pounds. And then that grand piano!"

Miss Bellamy reappeared. She had evidently heard Olive come downstairs. She said to Bobby:

"I have put soap and a towel in the scullery."

"Oh, thanks," Bobby said. "I was admiring your piano. I take it you are a musician?"

"It takes more than a grand piano to make a musician," she answered severely.

She sat down at the instrument and began to play, slowly at first. Then her hands flew along the keyboard and the room was filled with a roaring torrent of sound, threatening, ominous, and angry as thunder crashing overhead. Then it softened, it nearly died away and rose again in a long lament, so that one heard in it the wailing of all women sorrowing for those who would return no more. It grew louder again and muttered and growled, full of menace and distant, helpless rage. A crash of discords that violated every known law of harmony and yet made a kind of angry harmony of their own, succeeded and ended. Neither Bobby nor Olive knew how long they had listened. It might have been two minutes or an hour. In listening, time had ceased. Miss Bellamy rose and without even looking at them went back to her kitchen. Olive said:

"My gracious."

CHAPTER III

CROSSED FINGERS

IT WAS BOBBY who spoke next.

"Let's hope," he said, "she can cook as well as she can play."

"That's awfully Philistine," said Olive.

"Well, I'm hungry," Bobby defended himself.

"So am I," said Olive, hovering over the bowl of strawberries and fighting hard against the temptation to put in a finger and pull one out. "I wonder what it was she played," Olive added; and Bobby said simply that, whatever it was, it was a one-er.

An enormous limousine was drawing up outside. They both went to the window to look, saying to each other hopefully that perhaps this was Mr. Fielding. Before the car had well stopped a fat little man threw open the car door and hovered there a moment undecidedly, a small parcel in one hand, He put it back on the seat inside the car, jumped out, and came bounding up the path to the cottage, a little like an eager schoolboy running home. Without knocking he flung the door open and dashed in, crying:

"Tilly! Tilly! are you there?" Then he saw Bobby and Olive and stopped. "Oh, beg pardon," he said. "Oh, is it Mrs. Owen? And Mr. Owen? How nice of you to be so prompt. I do want to get the thing settled." He had rushed at them as he was talking and now was shaking hands vigorously. "I do hope you like it," he said and dashed away to the inner door, the one that admitted to the tiny kitchen. "Oh, there you are, Tilly," he cried and bustled back to the front door. "Biggs," he shouted. "Biggs, I've left a parcel in the car—Fortnum and Mason. Bring it along, will you?"

Miss Bellamy came in from the kitchen. This had originally been the scullery but a cooking stove had been inserted and the clothes boiler removed, so that now, with the addition of one or two cupboards, it made a fairly convenient kitchen. A small outbuilding had been added to serve as combined scullery and pantry.

"I was nearly giving you up, Mr. Fielding," she said, in her slow emotionless voice.

"Never do that, Tilly, never," he answered with an emphasis Miss Bellamy either did not, or did not wish to notice.

"I must see to the omelette," she said.

There was a knock at the door. Mr. Fielding rushed to it and tore it open. The chauffeur was standing there, holding a small parcel in one hand.

"Give it to Miss Bellamy," his employer said and bounded back to the kitchen door. "Tilly," he called. "Tilly. Biggs has got something for you. My contribution for lunch."

The chauffeur came into the room; a tall, dark, lean man, slightly disfigured by the scar of a wound that had ripped open his left cheek from eye to chin but had fortunately left the eye itself uninjured. He seemed to hesitate, as his eyes, as dark and deep as Miss Bellamy's and nearly as large, flickered uneasily about the room, apparently searching for her. She came to the door of the kitchen. Impassively he crossed the floor to her and held the parcel out. Impassively she took it, while, if Mr. Fielding did not actually hop round the two of them, he certainly gave the impression of being about to do so. There was the oddest contrast between his exuberant vitality and the machine-like and disciplined movements and gestures of the other two. The chauffeur turned away; and now for the first time that flickering and uncertain glance of his, again a contrast to the steady deliberation of his every movement, seemed to become aware of the presence of Bobby and of Olive. On Olive it rested for scarcely a moment, but on Bobby his gaze was as intent as it was swift. His head tilted a little to one side in what seemed a characteristic trick of attitude, he stood and gazed with an almost fierce intensity. It was only for the fraction of a second that this continued and Bobby was not sure how much of the impression he received was not due to his own imagination, a little startled as he was by that swift, direct, and searching glance. Yet the impression remained that he had seen both recognition and perhaps defiance flash for a moment and pass in the other's deep, dark, and hidden eyes, shadowed as they were by overhanging, slightly swollen lids.

"Caviare sandwiches," Mr. Fielding was saying, beaming with satisfaction. "I love 'em. First course, Tilly darling. Second course, one of your adorable omelettes, and do I see strawberries and cream? Not so bad, eh? Not so bad." He swung round to address this last remark to Bobby and Olive. The chauffeur was turning away after that brief exchange with Bobby of glance given and returned. Mr. Fielding called: "Oh, by the way, Biggs."

"Sir?" said Biggs, halting in the doorway.

"This lady and gentleman are going to be neighbours of ours. They are taking Fern Cottage—at least, they are thinking of it. That's your car up the road, Mr. Owen, isn't it? If ever you've trouble with it, you ask Biggs. Biggs knows it all. Don't you, Biggs? I mean, about cars?"

"I try to give satisfaction, sir," said Biggs and departed.

Mr. Fielding winked at Bobby.

"An excellent driver," he said. "First class mechanic, but he does keep me in my place. I'm afraid he thinks me vulgar. I suppose I am. Am I vulgar, Tilly?"

"No," answered Miss Bellamy, who had been occupied opening the parcel and arranging the contents on a plate, "no, but you like to pretend to be."

"Well, there's my character for you," Mr. Fielding said, turning again to Bobby. "You'll find it a nice quiet run to town— if you can make do with your petrol ration for the run, that is if you have to go to town daily. The train service isn't too bad and I hear there are to be more 'buses, soon. High time, too."

"If you'll sit down," said Miss Bellamy, in her far off distant voice, "we'll begin."

She had put the sandwiches on the table and had produced some fresh-gathered parsley to garnish the plate.
Whatever her air and manner of abstraction might be, she
seemed to be fully aware of all that needed attention and to
attend to it promptly and efficiently.

"Now, do tell me," Mr. Fielding asked Olive as soon as
they were seated, "what you think of Fern Cottage?"

"I think it's adorable," Olive said, and, throwing all the
prudence of the purchaser to the winds, she exclaimed: "Oh,
Mr. Fielding, I do hope you can let us have it."

"It depends," said Bobby, trying to be businesslike, "on
whether we can afford. What rent are you asking?"

Mr. Fielding popped a sandwich into his mouth. His
round little face puckered into a worried frown. He helped
himself to another sandwich. Olive told herself she would
simply have to scream if he took much longer to answer. After a thoughtful bite, he said: "That's been bothering me
more than a bit," and his candid, childlike eyes seemed to
ask Olive for sympathy and understanding. "The first thing I
want to be quite clear about is that whoever takes it must
promise to leave at the end of three years."

"We can promise that, can't we?" Olive said, appealing
to Bobby.

"Certainly," said Bobby.

"Good," said Mr. Fielding in a relieved tone. "You see
I've promised Fern Cottage to a very old friend out East. He
expects to be back at the end of three years —retired. He's
relying on me to let him have Fern Cottage—and I'm relying
on him, too. Nice to have an old pal living near you can drop
in on occasionally."

"There will be no difficulty about that," Bobby repeated.
"It could be put in the lease."

"Oh, so long as it's fully understood," Mr. Fielding said
deprecatingly. "My lawyer did suggest a clause to provide
for a fantastically increased rent at the end of the three-year
period. But people have really got to trust each other sometimes. The world would come to a standstill if we didn't.
Wouldn't work, you know, simply wouldn't work."

"Yes, and the rent, Mr. Fielding?" asked Olive, who felt she really couldn't bear the suspense any longer.

"It's difficult," Mr. Fielding said again, and he looked more like a worried child than ever. "I don't want to take unfair advantage of the way things are and yet as a business man"— he assumed a portentous scowl, as though he felt that for a business man a scowl was your only wear—"as a hard-headed business man I must consider the market. Frankly, I had no idea the demand was so great. I put an advertisement in all the papers—personal column, because they said if I didn't it might be weeks before the thing appeared. I wanted to get quick action. I couldn't believe it, the way the replies poured in. I couldn't face it. Not reading all that pile. Would have taken me a month of Sundays. So I left it to luck. I've always been a gambler. My profession. You ought to see our vicar's face when I tell him that. Well, anyhow, what I did was to shut my eyes, turn round three times, and make a grab. It happened to be your letter I got."

"Oh," said Olive, turning pale as she thought how easily it might have been another.

"I liked the way it read," Mr. Fielding went on. "Brief, business-like. To the point. Good references, too. Not that I took them up. I never take up references. I trust my instinct. A gambler has to. When I hired Biggs I never took up his references. Took him on the strength of my instinct—and his war service. You noticed that cheek of his? Egypt, the desert."

"You were saying about the rent?" Olive reminded him, and how she longed to shake him and shake him till he answered.

"Oh, yes," said Mr. Fielding. "Before the war, it was forty pounds a year. Cost of living doubled since then. That makes it eighty. But there's an extra demand for houses—market very short. Well, add another twenty for that and call it a hundred a year. What do you say to that? Or am I being greedy?"

Olive looked at Bobby, simply daring him to say 'No' at the peril of his life. But Bobby had no inclination to say 'No.' Instead he said:

"May we call it agreed then that we take the cottage on a three-year lease at a rent of a hundred a year?"

"You paying rates?" Mr. Fielding warned him.

"Oh, yes," agreed Bobby, and Mr. Fielding immediately and warmly shook hands with them both.

"Good," he said. "Glad to get it off my mind. But I'm afraid," he said, shaking his head at them sternly, "you aren't really good business people. I expected you to bargain. I should have been quite willing to take eighty or ninety. I suppose I oughtn't to tell you that, but I do rather feel as if I had done you down for ten pounds. We'll make it a non-repairing lease, shall we? Sort of compensation—to ease my conscience."

Bobby said that was a very kind suggestion; and Miss Bellamy appeared, carrying a superb omelette, as it were the apotheosis of all possible omelettes that ever were or could be. Mr. Fielding beamed on her, too.

"All arranged, Tilly," he told her, and seemed inclined to shake hands with her as well, had she not been fully occupied placing her omelette on the table. "These good people are going to be our neighbours," he went on, "and I'm sure we shall all be very happy together." Miss Bellamy said nothing but deposited the omelette before him. "Do I help it?" he asked and set to work. "Tilly," he demanded, "how many eggs did you use?"

"Twelve," she said, and her heavy and sombre voice sounded very different from Mr. Fielding's light, cheerful chatter.

"Twelve," repeated Mr. Fielding proudly, as if there were some great merit in the number.

"Twelve," repeated Olive in her turn; and this time pinched herself—she had no idea of trusting Bobby again—to make sure she really was awake, and that this incredible land where lovely country cottages were to be had for the asking and new-laid eggs were counted by the dozen, had actual material existence.

Under the table she crossed her fingers, having a vague idea that this in some way acted as a charm to ward off bad luck when good luck seemed as though it must be waking the wrath of the jealous gods.

CHAPTER IV

HOUSE AT LAST

THE CONVERSATION BECAME general. Bobby took occasion
to mention that he had recently resigned his position in a
provincial police force to accept an executive post at Scotland Yard. Mr. Fielding was very surprised and immensely
interested. He made two or three little jokes about how safe
they would all feel and how soundly they would all sleep,
safe and secure in the glow of the prestige of Scotland Yard.
At these jokes Bobby and Olive smiled wanly—few appreci-
ate jokes about their own profession—Miss Bellamy listened
with an unmoved countenance, and Mr. Fielding himself enjoyed them as much as most people do enjoy their own
pleasantries. And what a remarkable piece of luck it had
been that he should have happened to pick on Bobby's letter.
Pure luck. It might so easily have been that of someone else.
He would have to tell the vicar how well it paid to be a gambler and trust to luck.

"I do enjoy pulling his leg," explained Mr. Fielding looking more like a beaming happy child than ever, "though he's
a jolly good sort all the same. Isn't he, Tilly?"

"He dislikes me," observed Miss Bellamy in a tone of the
most complete indifference.

"Oh, you mustn't say that," protested Mr. Fielding earnestly. "No one could. Please don't think that," and both
Bobby and Olive noticed that in Miss Bellamy's dark, far-off
eyes there showed for the moment a gleam, a look, of a kind
of half puzzled, half resentful, wholly pitying tenderness. It
went as quickly as it had come and again she seemed to remove herself from all present surroundings. To Bobby and
Olive, Mr. Fielding explained: "It's Tilly's music. He

doesn't understand it. Called it pagan. Funny idea. My fault. I got Tilly to play the organ once when Mrs. Marks—she runs the Sunday school—was laid up. I suppose," admitted Mr. Fielding thoughtfully, "it was just a bit startling."

"I forgot," Miss Bellamy said, and again it was noticeable that however aloof and abstracted she might appear, however deep in a silence she seldom or never broke of her own initiative, yet she none the less seemed always aware of what was going on. "Sometimes I do. When I'm playing, I mean. I forgot it was church and they wanted a hymn tune."

Olive reflected that if instead of the expected hymn tune Miss Bellamy had treated a village congregation at morning service to such a display as she had just given, then it was no wonder the vicar had been a little startled. A remarkable performance and oddly disturbing. Olive said:

"I've been wondering ever since what it was you played just now. It was wonderful, I've never heard anything like it before, I do wonder what it was."

"It was nothing," Miss Bellamy answered carelessly. "Just what came into my head. That's all."

"Tilly's like that," said Mr. Fielding proudly. "She'll sit down and play something that makes you feel all turned over, if you see what I mean, almost as if you weren't yourself any more. And two minutes afterwards, she hasn't any idea what it was all about, just comes and goes."

"Oh, Miss Bellamy," Olive cried, "you ought to write it down, you ought really. It was wonderful."

Without answering, again as if she had not seen or heard, Miss Bellamy began to clear the table. Olive asked if she might help, but Miss Bellamy shook her head and went on alone with her task.

"Tilly says she doesn't want to be bothered," Mr. Fielding explained; "not with these scraps and bits of things. Just incidentals so to speak, if you see what I mean. What's really important, big, she puts down all right and when it's ready, I'm going to see it's heard by everyone. Everywhere. Worth waiting for."

"I'm sure it will be," Olive said with emphasis, and though Miss Bellamy made no comment there came again into her eyes as she glanced at Mr. Fielding that same expression of half puzzled, half resentful, wholly pitying tenderness they had shown before. She had finished clearing the table by now and she disappeared again into the kitchen. Mr. Fielding said with a little chuckle:

"Poor old vicar. What made it worse was he called next morning to talk it over, he said, and Tilly was at it again. Just playing, if you see what I mean, thinking at the piano she calls it. She says she hasn't an idea what it was she played, just letting her fingers do what they liked, she says, but vicar had the scare of his life. I can't make out exactly, but he says it was pagan—heathen, he says. Says he started by wanting to dance and what would the village have thought if they had heard of their vicar dancing in Miss Bellamy's garden at ten o'clock on a Monday morning?" Mr. Fielding stopped to indulge in his rich gurgling chuckle. "I expect they would have wanted him unfrocked or something," he went on; "what's more, he told me that wasn't the worst of it. I don't know what he means but he says he turned and ran and he didn't feel safe till he got to the church and that's half a mile away. Stories did get about because he was seen running like mad and people wondered. It's died down now."

"Odd," Bobby said thoughtfully.

"Well, I think her playing's simply marvellous," Olive declared.

"It's being out of touch with real things," Mr. Fielding explained. "Vicar, I mean. Unworldly, they call it. A real good sort and people love him, but I can't help pulling his leg at times now and then." Mr. Fielding paused and bubbled over with his rich infectious laughter. "When I tell him I'm a professional gambler, he gets worried. If I called myself a general agent, which is what I am, or rather was before I thought I had enough to retire on, it would be all right. Not that I've retired altogether. I've still my office and I keep my secretary on. Didn't want to sack her after all the years we've been together, so she goes every day to see to any correspondence. If there's anything special she rings me up and I toddle along. I don't often bite but I do sometimes. I bought some surplus government stores at auction the other day and sold the stuff at a good profit without even taking delivery. And just at the moment it's almost too easy making money on the Stock Exchange. You apply for a big allotment of any new issue of shares. You get a few. You sell 'em on the spot at a premium and there you are. I've made a thousand or two like that, but I've dropped it now. Not sporting enough. Of course, you have to keep your head. Most people don't and so they go smash. They hang on. I never do. As soon as I see my profit, I sell. But it needs discipline—self-discipline. It's rare."

He paused and beamed on them, his chubby little good-tempered face, his candid smiling eyes, his general air of a happy trustful child strangely unlike those supposed to mark the professional speculator he was describing himself to be.

He went on to talk again about Miss Bellamy's music and then to ask a few discreet questions about Bobby's work, which he thought must be very interesting. Bobby explained that it was ninety-nine and a half per cent dull routine and one half per cent violent action. Mr. Fielding supposed that at Scotland Yard they knew every crook in the country. He had heard about fingerprints and thought it very interesting. He supposed they enabled the Yard to trace anyone they wanted. He picked up a glass and pressed his own fingers on them, calling on Bobby to admire the perfect impressions resulting. Bobby's cigarette case was lying on the table and Mr. Fielding picked that up, too, and put his prints on it also. Not so clear, he pronounced, but he supposed the Yard experts could make them do if they had to. Bobby agreed that that was very possible and in response to further questioning explained that for the time he was chiefly occupied with instructional work—giving lectures, explaining new procedure, organizing tests of new methods and rehearsals of procedure to be followed in cases of emergency. He might for example send out an alarm of a supposed smash-and-grab raid somewhere, and see how quickly police cars arrived and if not why not? and how promptly and efficiently probable lines of escape were blocked and so on. Practice was necessary to make sure every man knew exactly what to do, once an alarm was given. Of course, care had to be taken to inconvenience the public as little as possible. The public expected efficiency but didn't expect the process of acquiring it to interfere in any way with the public's comfort or convenience.

Presently Miss Bellamy came back into the room. After some more general talk, wherein Miss Bellamy took small part, Bobby and Olive departed. An appointment in town for the next day had been made so that the necessary preliminaries to entering in possession of Fern Cottage could be completed; and as Bobby and Olive drove away they heard once more music flowing passionately from the cottage where Miss Bellamy was now alone, Mr. Fielding having left at the same time as Bobby and Olive. Involuntarily Bobby stopped the car to listen; and Oliver shivered and was not sorry when it ceased as suddenly, as abruptly, as it had begun. It was as though the player had risen in the middle of a movement and gone away.

Bobby still did not start the car. He sat thinking. He said:

"You could almost imagine the devil was in that playing of hers."

"Well, I don't wonder the poor vicar was upset, if that was how she played in church," Olive agreed, though reluctantly. "I don't know what it is—it's like telling you to do something, only you know you mustn't, but you will, and when you do, it's going to be awful. Warning you."

"Complicated," observed Bobby.

"Yes," said Olive. "What do you think?"

"I never think," asserted Bobby, "till I've got the material to start on. What do you think of Mr. Fielding?"

"Oh, he's most awfully sweet," declared Olive with enthusiasm, but then she would have said the same with equal enthusiasm of anyone willing to provide a house. "Just like a great big friendly school boy."

"Isn't he?" agreed Bobby; and Olive looked at him sharply, for she was not sure his voice had not been too readily acquiescent.

"Of course," she said after a pause, "it's quite plain he's in love with Miss Bellamy but I don't know if she is with him. I think she would like to be, only she doesn't dare."

"What on earth," demanded Bobby, "do you mean?"

"I think she is afraid," Olive said, "only what makes it funnier still is that I think he is afraid, too."

"Oh, come," said Bobby. "Unless you mean afraid the way every man is when it comes to getting married, because he doesn't know, poor devil, what he may be letting himself in for."

"I don't," Olive declared with emphasis. "That sort of being afraid is simply his being afraid of having to be a weeny-teeny bit less selfish, only of course he never is. But it did make me think there was something that held them together and something that held them apart, and that was what the music told."

"Oh, well," said Bobby, and Olive said abruptly:

"Miss Bellamy's a genius."

"That's a big word," Bobby said, and, after a pause imposed by the need to dodge two children playing tag, he asked: "Notice the chauffeur chap?"

"Mr. Fielding's? That tall, dark man? No. Why?"

"I just wondered."

"Bobby," said Olive severely, "you've got something on your mind. What is it?"

"Oh, nothing much," Bobby assured her, "only I never did like coincidence."

"What coincidence?"

"Bit odd it was our letter Mr. Fielding happened to hit on."

"That wasn't coincidence," Olive pointed out. "That was luck." She said: "It had to be someone's letter, hadn't it?"

"I suppose so," agreed Bobby, "though I think myself that things generally happen—because. And not by chance."

"Well, even if Mr. Fielding knew who you were and did it on purpose," Olive urged, "why shouldn't he? He might think you would be a responsible tenant and he might like the idea of having a Scotland Yard person living near. He might think it safer with all these smash-and-grab raids and crime waves and things."

"He might," agreed Bobby. "It wouldn't be, but he might be simple enough to think so. Anything else you noticed?"

"No," said Olive, though this was not quite true, because in fact she had, though she was determined not to think so. "What did you mean about Mr. Fielding's chauffeur? Why should I notice him specially? He's rather good looking, if that's what you mean."

"I'm pretty sure he knew me," Bobby said slowly. "I'm pretty sure seeing me was a bit of a shock—and I think Fielding himself was on the look-out to see if he did."

"Do you mean he might have a record?"

"Fielding might think so. It did strike me that might be behind all that finger-print talk of his. It might have been a kind of hint to check up on his chauffeur's dabs—Biggs was what he called him, wasn't it? I don't know, of course. It just struck me."

"It might be why he wanted you for a neighbour," Olive agreed. "Well, if it's like that, it doesn't matter. We've got a house at last. Are you going to?"

"Get his dabs? Certainly not. I've no right to, for one thing. Breach of Magna Charta and the liberty of the subject most likely. He may have recognized me, if he did, for a hundred different reasons, all perfectly innocent. And he can have all the record he likes if he is running straight now. Fielding went out of his way to tell us he took him without references. It is his own affair entirely. If he has any reasonable ground for suspicion of anything wrong, it's for him to say so."

CHAPTER V

INEFFECTIVE PURSUIT

THIS MORNING, SOME days later, Olive was very busy and very happy. Possession of Fern Cottage had been effected. Moving in had been successfully accomplished. The furniture had arrived in fairly good condition. Only quite a small piece had been chipped from the sideboard, and the bit broken off the best mahogany bedstead could probably be replaced without the mend showing too much. Nor had all the china been broken when the crate containing it had been dropped from the top of the van. Already a semblance of order was being created out of chaos, so that the house was at least beginning to look like a home. Miss Bellamy, dark, silent, and sombre as ever, had been in to offer help and had brought with her a Miss Rhoda Rogers, recently demobilized from the A.T.S., now living with her brother not far away, and anxious to make the acquaintance, and help in the settling down, of the newcomer. To them Olive confessed, a little effusively, for she was in a somewhat excited mood, that she could hardly believe in her good fortune in securing such a really pleasant and convenient residence.

Neither could Bobby for that matter. He was both less busy and less happy. At the moment he was driving slowly through a London suburb, seeking a suitable place from which to send out a test alarm of a smash-and-grab raid, He was still remembering the old tag about never fearing the Greeks so much as when they brought gifts, and he had the same feeling about the gift that fortune had recently dropped into his lap and Olive's. Or to use more modern language, he suspected there were strings to it, though he could not imagine of what sort or kind. A house handed to them on a plate, so to speak, when all the world was searching so eagerly and passionately and hopelessly for any sort of a roof for over-crowded heads. And then about the transaction, and the way in which it had been carried out, there were little things, small, disturbing things, very likely quite meaningless and unimportant, that yet remained uncomfortably in his memory.

For one thing he still strongly suspected that Mr. Fielding had known very well who he was, just as he believed, too, that there had been recognition, a disconcerted startled recognition, on the part of the chauffeur, Biggs. Was there any reason why Mr. Fielding liked the idea of having a Scotland Yard man as a neighbour? Was it just possible there was a wish he should be there and not somewhere else? Or was there some idea of keeping him under observation? It seemed unlikely—not much sense in either notion. Or was it just simply a vague belief that in these days of unrest and crime waves and so on, it would be a good thing to have a well-known Scotland Yard executive living in the district? Possible, Bobby supposed, though exceedingly silly, nor did Mr. Fielding, or Miss Bellamy for that matter, seem the sort of nervous type to whom such a notion would occur. Besides, if that were it, why not say so? But then if they had said so, would he have believed them?

There entered into his consciousness a recognition of the existence of a motor cyclist who seemed to be following the same rather devious route that Bobby himself had taken. And he began to be aware, too, of a certain resemblance between this man and Biggs, Mr. Fielding's chauffeur. He could not be sure; for the man's cap was pulled low over his eyes, his coat collar was turned up, he was wearing goggles. An effective disguise. Yet if this were disguise, odd that the man seemed more inclined to draw attention to himself than to avoid it. Once or twice, after disappearing for a time, he had turned up again with almost an air of saying: 'Well, here I am again, and what do you think of that?'

But Bobby did not know what to think of it, or whether to think of it at all.

He halted his car at the spot he had selected from the map as being suitable. It was near an important main road in which were various objectives likely to attract the interest of smash-and-grab raiders. But there was not much traffic and the streets were wide and convenient, so that possible inconvenience caused by a sudden rush of various police cars would be lessened and there would be a smaller risk of bitter complaints from a public demanding the solid bricks of security and protection but grudging the preparatory and necessary straw.

The motor cyclist had vanished now. There was a telephone box near where Bobby had halted. He was looking at his watch, waiting the hour settled with the Yard, when, by arrangement, certain police chiefs would be present to watch, profit by, and criticize the carrying out of the test.

At the moment decided on he alighted, went to the 'phone box, and rang up, giving first the code word by which the Yard would know this was the test and not the real thing. He got a prompt response. He answered, giving the locality, which had been left to his choice and discretion, and was told in reply that the general call had gone out. Nothing to do now but await the arrival of the police cars, note the time it took for their appearance, and compare the reports of the other cars whose duty it would be to try to block escape routes.

Then things, unexpected things, began to happen. Round the corner from the adjacent main road a woman came running. She was screaming something at the top of her voice. The motor cyclist seen before, appeared from a side street. Bobby turned towards the woman, now followed by two or three others, men and women, who also were shouting and running. One of them, still shouting and gesturing, excitedly pointed over Bobby's shoulder. Bobby turned, and was just in time to see the cyclist dart out of the 'phone box. He had a heavy spanner in his hand. He tore open the door of Bobby's car and Bobby heard the sound of heavy blows. He ran forward. The man drew back from the car and turned to meet him. Bobby had a momentary vision of a cap drawn down over the eyes, of a coat collar turned up, of goggles, of a huge spanner swung high in the air. He paused warily. The spanner came flying at him, vicious and angry. He dodged to avoid it. It missed him narrowly. In avoiding it he slipped and nearly fell. He recovered his balance, but the delay had given the other time to mount his cycle and go roaring away, round the corner, out of sight.

Bobby knew at once what had happened. The cyclist had put out of action both the 'phone in the booth and his own wireless. Any reports of what had actually happened—for Bobby at once guessed that a real smash-and-grab raid had coincided with the Yard test—would be set down, until he himself could get through with the code word required, as merely due to a natural confusion in the minds of spectators caused by the carrying out of the rehearsal.

Five minutes delay that would mean at least, or even more, till things got sorted out, and, in a smash-and-grab raid, five minutes start means an almost certainly successful getaway.

Evidently some gang, there were at least three the police were aware of as now operating, probably others as well, had known that these tests were being held, and had thought it would be a good opportunity for carrying out an actual raid, at the same time and place. Thus, they calculated, in the temporary confusion between the two, the actual performance and the police rehearsal, there would be an excellent chance of evading pursuit. The locality had been easy to guess, since similar tests had been held in every other London district, so that this neighbourhood had been plainly indicated as the scene for the next. Time, no doubt, had been more difficult. It had probably been the affair of the motor cyclist. Quite likely that the actual operators had also been following in a car, though at a greater distance, and that to them the motor cyclist had reported or signalled during the intervals of his disappearances. Bobby knew very well with what care and forethought and precaution these raids are organized. If this time a certain degree of improvization had been required, that was more than compensated for by the confusion certain to be caused between reality and test. Cars blocking the escape routes, for instance, would think they had done all that was required by taking up their positions as promptly as possible, and would pay no special attention to passing cars—or motor cyclists for that matter.

All this flashed through Bobby's mind as he was recovering his balance. He saw his car was pointing the wrong way, so that more time would be lost before he could turn it and start a hopeless pursuit, for already the motor cyclist would be far away, dodging and speeding through the streets. So, too, would be the actual raiders. Of course, the possibility of such a trick being played had been considered and discussed, but it had been decided that the risk had to be taken. All the same, the impudence of it. Using police training as cover!

Well, one had to do what one could. Bobby turned to the little group who had come running to give the alarm from the 'phone box where the instrument had just been smashed. One of the group was a serviceman, in uniform. Bobby made a grab at him.

"I am a police officer," he said hurriedly. "Find another 'phone, quick, and report. Dial 1212, but say Jake first, it's a code word. Understand? Good. Hurry. Oh, tell them—"

He added the registration number the cyclist's machine had shown, for almost unconsciously, from the sheer force of habit of noting and remembering apparent trifles, he had observed it and tucked it away in his memory. Then he ran to his car and started in pursuit. Quite hopeless, he knew. But possibly he might be able to gather some indication of the direction taken. He swung round into the side street from which the cyclist had emerged. At a corner, further on, a motor cyclist was lingering, one foot on a pedal, ready to start. He was waiting and watching, his head tilted to one side, in what might have been an unconscious trick of mannerism. The moment he saw Bobby he waved a hand and disappeared at full speed. Bobby stared, gasped, followed; incredulous and bewildered.

What on earth did that mean, he asked himself. Was it the same man? Was he deliberately inviting pursuit? A different registration number, Bobby thought, from the momentary glimpse he had caught of the number plate, but then these are easily changed when suitable preparation has been made.

But speculation could be left for the present. What mattered now was overtaking the fellow. Bobby trod on the accelerator, defiant of all speed regulations, and so began a wild and furious chase of which those who saw it still retain their memories. Bobby's car could do an easy eighty miles an hour. So could the cyclist's machine. Bobby sounded his horn. So did the cyclist.

Thus they roared through the quiet suburban streets while pedestrians stared and gasped and ran, and drivers stared and swore and wrenched their vehicles aside, out of the path of that wild race and pursuit, and every hundred yards or so a major accident was avoided by a fresh and ever repeated and ever more surprising miracle.

Bobby began to notice that the route they were following had rather the air of having been carefully chosen. There were comparatively few traffic lights to pass and few spots where traffic blocks were likely to occur. Nor did they once cross a major road at right angles, but always, when they came to one, joined it and left it by an easy approach and departure. Often there was a clear run, speed against speed, with the cycle holding well its own against the car. Useless now for Bobby to wish he had selected a larger, more powerful car. But larger and more powerful cars use more petrol, and that is a point which has to be considered, and is indeed over-riding when no need for any great extra turn of speed is reasonably to be anticipated. And when they came to busier roads the advantage was to the cyclist, for he could slip between other vehicles where Bobby's car could not pass.

Yet though two or three times this happened, though two or three times the fleeing cyclist thus gained an advantage that seemed as though it must enable him to throw off pursuit, yet there he always was, still visible, still following the same direction, still much the same distance ahead.

It began almost to seem to Bobby, incredible as was the supposition, that he was being led, deliberately and purposefully led, in a pre-determined direction. It seemed, too, certain that more than once the cyclist could have got away, and yet never had he taken advantage of any such opportunity. Indeed, once or twice it almost looked as if the fellow had deliberately slowed down in order to give Bobby a chance to make up the time and distance he had lost through interruptions the cyclist, with his handier machine, had been able to avoid. Why? In the name of all that is contradictory and absurd, why? The hunted fox, the hounds hard on its trail, is said to stop at times to play or gambol, but escaping gangsters seldom show any such inclination. Well, no time to think about that now, with every atom of concentration required to dodge the complete and final smash that threatened every few yards.

Bobby was, as a driver, in the first class. His life had before now depended on his skill and quickness in handling a car. But at present he had the feeling that he was like the highly competent amateur matched against the still more highly skilled professional. He was aware of a feeling that he was outmatched, in a way being played with, that the fellow could escape and disappear whenever he wanted to, that that wave of the hand with which he had greeted Bobby's first appearance in pursuit had been less defiance or invitation or greeting than deliberate mockery. The fellow, Bobby thought gloomily, must be strangely sure of himself. Nor were Bobby's chances improved when a zealous, competent, and courageous constable, warned by the general hooting and complaining of indignant drivers, came running just in time to see Bobby's car hurtling towards him. He jumped into the roadway, signalling Bobby to stop. Bobby responded by a frantic warning on his hooter that he meant to do nothing of the sort, and at imminent risk swerved. The constable was avoided, but he had his truncheon drawn and he hurled it with force and precision at Bobby's car as it whirled by. The truncheon smashed against the windscreen but fortunately that was of safety glass and held, though badly splintered.

All the same Bobby's chances of success in his pursuit, and his life as well, were nearly ended, for the momentary confusion, caused by the impact and loss of clear vision for a second or two, resulted in as narrow an escape from collision with a heavy lorry as can possibly be imagined. Indeed car and lorry actually touched and scraped, and how it was Bobby's lighter car managed to retain its balance, it is impossible to say. But so it was, and when Bobby had regained control and had left the indignant and protesting lorry driver far behind, there was the cyclist still, almost exactly the same distance ahead.

Once again there had been an easy opportunity for him to shake off pursuit, had he so wished. But instead he must have actually reduced speed, and now he was looking back as if to be certain Bobby was still there. The moment he was sure of that, he increased speed again, and again was resumed this inconceivable pursuit, this wild and desperate hunt in which the quarry seemed to take every chance and run every risk—to avoid final escape.

They were beginning to leave the town behind. Occasionally they left built-up areas for a time. Not that that made much difference as they roared and rushed along. Bobby noticed that they were now not far from the neighbourhood of his new home, where Olive was so busy getting furniture in place and curtains hung. Not more than two or three miles away, Bobby thought, not more than two or three minutes in time at the speed at which they were travelling. It was open country here and the driving as tricky and dangerous as ever, for if there were few or no obstructions, there were sharp and narrow bends and blind corners where tall hedges, untrimmed all through the war years, made observation impossible.

Here Bobby began to gain. The cyclist was only a few yards ahead now. It looked as if these twists and turns were affecting him, forcing him to slow down. For almost the first time Bobby began to think there really was a chance of overtaking him—and how he would enjoy, Bobby told himself grimly, getting within arm's length of this specialist in cheek and impudence who had led him such a dance. Straight ahead, in this lane as narrow as any they had traversed, a woman appeared, walking. She jumped into the hedge and stood there, screaming and half hidden by branches and foliage but making herself heard at least, even above or through the roar of the engines of car and cycle. A few yards further on, the lane, it was no more, turned at a sharp angle. Bobby swung his car round. Ahead was a long, straight stretch. It was empty. The cyclist and his machine seemed simply to have vanished.

CHAPTER VI

INEFFECTIVE SEARCH

IT WAS ONLY for the first moment that Bobby's bewilderment lasted as his eyes wandered up and down that long and empty road. Then he saw that in the roadside ditch on his right hand, half hidden by a great bank of nettles, lay the motor cycle. Two or three yards further on from where it lay was a low stile, in part hidden by the overgrowth of the untrimmed hedge. Bobby jumped from his car and ran to it. On the other side was a smooth, well beaten path, leading down a fairly steep slope to a small wood or copse a few hundred yards distant. Beyond this and a little to one side, so as not to be entirely hidden by the trees, stood a church and other buildings. Bobby recognized them. They were the church and cottages and farms of Much Middles, the village of which his new home, Fern Cottage, formed a part. Then the chimneys he could see further on must be those of Middles, Mr. Fielding's home, and nearer but hidden by the copse would be his own Fern Cottage and that other and smaller cottage where Miss Bellamy provided music and omelettes with equal skill, success, and éclat. And there would run the high road to and from London and the open country.

So all that wild chase and hot pursuit had brought Bobby back home, and there was the fugitive himself, now mounted on a pedal cycle and coasting easily down the slope of the hill. He turned as he drew near the copse. He saw Bobby at the stile, watching. He waved a gay farewell. Bobby waved back in acknowledgement of present defeat. He could almost hear the other's smooth, complacent chuckle, see his triumphant grin. Oh, well, the best laugh is always the last, and so far, in Bobby's conflicts with the underworld, the last laugh, and a grim laugh at that, had generally been Bobby's.

No good, though, for a man on foot to attempt to pursue a man on a cycle, and already the fugitive had vanished within the wood. He would come out, Bobby calculated, in Steep Lane, not very far from Fern Cottage, or perhaps nearer to Miss Bellamy's. As likely as not, so well organized did the whole thing seem, another car was waiting somewhere at hand, ready to pick him up. One of the conveniences modern progress offers to the criminal is easy and untraceable transport, since nothing is easier than to commandeer a car from some car park or another, make use of it, and then abandon it. If that was what had happened this time, the escaped cyclist would by now be comfortably driving back to town. Even if the police stopped him, he would have his stories and his papers all ready and convincing.

Bobby turned away. He remembered the woman screaming her terror in the hedge as he and the cyclist thundered by. He was not much surprised to find no trace of her. Probably an accomplice. He remembered how well she had been hidden in the hedge and he guessed that she had drawn closer twigs and leaves to form the effective screen that had hidden her features and lessened any chance of future recognition.

No doubt her job had been to provide a pedal cycle in readiness at a pre-arranged point where it could be used for escape along a path where no car could follow. Still more proof of the most careful, meticulous planning. Well, planning is the order of the day, and why shouldn't rogues plan as carefully as any of the rest of us? Bobby hauled from the resting place in the nettles the motor cycle that was the one trophy left him. A hundred, a thousand to one, though, that that had been stolen, too. He pushed it in the back of his car.

For some time it had been raining though only now did he notice it. He supposed that on his way back to the Yard he had better go through Much Middles and inquire if any one in the village had noticed a waiting car. No one had. Nor, so far as he could learn, had any cyclist been seen, not even by the members of a road gang busy on repairs. Not of course that that proved much. He went into a telephone booth, rang up the county constabulary—the village was just outside the Metropolitan Police area and police have to be careful not to trespass on each other's domains—and asked them to continue and complete inquiries about any motorist seen loitering, or any cyclist seen passing, in or near Much Middles village. Rather vague, he agreed in answer to the faintly amused, slightly troubled voice at the other end of the wire, but all police work meant not so much making bricks without straw as building houses without bricks or anything else.

The voice promised to do its best. Bobby got into his car again and drove slowly up Steep Lane, past Miss Bellamy's cottage, and Fern Cottage as far as Middles and a little further. He found he had been right in estimating that the path the cyclist had followed did in fact, after leaving the copse, join Steep Lane near the Bellamy cottage. A man was working in the field the path crossed. Bobby asked him if he had seen anything of a cyclist. He had but at a distance only. He had observed him with disfavour, for the path was supposed to be for pedestrians only, and he had noticed that when the cyclist crossed into the road he had turned, not towards the main road to the right but to the left, towards Fern Cottage and Middles. He had also noticed that after that the cyclist had not been again visible. This had not impressed itself upon him in any way, though now he did remember thinking it was odd. But the cyclist might easily have stopped to rest and smoke a cigarette by the wayside or indeed for any other of fifty different reasons. Consulting a map perhaps. Still it was a fact that after the Bellamy cottage had hidden him from sight he had not emerged into visibility again. For all Bobby's informant could say, though, he might, after resting for a few minutes, have either turned back unnoticed to the main road or gone on, equally unnoticed, towards Fern Cottage and Middles.

That was all Bobby could learn. Both uneasy and puzzled he drove on. At Miss Bellamy's cottage, he alighted and knocked. There was no answer. Everything seemed locked up, secure. He tried the front door. Securely fastened, and he noticed there was a new Yale lock. All the same, having some knowledge of country ways, he made sure there was no key hidden under a convenient mat or hanging on some supposedly inconspicuous nail close by. Not that he thought Miss Bellamy was likely to be so trusting, but country ways are apt to be infectious. His search was unavailing. He knocked again and still got no answer. Back door and windows were fastened, the cycle shed securely padlocked. The one or two other sheds were empty and undisturbed. The gravelled paths, splashed with the falling rain, showed no sign of recent footsteps. So far as he could see there was no possibility that the fugitive could be hiding here.

He went back to his car and drove to Middles. No one was at the house, except a young girl from the village, a kind of temporary housemaid. The cook-housekeeper was out on some household errand. Mr. Fielding was in town and wouldn't be back till evening probably. Biggs, the chauffeur, had driven him in and would wait to drive him back. Mr. Fielding often made use of the car in the city, during his visits on business. Convenient to have a car at hand, he used to say, in days when taxis were as rare as snowballs in summer.

Bobby, still unenlightened, went off to his new home where he found Olive, Miss Bellamy herself, and Miss Rhoda Rogers, whom he met for the first time, all very busy together. He explained that he had been following a suspicious character who had last been seen in the vicinity of Miss Bellamy's cottage. The three ladies all seemed slightly alarmed and Miss Bellamy wondered if she had better make sure he wasn't hiding in any of her outbuildings or even inside her home. Bobby offered to accompany her. He could run her there in his car in a minute or two and bring her back as quickly. Miss Bellamy said it was very kind of him and she would feel safer if he were with her. The other two approved. Miss Bellamy got in the car and Bobby drove her to her cottage. They both alighted and went to the door. Miss Bellamy produced her key from a purse in her bag, but not till after a brief search, and opened the door. She went in first, her wet and muddy shoes leaving traces on the boarded floor, for she had accidentally stepped in a puddle as she alighted from the car, and Bobby could not be sure, even though such had been his first impression, that till she reached it, trod on it, obliterated it, there had been a faint imprint of a wet and muddy, foot near the door. But certainly no trace now of any intruder's presence and the back door bolted on the inside, so no one could have slipped out there. Miss Bellamy led the way upstairs and he followed. There were two bedrooms; or rather there had been two, for the rear and smaller room was now only used for lumber. In it quite evidently no one could be hiding. The front room was Miss Bellamy's bedroom—a small, austere room offering no possible means of concealment. Even the small low iron bedstead had no valance to hide anyone lurking beneath and the wardrobe door was open.

To Bobby's secret amusement and surprise, Miss Bellamy displayed a somewhat outmoded Victorian modesty when showing him this room. She stood on the threshold, holding the door half open so as to let him sec within but not allowing him to enter. He even had the impression that she was trying to blush, as if she thought that was expected of at maiden lady allowing a strange man to peep into her bedroom, but that she did not quite know how to manage it.

"There's no one," she said with her new faintly embarrassed, old-maidish air that was so little consonant with Bobby's first conception of her character and personality, though of course, as he told himself, we all have these unexpected quirks and turns in our dispositions.

Bobby agreed with her and they went downstairs again. He offered to drive her back to Fern Cottage, but she explained that now she was back again, there were a few household matters she thought she would like to attend to. In any case it was only a few minutes to Fern Cottage, and it wasn't worth troubling Mr. Owen again. So Bobby said how kind it was of her and of Miss Rogers to help them in getting settled, and how much both he and his wife appreciated it, and she said how good it was of him to come with her to investigate and how terribly nervous she would have been had she had to come alone.

Bobby was not much inclined to believe this. He did not think Miss Bellamy was at all the nervous type. His own impression of her was that she lived in a world apart, a world of deep and hidden emotion where "nerves" played the smallest of parts.

CHAPTER VII

COSTUME JEWELLERY

BOBBY WENT BACK to Fern Cottage in a thoughtful and a troubled mood. Odd, he told himself, that that wild chase and fierce and hot pursuit should have ended so near the new home he had secured through such odd good luck. Odd that the fugitive cyclist should have reminded him, though certainly in a somewhat vague and undefined way, of Biggs, Mr. Fielding's chauffeur, and still more odd that both cyclist and chauffeur should seem to have an odd, unconscious trick of tilting the head to one side at moments of tension or expectation. Even more odd that the fugitive should have seemed at first so oddly willing to draw attention to himself and later so indifferent to possible chances of escape. Finally, most odd that in the end he should have vanished so completely in the vicinity of Miss Bellamy's cottage. To what reality then, Bobby asked himself, were all these separate oddities related? Nor to that question could he even begin to imagine any reasonable answer. But he made up his mind to have a chat with Mr. Fielding about Biggs as soon as might be possible, and then he wondered if that would be altogether wise.

At Fern Cottage he found Olive saying good-bye to Miss Rhoda Rogers, who was on the point of returning home to look after her brother. He would, she explained, probably now be clamouring for his lunch. Rhoda was tall and fair haired, with a thin body and a thin, eager, attractive face, though hardly one that could be called pretty, for the features were large, too large for the small, peaked face, and of no classic regularity. Her eyes, though, were striking and unusual, very large and of a bright clear blue. In them seemed

concentrated a queer energy of attention on each passing incident, however trivial, as it came to her notice. As Miss
Bellamy, an older woman, appeared to live her own remote,
interior life, so Rhoda Rogers seemed to live intensely in
each separate moment as it came and went. An odd contrast,
Bobby thought, and was annoyed to find once more that
word 'odd' coming into his mind.

Bobby joined his thanks to those Olive was expressing
for the help given to that process known as 'settling down,'
and Rhoda said how glad she was to have new neighbours.

"The vicar's a widower," she remarked, "and Mr. Fielding's a bachelor, and Miss Bellamy's a musician, and
George, that's my brother, spends all his time swotting at his
books, and it will be nice to have someone to speak to sometimes. I'll try not to be a bore," she added laughing.

Olive, of course, made polite protests that Rhoda could
never bore. Rhoda departed, and Bobby and Olive returned
indoors where Olive wanted at once to set Bobby to work.
Bobby, however, explained, trying to sound disappointed,
that he must return to the Yard to report on his adventure and
supervise the routine steps that would now have to be set in
motion. Not of course, he admitted, that there would really
be very much for him to do. It was all so well prepared, kept
in such readiness for instant action, that everything possible
had certainly been seen to already. But reports would soon
be coming in and they would require attention.

He returned from the Yard fairly early however. Nothing
of interest had come in, though the Yard seemed fairly confident of being able to find out soon whether one of the three
gangs known to be engaged in smash-and-grab activities was
responsible for this one or whether it was a fresh lot. Bobby
himself did not think that likely. The whole affair seemed to
him to have been organized with a skill and care that suggested considerable experience. The gang known as the Burden Gang, from its leader's name, was the one he himself
suspected. Olive listened to his story, looked uneasy at his
somewhat sketchy account of his chase of the motor cyclist,
supposed gloomily that he wouldn't be satisfied till he had

broken his neck and what was the good of being a deputy assistant acting whatever he was in the Yard hierarchy, if he had to do things like that? Why couldn't he leave them to young constables and sergeants, who, no doubt, enjoyed that sort of thing, as, personally, she had no doubt Bobby did, too?

From this aspersion Bobby defended himself hotly; and Olive said he might talk as much as he liked but she knew better; and then went on to explain what she had been doing, and did Bobby approve of her arrangements—which of course he did—and to tell how grateful she was to Miss Bellamy and Miss Rogers for their help.

"Miss Rogers is awfully nice," Olive said. "She lives with her brother in the bungalow we noticed near the church. Bobby, do you know what I think? I believe her brother—his name's George—is in love with Miss Bellamy and that's why Miss Rogers struck me as rather making up to Miss Bellamy. Because really I don't think she likes her awfully. I don't know about Miss Bellamy because you can't. I mean, you can't tell much about her, can you?"

"Cook and musician," Bobby suggested. "Alpha plus at both."

"That's not her," Olive said. "That's only how she tells you what she is but you've got to find out for yourself what the 'what' is. I think Rhoda is rather frightened of her."

"Don't wonder," Bobby remarked. "Anyone would be."

"Mr. Fielding's in love with her, too," Olive said. "Perhaps it's George Rogers who is pushing them apart all the time they're being drawn to each other. But I don't think it's that, it's more than just that," she added, half to herself.

Bobby smiled. Women were like that, he thought tolerantly. No woman could ever see an eligible bachelor and an unattached spinster without deciding they must be in love with each other— and if they weren't, then the sooner they were made to be, the better. Well, thank goodness, his business was with law and order, with crime, and, taking it all round, crime was less complicated, less dangerous, and less

violent than love. Most certainly, too, much easier to understand. But Olive was speaking again. She said:

"Mr. Fielding called for a few minutes this morning on
his way to town. He wanted to know if he could do anything
for us. Miss Bellamy was here and he was watching her all
the time." Olive paused and said slowly: "I think in a way
she fascinates him."

"The boa constrictor and the rabbit?" Bobby asked
lightly and when Olive nodded he looked puzzled and asked
her what she meant.

But that was a question she couldn't answer because she
didn't know. Instead she said that Miss Rogers was rather
frightening, too, or could be. She had been in the A.T.S. during the war. She had been given a special mention or decoration or something for something she did out East—Olive
didn't know what, Miss Rogers hadn't said—and then she
had been sacked, as she put it, for chasing a senior officer
round with a gun. That, she had admitted to Olive, was
largely cocktails added to fatigue and no sleep, and probably
she would have been let off more lightly if she hadn't told
the court that the only thing she was sorry for was that she
had fired up in the air. Because the senior officer had been
really most offensive—fatigue and no sleep again, most
likely—and she, Rhoda Rogers, would have loved to use her
as a target.

"Rhoda says," Olive explained, "that she's a first-class
shot and took prizes out there and she could have shot all
round the senior officer and scared her awfully without really
hurting her."

"I hope she won't try tricks of that sort here," Bobby said
uneasily. "She seems as if she might be a formidable young
woman."

"I think she is, I think she might be," Olive admitted.
"But she's very nice. She knew Mr. Fielding's chauffeur out
there. I think he had something to do with whatever she got
her decoration for. He was waiting outside with the car and
Mr. Fielding called him in for something. I said to Rhoda
after they had gone what a dreadful scar it was on his face

and what a pity because he would be rather good-looking but for that, and she said he had been in Egypt, too, while she was there."

"Was he?" Bobby said. Another coincidence? But not very surprising. When so many have served abroad, no wonder they occasionally meet again when they get back home. He said: "It may have been only fancy, and, of course, you must keep it to yourself, but the motor cyclist I told you I went after did look rather like Biggs. I couldn't be certain, or anything like. He had goggles on and his cap pulled down and his collar turned up, but there was something about the way he held his head that made me think of Biggs at once. I may have been quite wrong, imagination very likely. I haven't said anything about it."

"You've only seen him that one time here, haven't you?" Olive remarked.

"That's all," Bobby agreed. "I expect it was only fancy. It came into my mind the moment I saw him and the way he seemed to be almost wanting me to notice him. Very likely it was only some chance resemblance."

"Could you see if he had a scar on his face?"

"No. He was on my left and it's his left cheek."

Olive said she expected it really was only fancy. Biggs was probably busy at the time driving his employer somewhere or another. And now it was time she saw about the dinner. Bobby, a little surprised, asked if there were any? What with food shortages and 'moving in' and changing the retail suppliers and all the rest of it, he hadn't very much expected more than bread and margarine. Olive explained that she had managed to get some fish, and, she added with mild triumph, it wasn't cod either. It seemed there was a man brought fish round nearly every week and this had happened to be the day he came. In a severe voice, Olive added that dinner was more than Bobby deserved, and a wonder he hadn't to cook it himself—and both he and she and the powers above knew what his cooking was like—considering how easily she might have had to leave everything and rush off to hospital where it was a wonder he wasn't after the way he had been risking life and limb chasing about after motor bikes and things.

Bobby protested meekly that he had run no undue risks. Just an exhilarating ride, he said. Olive said she knew what she knew and went off to get her cooking done. Afterwards, during the meal, she extracted from Bobby a more detailed account of his day's adventures. When he had finished, he said;

"Now, tell me—was it a pure accident it all ended here?"

"Must have been," protested Olive, but uneasily. "Why should anyone want to bring you back home?"

"I can't imagine," Bobby admitted. "But there it is. It does look as though that had been the idea and I've still a sort of feeling that the way we got this house looks less like luck than plan."

"Very nice plan," declared Olive appreciatively.

Bobby went on to tell the story of the raid as he had learned it now from the full reports received.

The objective had been a small but flourishing and well stocked jeweller's shop. The day before the raid an imposing limousine—probably the one reported that same morning as stolen from a street in Mayfair and later found abandoned—had driven up. A showily dressed woman alighted. She explained that a friend had promised to buy her a diamond ring. So would they please have a really good selection ready for her to choose from? She was quite frank about it all. She made it plain that she used the word 'friend' in the technical sense in which it is employed in the profession she so plainly adorned—an appropriate word, this last. She made it plain, too, that she meant to choose a really expensive ring. So would care be taken, please, to make sure that no ring in the selection to be shown should be worth less than £100. From that up to £250, she said, admitting reluctantly that her friend was not likely to go even as high as £250, and no use hoping he would stand for more. But she would like, you could never tell, a few other pieces of jewellery to be on show on the counter. A necklace or two, for instance, that she could pick up and admire. Perhaps a few really good wrist watches as well. Her friend, she explained, had pots of coin, and when in the mood he could be really generous. But one had to catch him in the mood. If there did happen to be, say, a £500 or £1,000 necklace lying about that she could pick up in a casual way and exclaim about, her friend might not say anything at the time and certainly she wouldn't. But he might remember, especially if she put the thing down with the remark that only someone really rich could afford such a costly article. To hold a man back, she had remarked confidentially to the jeweller, as one wise guy to another, was often the best way of making him want to go on. Men were like that, weren't they? Wanted managing.

Bobby paused in his narrative at this point to remark that very likely it was the apparent frankness of this invitation to the shopkeepen to become a partner in plucking the pigeon, that had helped to avert suspicion. At any rate on the appointed day everything had been in readiness. Two trays of diamond rings were on the counter—not one ring priced at less than £100. So was a collection of wrist watches and a pearl necklace that had been borrowed for the occasion from another firm on a sharing basis, since this establishment was not one where necklaces of that value were a part of the ordinary stock.

At first everything had gone well. The lady was the first to appear. She explained that her friend was to meet her there and she had wanted to make sure all was in order. The beauty of the necklace pleased her greatly but she shook her head sadly when she heard the price. She hardly thought, she said with a sigh, that her friend would be willing to pay as much as all that. Then she brightened up and said that one could always try. Men were funny and they did so love to show off. At this point she gave a delighted exclamation. There was a 'bus stop close by and she explained that her friend had just alighted from a 'bus and that this was a very good sign. He always went economical in pennies when he was preparing to spend pounds freely.

"Oh, dear, his cold's worse," she added as a man appeared in the doorway and paused, sneezing violently into his handkerchief. "I must find his tablets he asked me to get."

She had opened her handbag and was fumbling within. It was then things began to happen. The two men behind the counter each received from her a handful of red pepper full in the face. One of them was still able to make a grab for the trays of rings but was laid out by a blow on the jaw from a gentleman suddenly recovered from his fit of sneezing. Then he grabbed the trays of rings and wrist watches, and so departed, bearing his sheaves with him. Simultaneously the lady opened the door at the back of the shop and smashed a bottle of pure ammonia on the table where two startled men were busy. Next she picked up the 'phone, threw it out of the window, ran back into the shop, collected the necklace, and disappeared into the street, where at that moment a powerful motor car was slowly passing by. Her friend, the trays of rings and watches, were all already inside. She and the necklace followed. The car shot away and all was over—except the tumult and the shouting, of which there was a good deal, as those within the shop struggled with the effects of panic, pepper and pure ammonia.

To all this Olive listened with increasing gravity. When Bobby had finished his story, she said:

"They got away with a lot of rings, all worth at least £100?"

"Some worth a lot more, I believe," Bobby agreed. "Quite a good haul. Only now they've got to be turned into cash and that won't be very easy or very safe either."

"You remember Mrs. Gregson?" Olive asked.

"The woman you got in from the village to help?" Bobby asked. "Yes. Why? what about her?"

"She went to the village for me this afternoon. When she got back she was full of a story about a jeweller's travelling salesman. She said he had been at the Much Middles Arms, and he had had too much to drink, and he was showing handfuls of diamond rings—handfuls, Mrs. Gregson said. He was offering to sell them dirt cheap, worth £100 each at least and take a fiver, he said. Mrs. Gregson said no one wanted them.

They thought it was all imitation costume jewellery. I wonder if—"

"So do I," said Bobby. "So do I, very much indeed."

CHAPTER VIII

THE REAL THING

A SCOTLAND YARD EXECUTIVE has to be careful about giving any appearance of wishing to interfere outside his own Metropolitan police area. The Yard itself is very conscious, if the rest of the world is not, that it is only one among many local police forces, none of whom intend to put up with any meddling from any outside body. Even in London the Yard holds no complete dominion, for the City force is entirely independent. Bobby, therefore, though disturbed and worried by this tale of what it seemed might be the loot of the smash-and-grab raid displayed in the local public house, was in some doubt as to what to do, or even whether there was at the moment anything he could do usefully.

Another oddity, certainly, to add to all the others and perhaps the greatest oddity of all. For who has ever heard of a smash-and-grab raider the worse for drink or making a display of his booty in public immediately on the conclusion of the job. A cautious, disciplined, and temperate race while working, are smash-and-grab raiders. It simply didn't make sense, Bobby told himself.

The story appeared to be common property in the village so certainly the local police force, consisting of Constable Jonathan Taylor, would know of it, and would, of course, have at once informed his superiors. And they in their turn, would, no doubt, as a part of the ordinary routine, have already informed Scotland Yard of this new and puzzling development.

He decided finally as he helped Olive to wash up that he would stroll along to Middles, Mr. Fielding's residence, find out if Mr. Fielding knew anything of this spate of jewellery

in the Much Middles Arms, and take an opportunity to say
half-jokingly and wholly confidentially, that the fugitive motor cyclist who had evaded him so successfully had been
oddly reminiscent of Mr. Fielding's chauffeur. It might then
appear whether or no Biggs had a completely satisfactory
alibi. If so Bobby decided he could then dismiss the supposed resemblance as imaginary or merely coincidental. As,
he felt, most likely it was. Afterwards he would go to the village, possibly look in for a drink at the Much Middles Arms
and then try to find Constable Taylor in case he had anything
to say and was willing to say it. Almost certainly, too, a sergeant or inspector of the county force would be appearing
soon for further inquiry into this queer tale of the man of too
many drinks and too many valuable pieces of jewellery. In
which case, a chat seemed indicated and might be useful.

He announced this decision to Olive, who, stopping him
just in time from putting the very, very best china on the
scullery shelf, sighed resignedly, and remarked that she supposed it was no use saying anything about the piano that
wanted moving, because the men had put it in the wrong
room, or about the pictures that wanted hanging, or the din-
ing-room carpet that wanted laying, or the curtains that—and
Bobby was only able to check the list by promising faithfully
to get up at five next morning to help. Therewith he departed
and on arrival at Middles, a comfortable-looking, medium-
sized house in the Queen Anne style, was at once hailed by a
beaming Mr. Fielding who seemed to be pottering about his
large and well-kept garden, pulling up a weed here or tying
up a shrub or a plant there.

"I was just thinking of toddling along," he explained, "to
see how you and your good lady were getting on. Getting
settled?"

"Chaos subsiding slowly into order," Bobby said and
added sadly: "I expect as soon as it's all over, spring cleaning or something will begin."

Mr. Fielding offered a grave masculine sympathy, and
Bobby said what a lovely garden Mr. Fielding had, and Mr.
Fielding beamed afresh and insisted on taking Bobby round.

There was a rosary, a rock garden, a kitchen garden, a small orchard, in which last stood an air raid shelter in course of demolition.

"An eye-sore," declared Mr. Fielding severely. "I want to get rid of it. Not too easy. An eyesore, a funk hole. I'm beginning to be a little ashamed of it."

"Good Lord, why?" Bobby asked. "It's only silly to run unnecessary risks."

"Well, yes, I suppose so," agreed Mr. Fielding. "All the same, I shall be glad to get rid of the thing."

Bobby remarked casually that that would take some doing. It had been solidly built; and Mr. Fielding observed that the workman from the village engaged for the job seemed to be of the same opinion, for he had not been near for two or three days. The north end of the erection, which was oblong in shape, had been nearly levelled however, and demolition had begun on the two side walls, though only to a slight extent on the west wall. The resulting debris was being used to fill up the interior. At the southern end the wall was still intact. The two men turned away, and as they were walking back to the house Bobby said he wondered how, when help was so difficult to get, Mr. Fielding managed to keep so large a garden in such good order. It looked like a full time job for one or two men.

"Oh, we all take a hand," Mr. Fielding explained with his jolly laugh. "Biggs—that's my chauffeur, you know, you've seen him—and me—and sometimes I think it's all me—and now and again as a great favour someone from the village. Even Mrs. Hands joins in. She's my housekeeper, an excellent woman though she's getting on. Nearly seventy and as brisk as any seventeen. She's quite keen. Biggs isn't. He does it when he's asked, but that's all. His idea of a garden would be one growing spanners and plugs. Not like the man I had before him. He was a really good gardener and I was sorry to lose him. Cann was his name, Alf Cann. He went off at a day's notice, and I never knew why. I hear he is back in the village now, so the game-keepers round here will have to pull up their socks again. I'm afraid he was a bit of a

poacher. Sort of spare time job with him. Nothing but suspicion, of course, and I wasn't going to get rid of him merely
on suspicion. I can't have him back in his old job, though, if
that's what he wants. No reason to sack Biggs. Good driver,
knows his job, and I should make myself very unpopular
with the darts team at the local. I'm told he's about their best
man. Ever play?"

Bobby said very occasionally and anyhow he wasn't
much good at it. He asked casually if Mr. Fielding had heard
the queer story about the visitor to the Much Middles Arms
who had been offering apparently valuable jewellery at almost 'giving away' prices?

Mr. Fielding said he had heard something of the sort.
Mrs. Hands had been in the village and had picked up a story
about a pedlar who had been trying to sell artificial jewellery
at prices no one wanted to pay. He had offered what he
called a lovely real opal for ten pounds, and who was going
to give that much for sham stuff not worth as many shillings?
Finally, Mr. Sadler, the landlord, had told him to clear out as
he was making a nuisance of himself. At the time Mr. Fielding had not paid the story much attention. No doubt the man
had had too much to drink, but then to-day even artificial,
now 'costume' jewellery was fetching absurd prices. But he
looked grave and troubled when Bobby told him the story of
the smash-and-grab raid in town and of the pursuit of the
motor cyclist who had finally disappeared near Miss
Bellamy's cottage.

"Miss Bellamy was out at the time," Bobby explained,
"so I got her to come back with me for a look round her
place in case the fellow was hiding there."

"He wasn't, was he?" Mr. Fielding asked anxiously.

"Not a sign," Bobby answered. "I made sure of that," but
Mr. Fielding still looked worried and anxious.

"Very queer," he said, half to himself, half to Bobby.
"Very queer. I don't think I like it. I think I'll toddle down
and see if she's all right."

"Oh, I think she is," Bobby said. "We had a good look
round. By the way, the motor cyclist fellow reminded me

somehow of your man, Biggs. Not that I ever saw his face clearly. He was wearing goggles for one thing. It was just something about his build and a trick he had of turning his head sideways. I wonder if your man has a brother?"

Mr. Fielding had no idea. All he could say was that he had never heard of one. He was clearly very interested, more than interested indeed. Intent and excited. His whole expression had changed, even his way of holding himself had altered, had changed from an easy carelessness to a tensity of poise like that of the sprinter waiting for the starter's word. Gone, too, like a dropped mask, was his former air of good humour and bonhomie. Vanished, the almost childlike trustfulness of his candid eyes and cheery smile, his general manner of happy, friendly confidence. The eyes had grown small and bleak, the mouth tight closed, the whole expression watchful, hard and dominating. All of us have two or three or more different personalities, but never had Bobby seen a swifter transformation than that of the jolly, friendly Mr. Fielding he had known before, beaming like a happy child upon a friendly world, to this of an Ishmael whose hand was against every man as every man's hand was against him. It was like an instant change from dove to vulture.

Next moment the former friendly beaming smile was back. No trace of the vulture now, only the dove all peace and gentleness and good will. But Bobby knew, and did not forget, that behind that happy, jolly façade lay a strong and formidable self, one that, he supposed, accounted for the success Fielding had apparently achieved in that jungle without pity or scruple wherein the city of London speculators match themselves against each other and against fate.

"You gave me a shock for the moment," Fielding was saying now with his jolly laugh. "I have been a bit worried about Biggs at times, things I noticed, little things. I hardly know what they were but I was beginning to wonder if I had been quite wise in taking him on without references. But I was in a bit of a hole with Cann leaving me so suddenly and then that scar! You felt he had done his bit in the war. And I can generally trust my judgment. All the same I was getting to feel that he wasn't quite open, something he was holding back, a hidden man, not candid, not frank. It's what I value more than anything else—candour, complete frankness, everything open and above board," and he paused to look up at Bobby with a childlike certainty of sympathy and understanding. He went on: "Gave me quite a shock when you said that about Biggs. For the moment I wondered. Then I remembered. He drove me to Reading. I had to see a man there about a business deal. An old pal of mine who has got into difficulties and needed a little ready cash to tide him over. Not much, a couple of thousand. It'll pay me all right in the end as I told him when he began to get sentimental, poor chap. So whoever it was you saw, it couldn't be Biggs unless he's like the Irishman's bird and can be in two places at once." Mr. Fielding stopped to laugh at this remembered jest and then looked very grave and shook his head in self-reproach. "A lesson to me," he admitted, "to think ill of no man. Really, I shall feel quite uncomfortable next time I see Biggs."

Bobby said he hardly thought Mr. Fielding need feel like that, though it was very nice of him, of course, and Mr. Fielding said seriously that in his experience it was always better to think the best of everyone—best and generally right as well. Bobby said he was afraid that wouldn't always work out very well in his job; and after a little more talk, during which Mr. Fielding mentioned that Biggs had gone off for the evening and would probably be at the Much Middles Arms, playing darts, he and Bobby parted. Mr. Fielding "toddled off," as he expressed it, to call on Miss Bellamy and assure himself she wasn't feeling nervous. If she seemed so, he told Bobby, he would ask Mrs. Hands to spend the night with her. Bobby, for his part, made his way to the village where he went first to the cottage that served both as the Much Middles police station and as Constable Taylor's residence. At this time Constable Taylor had generally relaxed into shirt sleeves and domesticity, but to-day he was still evidently considering himself on duty and he was hovering near the telephone in a way that clearly indicated an expected call.

Even though he knew Bobby's identity Taylor seemed at first reluctant to talk, but he admitted that he was expecting a message to say when the head of the county C.I.D. would arrive.

"I suppose then," Bobby remarked, "you are taking seriously this story about the jeweller's traveller and the diamond rings he was trying to sell?"

"Well, sir," Taylor answered, though still with a touch of hesitation in his manner, "seeing it's you, I suppose there's no harm in saying, but I haven't said a word and told special not to when I rang up to report, even though at first I didn't reckon it amounted to much—just one of those travelling salesmen and cheap stuff he wanted to get rid of, I thought. But there's nothing cheap about that"—and as he spoke he opened a drawer of his desk and took out a lovely opal ring, as fine a stone as Bobby had ever seen. "That's the real thing," he declared. "Wouldn't you say so, sir?"

Bobby agreed. He had picked up some slight knowledge of jewellery during his varied career and at a rough estimate he was inclined to put its value as well over £200. And the supposed travelling salesman was said to have offered it in the bar of the Much Middles Arms for £10. A sum that apparently no one had been willing to pay because they had all taken this lovely shining stone for a worthless imitation. It seemed to Bobby that everything was becoming more and more incredible and contradictory.

"Where did you get it?" he asked.

"Vicar picked it up this evening, round about seven," Taylor answered. "Just inside the drive at Middles."

"Middles? Mr. Fielding's place?" Bobby asked.

"That's right, sir, and just as well it was Vicar saw it there, for there's some in this village I wouldn't have trusted not to pocket it and say nothing. But Vicar brought it straight along; just inside the drive gate it was, shining like the full moon, Vicar said."

CHAPTER IX

SUPERINTENDENT BELL

BOBBY WENT BACK home feeling more puzzled than ever, and more convinced than ever that some strange, complex plan was being worked out to a conclusion that he felt might well be tragic.

For in all this that was happening he seemed to see a dark and sombre threat, a hidden menace that was, he felt, beyond and different from any mere tale of theft and robbery.

Obviously the first thing to do was to try to trace the travelling salesman, as he had called himself. But that was a job for the county C.I.D., and no doubt they would do their best. No easy task though, for by now, the fellow was very likely back in the east end of London, that human warren, the best of all possible hiding places. Only in that case, how had this opal ring come to be where it was found? Difficult to believe it could have been lying there long, shining like the full moon, or so the vicar said. And why was it there, just within the Middles drive? Had it been dropped accidentally by someone on the way to the house? If so, did that again point to Biggs, the chauffeur, as being in some way concerned?

Bobby had intended to pay a visit to the Much Middles Arms, the one public house in the village. But by now it was late and closing time. As he passed a stream of customers was issuing from the inn, some walking away, others lingering to discuss what had apparently been an exciting and hotly contested darts match. Bobby noticed that Biggs was there, in the middle of one of the groups. He was holding forth with great vigour and decision on some aspect of the game in which seemingly he had been taking a leading part.

One or two of the men looked at Bobby curiously as he went by, and one or two wished him good night; for his identity was already known and his arrival in the village and occupation of Fern Cottage had caused a good deal of talk and mild excitement. Bobby responded pleasantly to these greetings and went on his way home, there to find Olive as busy as ever.

"Nothing useful I can do," he told her, looking very depressed. "I'm out of it. I can't interfere here, and at the Yard we shall just have to wait and see what reports come in. There may be something in the morning."

"Well, we had better get to bed," Olive suggested. "If you are getting up at five—"

"Getting up at five? Me?" protested Bobby, appalled. "What for?"

"To get on with hanging those pictures," said Olive, relentless and stern. "That'll be something useful."

And it was so. Even Olive admitted that he had put in a good early morning job when she came to tell him breakfast was ready. He was busy doing it justice and nursing an injured thumbnail he had confused with another sort of nail when the 'phone rang with a message that Superintendent Bell, head of the county C.I.D., was on his way to the village and would like to have a talk with Mr. Owen, if convenient. Bobby, secretly very pleased, answered that it would be quite convenient. It seemed a puzzling affair and he would be very glad to know what Mr. Bell thought of it.

Years before, when Bobby had been newly posted to the detective branch he had known Bell, then a sergeant not very highly thought of by his superiors and with apparently small prospect of ever achieving promotion. A sensational case, however, brought to a successful conclusion, had attracted attention to him and earned him an inspectorship. Since then his rise in the service had been rapid, culminating in a recent appointment as superintendent in charge of the county C.I.D., though without in any way alleviating his congenital melancholy. But he had acquired a certain air of authority; and if he still gave a general impression of expecting some disaster he knew he was helpless to avert, he nevertheless managed to produce very successful results.

Breakfast was over and Bobby, unable to think of any excuse for delay or avoidance, was perched on the top of a rickety step-ladder, making measurements alleged to be required anent the hanging of curtains, when Bell drove up. Bobby, descending, told Olive how sorry he was to have to leave the measuring unfinished, and Olive said that was all right. She would get on with something else, leaving the curtain question till he had more time to spare. Bobby said in a dispirited way that that was a good idea, wasn't it? and went to find Bell.

They began by a few reminiscences of old days at the Yard and Bell offered his congratulations on Bobby's recent return there. Bobby remarked that Bell, too, had risen considerably in rank, and Bell admitted that that was so, but observed that rockets that went up in a hurry came down more quickly still, nor had he any such record behind him as had Bobby. It was the war, he said, that had jockeyed him into his present job while better men were being killed or maimed all over the world—and would be again before long, judging from the present state of international affairs.

After these preliminaries they settled down to a discussion of recent events, going over the whole story again and in every detail.

"I have the feeling myself," Bobby said, "that all this is only a preliminary, that it is all leading up to something that has been very carefully planned."

Bell nodded.

"Something pretty bad," he said slowly—it would be unfair to say with relish, but certainly with conviction.

Indeed both men felt that so much careful planning, combined with such apparent recklessness as the display of what was apparently the stolen jewellery in public and the manner in which the motor cyclist had behaved, all pointed to some intended development whose nature they could not even guess at but which intuitively they felt was likely to be grim.

"We can't even be sure," Bobby said, "that it centres here. All this may be a sort of red herring, though I don't think so. Do you know anything about Mr. Fielding?"

Bell, consulting some notes he had, said that Fielding had bought the house known as Middles four or five years before the second German war. After the usual interval of suspicion and hostility that is the lot of every newcomer in an English village, he had been accepted as one of the community and was now well liked and much respected. He subscribed liberally to all village funds. He took part in all local activities and was always friendly and amiable, a peacemaker when squabbles and small rivalries broke out, as they always do when human beings meet together. He was a good churchman, and, though he was thought to be a somewhat exacting employer, he paid good wages. The village had been surprised when his former chauffeur, the man named Cann, Alf Cann, of whom Mr. Fielding had made casual mention to Bobby, left without apparent cause. Gossip had resulted but had soon died down for lack of fuel.

"I understand Cann has turned up again," Bobby remarked.

"So Taylor tells me," Bell said, consulting his notebook. "Staying with his aunt, Miss Cann. She keeps a small shop. Sweets and odds and ends generally. Provides teas as well. I think I'll try to have a chat with Cann. Nothing in it probably, but he does happen to turn up again just now after leaving suddenly."

Bobby remarked that he, too, had arrived in the village just as all these unexpected things began to happen. He and his wife had thought it a wonderful stroke of luck to find a vacant house so convenient in every way as Fern Cottage. At a very moderate rent, too. Did Bell know who had lived there before? Bell, once more referring to his notes—he seemed to have compiled that morning a complete 'Who's Who' of Much Middles—said it had been a Mr. James, a rubber planter, now on his way back to the Far East. The village people had expected that the next occupant of Fern Cottage would be Miss Bellamy, preparatory to the announcement of her engagement to Mr. Fielding. For that the pair of them would, sooner or later, get married was the general conviction. It was obvious that Mr. Fielding could not keep away from her, and though Miss Bellamy seemed so entirely wrapped up in her music—of which the village had a poor opinion— it was taken for granted that his persistence would in the end be rewarded. After all, she did nothing actively to discourage him, though she did show some tendency to keep him at arm's length. It was an attitude generally approved. Even to-day, still the man's business to make the running. Because in spite of all modern progress and the rate for the job and all the rest of it— including slacks—men and women still remain men and women and probably always will.

All the same it had been a surprise when Fern Cottage was let to a newcomer and Miss Bellamy remained in her extremely inconvenient cottage to which only a very few modern amenities had been added. She had arrived a year or two after the outbreak of the war when the elderly London lady who had occupied the cottage to escape the threatened air raids, and who had had made a few necessary alterations to render it more habitable, had decided it would be wiser to go further afield. And Mr. Fielding had almost immediately on Miss Bellamy's arrival begun to pay her marked attention.

"Near her cottage the chap you were chasing disappeared, wasn't it?" Bell remarked thoughtfully. "I take it the likeness you thought you saw to Fielding's chauffeur can't have meant anything?"

"Mr. Fielding provides a complete alibi. Biggs was driving him to Reading," Bobby answered. "I did wonder if Biggs had a brother or anything like that. It was the way he cocked his head to one side that I noticed as much as anything. Just possible they had been pals in the army and caught the trick from each other."

"Possible," agreed Bell. "Or the cyclist bloke may have made up deliberately to look like Biggs. Just to muddle things up." He paused and looked resentful. "Sort of thing they would do," he complained. "Making it difficult."

"That would show," Bobby remarked, "that Biggs was known to them. Gives a bit of a starting point."

"We shall have to see if Biggs can suggest anything," Bell said. "Looks as if it might be an attempt to compromise him, so he ought to be willing enough to help."

There was a knock at the door. It was a sergeant of the county police, one of the helpers Bell had brought with him. To this man had been assigned the task of trying to trace the travelling salesman's movements after he had been more or less ejected from the Much Middles Arms. The sergeant had ascertained that he had been seen to leave the village on his pedal bicycle, taking the London Road, but must have returned, since later he had appeared at Miss Cann's, asking to be served with tea. After that he had been seen sitting by the roadside near Middles. That was about an hour before the discovery of the opal ring. Nothing had so far been learned of his subsequent movements.

The sergeant also reported that headquarters had rung up to say that the opal ring, sent by special messenger to London the night before, had now been identified as one of those stolen in the smash-and-grab raid. Its value was put as somewhere about £250. The jeweller, told that it had been offered in vain in a public house for £10, had expressed horrified amazement and had refused to believe it. No one, he protested, could possibly have failed to recognize the ring's value, and indeed its finder, the vicar, had described it as shining like the full moon.

"It's a point to remember," Bobby observed, and Bell nodded and looked thoughtful; but the sergeant opined that there were plenty who wouldn't be able to tell the difference between the crown jewels and Woolworth stuff.

Then he departed to make further inquiries and Bell said he thought he would try first to have a chat with Cann, the former, and then with Biggs, the present, chauffeur at Middles, and would Bobby like to come with him, if he could spare the time? Bobby accepted with alacrity and a gratitude he strove not to make effusive. But he did feel as if he could not have borne it if the county police had shown any disposition to push him out of an investigation in what seemed as bewildering and strange an affair as he had ever known, one that he still felt was likely to develop still more strangely and perhaps more tragically.

Bell's car was outside. In it they drove down the lane and Bobby, as they reached Miss Bellamy's cottage, showed where the escaping motor cyclist had left the copse higher up in the fields behind and then had vanished near here.

"Can't imagine what became of him," Bobby said. "It's all open field here and yet he seems to have vanished completely."

Bell had brought the car to a halt while Bobby talked and now abruptly there came a burst of music from the cottage, roaring out through the open window in great waves of passionate, angry sound. The two men listened. Indeed the music was so clamorous in its demand on their attention they had no other thought. It changed from its loud anger and thunderous menace into what seemed like an equally passionate protest, an appeal for a mercy and for a help there was no hope would be granted, a wild and anguished cry as it seemed against the cruelty of destiny, an appeal against a doom felt nevertheless to be inevitable. It changed again. Now it was not lament, not protest, but merely a faint unhappy crying in the dark, as of a lost child, or of one knowing himself abandoned for ever. It died away, and yet even the silence that followed seemed vibrant with a feeble, protestant despair.

"Ended with a whimper, not with a bang," Bobby said, half jestingly, trying to shake off an impression he did not fully understand.

"Kind of shook you up, didn't it?" Bell said. "Gripped you in a way. What was it, do you think?"

"No idea," Bobby answered. "I expect she would say she was only talking to herself. That's what she told us once."

"Talking to herself?" Bell repeated. "I saw a woman at the window just before it started." He paused, "Perhaps not to herself but to us."

"If she was, what was she saying?" Bobby asked.

But that was a question to which there was no answer.

CHAPTER X

MURDER BEGUN

MISS CANN PROVED to be an elderly woman with a thin, intelligent, slightly discontented face; a woman, Bobby guessed, who felt that circumstances had deprived her of opportunities of which she believed, had they come to her, she would have been able to make good use. To the questions her two visitors put to her she replied warily, evidently suspicious of where her answers might lead her, but it soon became plain that she had in fact little information to give. She had paid no special attention to her customer of the previous day. He had asked for tea, he had been served, he had paid and departed. Her nephew was out. He had had his breakfast and then had gone out without saying where or when he would be back. Looking for a job, she hoped, since he had lost the one with Mr. Fielding he had been fool enough to throw up. She added that she had sat up late talking to her nephew the previous night. They had not gone to bed till after twelve.

"And one o'clock before he got there," she added, "the way he was fiddling about."

The remark puzzled both Bobby and his companion. It sounded like an attempt to establish an alibi, and yet there seemed no reason why an alibi should he needed for that time of night. It was, however, easy to see that Miss Cann's attitude towards her nephew was strongly protective as against the rest of the world and equally strongly disapproving as regarded himself. His sudden arrival and announcement that he had lost his new job had not been welcome, but Bell's suggestion that perhaps he owed Biggs a grudge for having supplanted him, brought a sharp retort.

"Why should he?" she demanded, "seeing he left on his own? Mr. Biggs had nothing to do with it and if you've been hearing anything about them having a fight, it's a lie. It wasn't Alf at all, it was that young Rogers at the bungalow near the church, and serve him right if he got the worst of it, and so I told that sister of his. Them as call themselves gentlemen have no call to go round fighting and such, like the riff-raff of a Saturday night."

Evidently Miss Cann's sense of the social proprieties had been outraged by the idea of a 'gentleman' engaging in fisti-cuffs with a chauffeur. Bobby was inclined to guess that she upheld the social conventions and barriers the more strongly because in her youth they had been so much stronger and she had been unable to break through them. No reason therefore why others should escape or ignore what had hampered her own development so grievously.

Bell said:

"What was the fight about?"

Miss Cann said she wasn't one to gossip. Bobby intervened to remark that both he and his friend had noticed that at once, indeed Constable Taylor had told them as much. He had also told them that Miss Cann let nothing escape her but never said a word. This mendacious statement produced a considerable improvement in the social atmosphere. Presently it came out that the cause of the quarrel was that young Rogers was sweet on Miss Bellamy and had discovered that Biggs visited her late at night.

Bobby expressed polite incredulity on both counts. Miss Bellamy was much older than Mr. Rogers and much superior in social standing to Biggs. Miss Cann retorted that Miss Bellamy wasn't as old as all that and anyhow age had nothing to do with it, and that she herself had seen Biggs entering Miss Bellamy's cottage at a late hour.

"But I thought," Bobby put in, "that most people round here believed Miss Bellamy and Mr. Fielding were likely to get engaged soon. Hasn't he made it pretty plain that he's in love with her?"

"Not him, he's afraid of her," Miss Cann retorted.

Bobby asked her what made her think that but she refused to say more. Evidently she felt that already she might have said too much and she began to be busy, unnecessarily re-arranging shelves behind the counter and inventing errands to take her into the back regions of the shop. But one cryptic remark she did throw over her shoulder just before the last of these disappearances.

"If you want to know more about Miss Bellamy," she said, "listen to her playing when she doesn't know anyone's there. That'll tell you."

But she refused to say more or to explain herself; and, as it was plainly useless to prolong the interview, the two men returned to their waiting car. As they settled themselves in it, Bobby remarked: "Odd she should say that about Fielding being scared of Miss Bellamy. My wife said almost the same thing the first time we saw them together."

"Being in love and being scared out of your life are much the same," observed Bell wisely. "What do you think she meant by that about Miss Bellamy? How in blazes can hearing her play the piano tell anyone anything?"

"I don't know," Bobby answered, and would have rubbed the end of his nose in perplexity had not severe domestic criticism cured him of the habit—almost. "Somehow," he went on slowly, "I've got an odd sort of feeling that in Miss Bellamy's music is the explanation of everything."

"Oh, Lord," said Bell, and had an air of being about to cry. "That about puts the lid on it. Wasn't it all mixed up badly enough before," he asked reproachfully, "without dragging music in?" As Bobby made no effort to reply to this question, he went on: "I think it's pretty clear though that this man, Cann, comes into it somehow."

"Or else it's just that his aunt is afraid he does," Bobby said. "It's certainly odd, suspicious, too, that she was so anxious to tell us he was with her till after twelve and she heard him moving about till much later. I can't see any connection at present."

"She may have wanted to make us understand he didn't go visiting the Bellamy woman late at night," Bell suggested.

"Might be that," agreed Bobby. "So perhaps she knows he has at other times and there really is ill-feeling between him and Biggs because of that. Do you know anything about the Rogers brother and sister, she talked about? I've met the sister. She came in to see if she could help us settle down. An attractive girl— of many possibilities I should say."

Bell stopped the car and consulted his notebook.

"That's right," he said. "Lots of possibilities. Father a vicar in the East End. Killed in one of the air raids. She was injured at the same time, but not badly, recovered, joined the A.T.S., served in the Middle East. She was given a decoration for saving important secret documents from Egyptians in German pay. She found them making off with the papers on forged authority. When she challenged them, they tried to knife her. She opened up with a tommy gun and killed two. Later on she got into trouble. She was court martialled for insubordinate conduct, including threatening a senior officer with a revolver. She had to resign and there seems to have been a general idea that there was something behind, or she would have got off more easily. Natural for her to be in a state of nerves after what had happened. That was the line the defence took; and it seemed rather hard to throw her out after her saving papers it would have been pretty serious for the enemy to get hold of. The general idea was that she ought to have been let off with a reprimand and six months' leave."

"Rather an interesting story," Bobby said thoughtfully. "You can understand her brooding on the killing of the two men, but if she got chasing other people round with revolvers, I suppose it did rather look as if she might be going to make a habit of it. I suppose that's what the court martial thought. What about the brother?"

"Pacifist. Conscientious objector," Bell said. "Never trust conscientious objectors myself—they're so conscientious you never know what they'll be up to next. Cut your throat as soon as look at you if their conscience works that way."

"Not so much of a pacifist," Bobby observed, "if it's true about the Biggs fight."

"Pacifists," Bell reminded him, "are the most belligerent and quarrelsome lot going. It's only their country they don't want to fight for—anything else and their coats are off in a minute."

"Yes, I know," Bobby agreed. "What did this chap do during the war?"

"Oh, work of national importance—on a farm. I believe he asked for a guarantee that none of the food he helped to produce should go to the army, but he gave that idea up. Now he's working for some examination or another. Very bitter about it all. Says his career has been set back for years. What about having a look at him? It might be as well to check up on Miss Cann's story. She may have invented it to put us off her nephew."

"Good idea," Bobby approved. "Miss Cann is on her nephew's side first of all. After that I'm not so sure. But in any case I don't think she's negligible."

The Rogers bungalow was on their way and distant only a few minutes' drive. They alighted there, but to Bell's knock there was no response. Bell knocked again and waited. Bobby strolled along the gravelled path that ran by the side of the bungalow to the garden in the rear, and came back to the patiently waiting Bell.

"He's there all right," Bobby said. "You can see him sitting writing. Working for his exam most likely and doesn't want to be interrupted."

"It's always," said Bell with melancholy sympathy, "what we don't want that's sure to happen. My experience anyhow."

He went down the path to the window Bobby had indicated and looked in. Rogers heard him and glared back. He was a short, dark, thick-set young man, with a Hitler moustache he had affected because he had hoped it would be unpopular, and with a certain nervous and strained expression that reminded Bobby of his sister. He showed no indication of taking any notice of Bell beyond his baleful glare. Bell tapped again, and then a third time and more loudly. Rogers rushed to the window and threw it open.

"Get out," he shouted. "Can't you see I'm busy? Clear out or I'll knock your head off."

"Police," said Bell.

"I don't like police," said Rogers.

He tried to close the window. Bell held it open. Rogers tried again and managed to trap his finger. He used language unbecoming to a conscientious objector. Bell said, sadly acquiescent:

"Lots of people don't like us."

From behind Bobby said:

"It's why we are. If everyone liked us we should fade away. Services no longer required, as they say when they give you the sack."

Rogers transferred to Bobby that baleful glare of his.

"I suppose you think that's clever?" he snapped.

"Good gracious, no," said Bobby, shocked.

"Well, now, you've ruined my morning's work, what do you want?" demanded Rogers, just a trifle less belligerently.

"Smash-and-grab raid in London," Bell said. "Alleged participants traced to this locality. Alleged seen near here. Alleged stolen property seen. Can you give us any information?"

"No. I can't. I saw the stuff l suppose you mean. Fellow was showing it off in the pub. Cheap stuff, most of it, not worth tuppence. Not at all what smash-and-grab raiders go for I should think."

"Are you sure?" Bell asked.

"I've got eyes in my head."

"One ring has been identified as valuable and as part of what was stolen." Rogers shrugged his shoulders.

"I don't know anything about that," he said. "In my opinion, what I saw wasn't worth anything. That's all I can tell you. Now will you please go away. I've got some work to do and it happens to be important. It's been hampered enough already by people like you."

"Sorry about that," said Bell amiably. "Most unfortunate.

Quite a lot of things have been interfered with these last few years. One thing more. We have information that there was a fight between you and a man named Biggs. If that's true, it may have some bearing on our inquiries. Will you confirm or deny?"

"No, I won't," snapped Rogers and banged the window to, though this time with more regard for the exact position of his fingers.

"Nice pleasant-spoken young gentleman," observed Bell.

Bobby was still looking through the window. Rogers shook a fierce and angry fist at him. Bobby turned away and remarked:

"I think it's true."

"What is?"

"About the fight."

"Why?" asked Bell. "Miss Cann said he got the worst of it and his face isn't marked."

"No," agreed Bobby, "but I noticed there's a pillow, not a cushion, a pillow, on his chair, and when he sat down again he did so with care and precaution. I imagine a medical examination would reveal extensive bruises, probably inflicted by a boot. Besides, if it hadn't been true, he would have said so."

They went back to their car. As Bell was preparing to start, he said:

"We had better try to get a chat with Biggs and his boss, too. I think Mr. Fielding will have to be told that a part of the stolen property has been found on his premises."

Bobby was inclined to think that in Bell's place he would prefer to keep that piece of information to himself a little longer. But he was not in charge of the inquiry and the decision was not in his hands. They turned into the road that led from the village to Middles and almost at once overtook the local constable, Taylor, pedalling for dear life. When he saw who was coming he jumped down and signalled furiously. They drew up and he ran to the side of the car.

"Just been rung up from Middles," he said. "Dead man found."

CHAPTER XI

DUD STUFF

BOTH BOBBY AND his companion were conscious that it was some such development as this that they had been expecting —or, if expecting is too strong a word, that in a way they had been prepared for. The old saying that coming events cast their shadow before seemed now to be justified in the vague impression of approaching danger and present menace of which they had both been recently aware.

To the excited, breathless Taylor, Bell said;

"Try to find—" he named his two assistants he had brought with him that morning. "Tell them to drop everything else and report at once to me at Middles. Ring up H.Q. first, though, and ask for more help. Then go on duty at Middles, at the entrance to the drive. Don't let anyone through except our own men on duty. We don't want all the neighbours milling round. Understand?"

A crestfallen Taylor saluted and said he did. Hard luck to be warned off like this, kept away from such an exciting, sensational affair. With only a modicum of luck he might easily have been first on the spot and perhaps have had the murderer under arrest by now. Glory and promotion missed by minutes! Just like the high-ups to keep all the chances to themselves. As it was, he didn't even know who the dead man was—Mr. Fielding, Biggs, one of the neighbours, a stranger? Mr. Fielding he expected. In his secret heart, he rather hoped so. Quite without malice. But if so, everything would become all the more exciting and thrilling.

It was the same question, whether the dead man would turn out to be Mr. Fielding himself, Biggs, or someone else, that was in the minds of both men in the car. It was soon answered, though, for as they swung into the short Middles drive they saw Mr. Fielding himself hurrying towards them. He was wearing the old raincoat it was his habit to put on when gardening, or doing any odd job, in order to protect his other clothes. Bell stopped the car. Mr. Fielding ran up.

"Thank God you've come, Owen," he panted. "You've heard? I rang up. I've been looking for Biggs. I can't find him. I wanted to send him for help. I've called Dr. Stevens. I can't think what's become of Biggs. Mrs. Hands is in hysterics. It's awful, awful," he repeated, mopping his brow, and indeed he looked distraught, his chubby cheeks like chalk, his mouth quivering, his big child-like eyes full of wonder and terror. He dabbed at his face with one of the nice clean handkerchiefs just returned from the laundry and thrust it back into the pocket of his deplorable old raincoat. "Awful," he repeated. "I couldn't believe it. I stood there staring. I thought I was going to faint."

"Who is it?" Bell asked.

"I don't know. No one I ever saw before. He's just lying there."

"Could it be suicide or does it look like murder?" Bell asked.

"I don't know. I've no idea. Shot dead. I didn't stop to look. Shot three times. To make sure, I suppose." He laughed hysterically. "I thought I had better get help. I rang up Taylor. He said something about informing his chief. I suppose he told you, Owen," Fielding added, speaking directly to Bobby. "Thank God you are here to look after things."

He was evidently taking it for granted that Bobby was the responsible officer and would conduct the ease. Bobby said:

"This is Superintendent Bell of the county police. He will be in charge. By good luck, Mr. Bell happened to be here this morning."

"Where is the body?" Bell asked.

"In the air raid shelter."

"The air raid shelter?"

"That's right. We've suspected sometimes tramps used it

for sleeping in. One reason why I wanted it pulled down."

"Is it a tramp, do you think?"

"I don't think so. I don't know. I didn't stop to look. I felt I might be sick and I wanted to get help. I can't think what's become of Biggs. I haven't seen him since last night just before I went to bed. I told him I shouldn't want him this morning and he said he would give the car a look over. Said it needed it. Now I can't find him anywhere and Mrs. Hands is in hysterics. I've had to do everything myself—everything."

"Who found the body?"

"It was the dog barking," Fielding explained. "Mrs. Hands heard it. She went to see what was the matter. She thought perhaps it was a tramp and she had better send him away. The dog was near the air raid shelter, howling. Mrs. Hands took a look and bolted back to the house. I don't blame her. I didn't believe it at first. I thought it must be some drunk or someone sleeping out. I went to look. It was an awful shock." He paused again to dab at his perspiring face. "An awful shock," he repeated.

"I'm sure it would be," Bobby murmured sympathetically.

"Where is the air raid shelter?" Bell asked.

"In the orchard, at the back of the house," explained Bobby. "Mr. Fielding showed it me the other day."

"You won't want me?" Fielding asked. "Mr. Owen can show you. There's Mrs. Hands, too. In the state she's in she's not fit to be left. I must try to get hold of someone from the village. I'll send Biggs if I can find him. You're sure you won't want me?"

"No, that's all right," Bell said. "You'll stay around though, won't you? I shall want to take a statement later. You didn't touch anything, I suppose?"

"I took one look," Mr. Fielding assured him, "and then I got away as fast as I could."

He went back to the house and Bobby led the way round to the small orchard where the air raid shelter stood. It had been dug out to a depth of about five feet below the surface of the ground, with surrounding brick walls another five feet in height. This had given space for three tiers of bunks, with three feet or so between each, on each side. At the north end, where the entrance had been, the wall had been completely levelled. At the south end, it was still intact, but demolition had made good progress on both side walls. On the west indeed demolition was nearly complete. The resulting bricks and rubble, together with the earth that had been piled on the corrugated iron roof for further protection had filled up the interior of the shelter to within a foot or less of ground level. On this piled-up mass of debris lay a man's body.

It was that of a man of middle age, certainly not a tramp, though somewhat shabbily dressed. But that is little to go by in days of clothes coupons. Well nourished, Bobby thought. Probably a member of what is called the lower middle class, a shop assistant perhaps, or one of the more poorly paid clerical workers. Almost certainly not a man who worked with his hands. The face had acquired something of that repose and dignity that death often gives, though still the glazing eyes stared upwards as in wonder and surprise, as though those had been the last impressions of the departing spirit.

There were, close inspection showed, three wounds. One was apparent, for a bullet had drilled a hole right through the centre of the forehead, a small, neat aperture that had bled only a little. From his knowledge of gunshot wounds, Bobby suspected that the exit wound would be much larger and have bled much more freely. The bricks and earth and rubble, near where the head lay, showed signs of this, though much of the bleeding that had occurred had evidently soaked away through the interstices of the debris.

The other two wounds were much less apparent. They were in the chest and again bleeding had been small. Bobby expected that with both of these there would be no exit wounds, the bullets being probably still in the body. One wound was nearly hidden by a fold of the coat, disarranged by the fall. Both Bobby and his companion agreed that the weapon used had probably been a small automatic. If so, it was likely the thrown-out cartridge cases would be somewhere near.

All this was noted and observed from the edge of the shelter. The two detectives did not wish to go nearer, to disturb either the loose debris on which the body lay or the body itself, till further help arrived. At one time, though, Bell, catching his foot on a course of bricks where the west side wall had been nearly levelled, had a narrow escape from overbalancing to fall headlong into the shelter on top of the dead body. Fortunately Bobby was able to catch him just in time, so preventing a fall that would have considerably affected their decision not to move or touch either the body or the environment until both a doctor and further technical help arrived.

In the meantime they began a close search of the ground near.

It was not very rewarding. The long, thick, overgrown grass had preserved no trace of footsteps and showed no sign of any struggle. They did indeed discover three thrown-out cartridge cases to confirm their belief that the weapon used had been a small automatic. Expert examination would probably reveal the actual type and make. The position of the cartridges seemed also to suggest that the victim, when shot, must have been standing where his body now lay, that is, within the limits of the half demolished shelter.

"Only, if that's so," Bell asked, "what was he doing there? He can't have been meaning to sleep in the place. No roof and all that rubble to lie on."

"No," agreed Bobby, thoughtfully. "No, difficult to say."

"Might have used it before and came to have a look," suggested Bell. "Mr. Fielding did say tramps sometimes slept there. But this chap doesn't look like a tramp. Might have been trying to hide, perhaps."

"That's possible," Bobby agreed, but with little conviction.

"Got to get identity established first of all," Bell said. "Any ideas?"

"Same as yours, I expect," Bobby answered. "Seems to answer to the description given of the travelling salesman we've been told about and his dispatch case full of jewellery young Rogers was so sure wasn't worth anything, All the same, it does seem to have included an opal ring of worthwhile value."

"That's what I was thinking," Bell said. "Fielding says his chauffeur can't be found. Looks like motive and murder both pretty plain?"

"So it does," agreed Bobby, but with doubt in his voice, and now Bell shook a despondent head.

"You don't get things handed to you on a plate like that," he admitted. "At least, not if you're me, you don't. When things look dead easy, you may be dead sure there's a snag in it somewhere."

Bobby could not have been more heartily in agreement.

"But this chauffeur chap has got to the found," Bell added, and again Bobby was in hearty agreement.

"It looks to me," he said, "as if there's a bag of some sort under where the body is lying. I should say that when the chap was shot he fell on it and pressed it down into the loose rubble where he had been standing."

Help arrived; the Dr. Stevens summoned by Mr. Fielding; Bell's two assistants; the technicians, photographers, finger-print experts and so on, sent in haste from headquarters. The body was moved and under it was in fact a dispatch case. Bell opened it. Within was a glittering mass of jewellery. Rings chiefly, but other articles as well. The doctor left his examination of the body to stare. One of Bell's sergeants said:

"That's the smash-and-grab loot. This bloke must have been trying to hide it on his own and his pals knew. So they put him out but hadn't any notion the stuff was there, waiting for them."

Bell had been looking more closely at the contents of the dispatch case. He said in a voice from which tears were not far distant:

"All dud stuff, and fourth rate at that. The whole lot's not worth a fiver."

CHAPTER XII

NIETZSCHE IN MUSIC

THE TECHNICIANS WERE by now all absorbed in their respective tasks. An ambulance had arrived to remove the victim's body for the post-mortem the doctor was to carry out. Bobby suggested to his companion that as there was nothing much more they could do until the routine work had been completed, and more information was available, it might be as well to find out if Biggs had put in an appearance yet. Bell agreed, and they moved away towards the house. Emerging on the drive, they saw hurrying towards them an elderly man and, at a little distance behind, Taylor apparently in pursuit. Seeing them in front of him, the elderly man paused. Taylor came up, looking very red and angry.

"I told him there was orders against it," he explained, "and off he went and sneaked in, he did, behind my back, through the fence somewhere. You come along back with me, Tom Sadler, and don't try any more of your tricks."

"Free country, ain't it?" retorted the man addressed as Tom Sadler. "No one's got no right to stand between a bloke and his work."

"Does he work here?" Bell asked Taylor.

"Odd job man and helps in the garden when he feels like it," answered Taylor, still indignant, "and that isn't often. Mr. Fielding was asking me only yesterday about him and what he was doing, because of his having promised a week ago to help pull down the air raid shelter but he hadn't been near the place."

"That was my rheumatics, that was," said Sadler with dignity. "Pulling down air raid shelters isn't no work for rheumatics."

"Too much like hard work, you mean," retorted Taylor. To Bell he said: "All he wants is to get to know what's going on, so he can tell about it at the Much Middles Arms and get stood a pint or two in return."

"Well, you clear out now," Bell said to Sadler, "and mind what you're doing. If I want to see you later, I'll send for you."

Sadler retired, grumbling, and as he moved off there arrived a newcomer, a tall man in clerical dress, the vicar, Mr. Gayton, as they guessed at once. He was thin and emaciated-looking, with a thin ascetic face; of him indeed Olive was moved to remark thoughtfully at a later date that in her considered opinion he ought to be fed forcibly at least twice a day. He had a loose-lipped, sensitive mouth, large dreamy eyes, and long beautifully shaped hands. An imaginative type, Bobby thought, and was inclined to guess that what the Church had gained, Art had lost. A difficult type, too, he reflected. Neither artist nor priest ever looked at things quite as did other men, and the combination would probably be more unpredictable still.

Mr. Gayton seemed to know, or guess, the identity of Bobby and his companion. He greeted Bobby by name as a newcomer in the parish on whom he had been meaning to call immediately, and he had heard of the arrival that morning of an officer of the county police. He went on to explain his appearance. Mr. Fielding had asked him on the 'phone to come across. He hoped there was no objection. At the entrance to the drive there was a small group of gaping, staring villagers. They had told him that Constable Taylor had warned them against entering the Middles grounds and was at the moment engaged in fetching back old Tom Sadler who had tried to sneak in. Mr. Gayton had, however, ventured to assume that these instructions did not apply to him. Bell said that was all right. The only object had been to prevent the intrusion of a crowd of merely curious spectators. Indeed, he and his friend and colleague, Mr. Owen, of Scotland Yard, had been meaning to call on Mr. Gayton to ask if he could give them any information: first, about his discovery of the opal ring, and, secondly, about anything that might be useful concerning the village and its inhabitants.

Mr. Gayton didn't think he could tell them anything. Nothing useful, that is. On either count. He had called to see Mr. Fielding on some small point of parish business. Mr. Fielding was kind enough to act as treasurer to one or two parish funds. He had stayed only a few minutes. When leaving he had seen the opal ring lying right in the middle of the drive, near the gate. He could not be sure it had not been there before, but that did not seem likely. Moreover, as it happened, when he arrived the laundry delivery van was standing at the entrance to the drive and he had stopped to say a word or two to the driver, who was just returning from the house where he had left Mr. Fielding's long delayed, long awaited, much desired laundry. Mrs. Hands, the housekeeper, had been ringing up to complain that Mr. Fielding hadn't so much as a clean sock or a clean handkerchief left. So if the opal ring had been there at that time, not only he himself but the laundry delivery man must have failed to notice it. That seemed highly improbable. He had seen and heard nothing to suggest that any third person was near by at the time, but agreed that there were rhododendron bushes near that would have provided ample concealment for anyone wishing to remain unseen. He had thought it best to take the ring at once to Constable Taylor, an admirable man and a member of the church council. Taylor had asked him to say nothing about it for the time being and so of course he had not done so.

"Mr. Fielding," added the vicar, "was evidently much distressed when he spoke on the 'phone. I felt bound to come immediately. He seemed disturbed about his chauffeur. I couldn't quite understand why. The unhappy victim is a stranger here, I'm told. Surely there is no suggestion that Biggs . . . it surely isn't possible . . .?"

"No suggestion about anything so far," Bell answered crisply. "Mr. Fielding did mention that he didn't know what had become of his chauffeur. That's all the information we have at present."

"Possibly," Bobby suggested, "Mr. Gayton could tell us whether he thinks there is any truth in the story we've heard that there has been trouble between Biggs and a resident in the village, a Mr. Rogers, and that recently it resulted in a fight between them?"

"Oh, have you heard that?" Gayton exclaimed. "Who told you? I don't know if it's true. There has been some such talk but I think they both deny it,"

"Do you know anything about Mr. Rogers?"

"No. No. He and his sister have not been here long. They bought the bungalow you may have noticed not far from the church. I called, of course, but I was not made very welcome. Indeed I might almost say they were not very civil. Mr. Rogers kept turning to his books. He let me see he wanted to get on with his work. I understand he is reading for an examination. Miss Rogers was cleaning a pistol. She did offer me a cup of tea, but she seemed unwilling to leave what she was doing. They have not seen fit to become members of my congregation and they take no part in village life. I did make another attempt. I thought perhaps my first call had been at an unlucky moment. But my knock was not answered, though I am under the impression that there was someone in. I may say I am sure of it, for I saw the young man at the window behind the curtain. I believe he was a conscientious objector during the war. A mistaken point of view in the opinion of the Church but one that must be respected."

"We can take it anyhow," Bobby said, "that there has been gossip about a quarrel between Rogers and Biggs. Do you know what is supposed to have started it? There seems no obvious reason why there should be any trouble between a young man reading for an examination and a chauffeur in somebody else's employ."

"I'm afraid a good deal of very foolish gossip goes on here," Gayton admitted in a distressed tone. "I try to check it as much as I can."

"Quite right, too," declared Bell. "Very mischievous is gossip. Leads to a lot of trouble. But there's been a murder done and if there has been gossip, it may help to give us a line, if you would tell us what it is."

"I should not care," Mr. Gayton answered firmly, "to repeat any story of the truth of which I was not sure. It might do grievous wrong."

"If people are innocent, they've nothing to fear," Bell argued, but Mr. Gayton seemed unconvinced, pressing his long, mobile lips closely together.

Bobby said:

"We quite understand your point of view. Our duty is to try to get hold of any piece of information that may help to bring a murderer to justice. I am sure we may depend on your help."

"It is less important," Mr. Gayton answered, "to bring a murderer to justice than to bring him to repentance."

"In my experience." said Bell gloomily, "they only start repenting when they're caught."

"All that's a bit outside our province," Bobby interposed. "What we have been told is that there was jealousy between Rogers and Biggs and that the cause was Miss Bellamy."

"Who told you that?" demanded Mr. Gayton, startled.

"I don't think we must give names," Bobby answered. "We always say 'From information received.' In this case there is information that Biggs was seen entering Miss Bellamy's cottage late at night."

"Was it Miss Cann?" insisted Mr. Gayton.

"What made you think of her?" Bobby countered.

"She told me the same story. I could not believe it. I questioned her closely. She was quite positive and clear in what she said. I suggested that possibly Biggs had brought a message from his employer. It doesn't seem very likely, I know, at that time of night. It was midnight, Miss Cann said. She said he didn't come out again while she was there. I am inclined to think she waited for some time. I laid it upon her very strictly that she should say no word about it to anyone else. We must not be ready to think evil of one another. She promised faithfully. I am distressed she has spoken now."

"She might have got herself into trouble if she hadn't," Bell interposed, and added, not without intention: "It's a serious criminal offence to keep back information. Liable to imprisonment. I must really ask you, sir, to distinguish between repeating gossip and giving information to the police."

"Especially," Bobby added, "in a case of murder. If murder goes unpunished, it is apt to be repeated. Once a man has killed, it sometimes seems as if he were the more ready to kill again. It is as though the blood guilt, once incurred, is easier to endure another time. I have even heard it suggested that it's a kind of despair. The blood guilt cuts the murderer off so completely from his fellows that he feels he may as well incur it again. Perhaps that is why Cain bore the killer's mark, so that others might beware. The only safety for the rest of us seems to lie in sure punishment."

"The worst punishment of all," said Mr. Gayton, "is—immunity."

"What they would like best, anyhow," grumbled Bell.

"We mustn't argue about it," Bobby said. "All that is outside our duty. I believe Miss Bellamy is a newcomer, too?"

"Yes," agreed Mr. Gayton. He added slowly: "A strange, disturbing personality, but certainly not one in any way likely to be mixed up in a vulgar intrigue with it neighbour's chauffeur. No, that I do not believe, whether Miss Cann's story is true or not. Whatever the explanation I am sure it is not that."

"In what way—disturbing?" Bobby asked.

"Have you heard her play?" Gayton asked.

"Once or twice."

"Well, then," Mr. Gayton said as if no further explanation were required. Then he repeated: "A disturbing element. Not, I fear, a good influence. Ever since she came, there has been—what shall I say? Unrest. Definitely. A kind of pagan element. I shall never forget the Sunday she played for us in church. It seemed as though what she played was a denial of the whole body of the Christian faith, as if she were telling us that hate is stronger than love, and that pity and mercy were no more than foolish weakness." He paused and then as his two listeners watched him in wonder and surprise at this outburst, he said loudly: "Nietzsche in Music."

"Well, I don't know if all that has anything to do with us," Bell said, a good deal puzzled.

"I think perhaps it has," Bobby said thoughtfully.

"Why? How? How can it?" Bell demanded.

"I haven't the least idea," answered Bobby.

Bell grunted. Mr. Gayton began to walk on towards the house, saying something about not keeping Mr. Fielding waiting. The two others turned to accompany him and Bobby said to him:

"Would you say it is likely to affect everyone in that way? Or is it merely personal? In your own case, for instance?"

Mr. Gayton flushed. Possibly he had detected a hint of hidden meaning in Bobby's last words, for indeed Bobby was thinking of the story Mr. Fielding had told of the vicar hurrying away from Miss Bellamy's cottage, lest her playing should set him dancing on the lawn.

"I think it affects most people more or less strongly," he answered now. "I can't say it's so with everyone, of course. You have heard her yourself, you say."

"On our first visit," Bobby agreed. "I remember it did suggest —the word my wife used was 'warning,' I think. I thought it more like a kind of sending round the fiery cross, so to speak. A sort of summons to action—or to readiness for sounding action. One could almost hear the trumpets."

"If she meant there was trouble coming," Bell remarked, "she hit it all right. But how did she know?" Then he added: "Of course it's generally a safe bet that there's trouble on the way."

"Is that how it affected you?" Bobby asked Mr. Gayton.

"I think," Mr. Gayton answered in a low, abstracted voice, almost as if he were thinking aloud, "I think somehow it calls out the deepest, most hidden instincts of our nature. What is buried there, even beyond our own knowledge, it calls forth and brings to life. After that Sunday I mentioned I went to—well, to remonstrate. It had not been seemly. Whether intended or not, it had sounded like a challenge to the Church and all that the Church stands for. I don't know if she saw me coming. As I opened the garden gate, she began to play. I had to listen. There is a strange force in her play-ing. I became conscious once again of feelings and desires and wishes I had thought long ago expelled from my life. Not evil in themselves, I hope and pray, but unseemly. A young man may quite rightly seek outlets for his energies that would be most improper and unseemly in one of my age and profession. A stricter discipline is required. It seemed as though an attack were being made upon it. I—I went away. I confess—" and Bobby, watching him closely, saw that his forehead was damp, that his full, loose lips were twitching nervously. "I confess I fled as from the accursed thing."

"You would say," Bobby persisted, "that others often have much the same experience?"

"Each according to his temperament and his tempta-tions," Mr. Gayton answered. "I do not suppose Miss Bellamy knows what her playing does. 1 do not think we must blame her. I do not think she understands. But I did feel—I do not think it was merely fancy—that after that Sunday there was less desire in the village to be friendly, to meet others half-way. I seemed to find an unhappy inclina-tion to stand upon strict rights, to claim the utmost possible, to show a hardness towards others no practising Christian should show to any but himself—or to open and acknowl-edged sin. I remember well how one evening I found two of the village lads who had always been good friends fighting outside her cottage. Miss Bellamy was playing. It was as if she were playing to them. I've no reason to suppose she even knew they were there, much less what was going on."

"What were they fighting about?" Bell asked.

"They couldn't tell me. I don't think they knew. My own belief is that Miss Bellamy's playing had brought out the pugnacity and love of violence that does seem to be an innate evil in the young man. A form of original sin only to he con-quered by discipline and prayer."

"Well, I don't see," protested Bell in a perplexed voice, "why listening to a lady playing the piano should make two boys want to fight each other."

"It is strange music," Mr. Gayton said.

CHAPTER XIII

CROSS-EXAMINATION

MR. FIELDING HAD seen them coming and was standing waiting at the front door. He looked, as was natural, pale and
worried, changed indeed from the perky, self-confident little
man Bobby had met before. He said there was as yet no news
of Biggs. Biggs had not come to the house for his breakfast
as usual, but Mrs. Hands had not worried. Her attitude had
been that what he didn't want, he could go without. Mr.
Fielding said with a faint smile that Mrs. Hands was a stick-
ler for the proprieties, and that once or twice, when Biggs
had appeared in his working clothes and with oily or greasy
hands, she had packed him off again to tidy himself. So, al-
though the terms of his engagement provided that he should
have his meals in the house, sometimes in the morning he
contented himself with what he could prepare on a gas ring
in his own quarters. There seemed indeed, Mr. Fielding explained, a kind of private feud between housekeeper and
chauffeur, and there had been some bickering over the disposition of Biggs's rations.

"Mrs. Hands was friendly with the man I had before
Biggs," Mr. Fielding said. "I think she thought Biggs was in
some way responsible for Cann's leaving. I don't know why.
Cann left entirely on his own account as far as I know. I was
sorry to lose him, though very glad to get as competent a
man as Biggs in his place."

Bell asked where Biggs's quarters were. Mr. Fielding
explained that Biggs occupied two rooms over the garage.
The only possible arrangement, for there wasn't a spare bed
in the village. Mr. Fielding agreed at once to the suggestion
that it might be as well to have a look at these rooms. Ac-

cess, he explained, was by stairs at the back of the garage. The garage door was open. If that admitting to the two upper rooms was locked, they must do as they thought fit about breaking it open. For himself he gave his full consent. But Biggs wasn't there. There was no answer when he was called on the house 'phone. He couldn't, Mr. Fielding said, imagine what had become of the fellow, but he would give him a good talking to when he did turn up. And then very likely Biggs would give notice and competent chauffeurs were hard to get.

Therewith Mr. Fielding retired indoors, taking the vicar with him, and the two detective officers made their way to the garage.

"Is that vicar," Bell asked doubtfully, as they walked along, "as simple as he seems, or did he put in all that about the Rogers girl and her pistol as a hint where to look?"

"It's a possibility," Bobby agreed. "She's a bit handy with firearms apparently," he added, remembering the story Bell had told him of what had happened during her term of service in Egypt.

"We'll have to go into Mr. Gayton's story," observed Bell gloomily. "Bit difficult."

"Hard to see," Bobby agreed, "how either of the Rogers pair come into it. It's hardly likely they can have had anything to do with the smash-and-grab raid."

"Only thing you can be sure of," pronounced Bell, and even more gloomily, "is that there's a lot more to come out—and won't, if it can help it. Got to be dug out and that won't be easy—not by a long way it won't. And what's all this about some woman or another and her piano playing? Where's that come in?"

"Miss Bellamy? Probably it doesn't come in at all, though I think it does—somehow, somewhere. There are times when I feel as if the whole explanation lies in her playing."

"Oh, well, now then," Bell muttered. "I suppose she'll have to be questioned," he added with a sigh, "but I don't know anything about music. Noisy," he complained.

They had reached the garage now. It was large, with ample room for three cars. At the back was a small partitioned off space, used apparently as an office. There was an old roll-top desk, a chair or two and some shelves, holding various guides, maps, motoring manuals, a few paper-covered novels, and a number of odds and ends. The roll-top desk was open and a hasty inspection revealed no more than accounts, expense lists, bills paid and unpaid, and so on. Nothing apparently of any immediate interest. At the back were the stairs. The two men ascended these and entered first a small room, half sitting-room, half kitchen. Opening from this was the bedroom. The bed had not been slept in, and no toilet articles appeared to be missing or to have been used that morning, There was an empty suitcase, clothing in a wardrobe and in a chest of drawers. Everything in fact was as if the occupier might return at any moment. They began a swift methodical search and found nothing till Bobby, turning again to the wardrobe, discovered there a cash box tucked away to one side, out of sight.

"Locked," he said, showing it to Bell.

"I suppose we had better leave it for the time," Bell said. "We'll have an independent witness present if we do have to open it. Biggs may turn up yet, but it's beginning to look bad. I'll send one of my chaps to wait here. If Biggs does show up, he can bring him along. I don't like it very much," he added.

"Nor do I," said Bobby.

They left the garage then, taking the precaution to lock the door behind them with a key they had found hanging on a nail just inside. First they returned to the air raid shelter where the routine work was still in progress. More help had arrived, so it was possible to detail a man to stand guard at the garage, there to await the possible but now hardly expected appearance of Biggs. There were other matters to be attended to, other directives to be given, and then, Bell having satisfied himself that all was being carried out properly, he and Bobby returned to get their car and drive to the Rogers bungalow. Rhoda heard the car stop. She came to the

door and opened it, standing there to watch them as they
alighted. She stood very still. Her brother came to her side
and said something. She took no notice. He went away.
Bobby, coming with Bell up the garden path was aware
again, and even more strongly, of the impression she somehow conveyed of an intense and passionate nature, held in
fierce yet uncertain control.

"If she ever lets herself go . . . ." he said to himself and
then he thought: "Well, suppose she has . . ."

"Miss Rogers, I think?" began Bell, raising his hat. "I
hope you'll excuse . . ."

"Is it true a man's been murdered?" she interrupted. "Is it
true? Is it true Mr. Fielding's chauffeur can't be found?"

"Why, yes," Bell answered.

Rhoda's brother appeared abruptly at her side.

"That travelling salesman chap, isn't it?" he said. "Well,
we don't know anything about it."

Rhoda cut him short with a gesture that was only a lifted
hand but nevertheless conveyed a passionate command for
silence. He seemed to understand.

"Oh, all right, all right," he muttered and went away
again.

"Do you think he is the murderer?" she asked, though indeed she made her words sound less like a question than a
challenge and a defiance.

"Do you, miss?" Bell asked.

She did not answer but went back into the house. She
seemed to expect them to follow and they did so. They entered the large sitting-room or lounge that occupied almost
the whole frontage of the bungalow. George was there. He
had ensconced himself at his writing table, behind a barricade of books, papers, an old and battered typewriter and so
on. Over it he watched them moodily as they came in.
Rhoda, looking almost as sulky—or was it frightened?— sat
down and pointed silently to two chairs for the two visitors.
Bell apologized for disturbing them. It was, he said, as he
well knew, having suffered himself, bad enough to have to

face exams without having to suffer interruptions as well.
George looked contemptuous.

"I suppose you picked up that exam story in the village,"
he said with his most superior smile. "People simply can't
understand research work. If they see you with a book in
your hands they take it for granted you must be reading for
an exam so as to get a good job. The only idea in their
heads."

"Oh, yes," said Bell, slightly puzzled.

"Research?" repeated Bobby, interested and trying to
make his voice sound as impressed as he didn't feel.

"Research," confirmed George in such a tone as Mount
Everest might use in speaking to a mole hill. "As a matter of
fact, I'm engaged on a most interesting inquiry into the
meaning and origin of the O.S.T."

"O.S.T.?" repeated Bobby inquiringly, trying to remember what in the present world plethora of initials those particular letters referred to.

"Old School Tie," George explained, still in his Mount
Everest voice. "Many relate it—and I admit at first sight the
idea seems plausible—to the ancient tribal totem by which
the members of the tribe distinguished their semblables from
others who of course in a hostile world had to be regarded as
hostile. But I think I can show that in fact it is an unconscious symbolism of the infantile desire to return to the
safety and comfort of the maternal womb."

"Oh, come," said Bell, and looked uneasily at Rhoda
who was not listening and had no need to, since she had
heard it all so many times before.

"The proof," George went on, "lies on the surface. It can
be seen in the brilliant colouring and loud pattern of the
O.S.T., which is an expression of the need the infant feels to
utter as loud a cry as possible so as to attract the attention of
the protective mother."

"Good God," said Bell.

"Shut up, George," said Rhoda suddenly.

"Well, I daresay they don't understand a word of what I'm saying," remarked George, still very much Mount Everest.

Bell agreed. Bobby, he supposed, might understand, but he certainly did not—nor saw any need to. He turned to Rhoda and repeated his earlier question.

"Do you think Biggs may be the murderer, miss?" he asked.

"No. Why should I? Why do you ask? Why should I think anything when I don't even know what's happened. Tell me."

"We don't know much ourselves at present," Bell admitted. "An unidentified man has been found shot dead in the grounds of Mr. Fielding's house. Biggs can't be found and his bed hasn't been slept in. We should like to find him and question him. Can you give us any information?"

"Of course not," interrupted George. "What on earth have we got to do with it? Nobody with any sense—I mean we only heard by pure chance . . . it's . . . it's idiotic . . ." He seemed to be about to launch into a tirade but Rhoda turned and looked at him and he stopped. "Oh, well," he said angrily.

"I don't know what there is you think we can tell you," Rhoda said in those careful, restrained tones of hers that seemed to put into each word, even the simplest, a strange, deep significance. She was staring at them with passionate intensity. "Tell me what you know," she said, or, indeed, commanded.

"No more than I've said already," Bell answered.

"Well, that's not much," she retorted, and seemed to retire into her own thoughts, and it was as though they were thoughts that burned and throbbed as with an inner life of their own, as if indeed they were almost tangible in their intensity.

"There's this," Bell said. "The dead man was shot. The firearm used can't be found. It is necessary to check up on all reported in the vicinity. Our information, miss, is that you are in possession of a pistol and that you've been seen cleaning it."

"Doing what?" George exclaimed from behind his barricade of books and then he began to laugh. "That old woman told you, I suppose?"

"What old woman?" Bell asked.

"The one going about in trousers and calling himself the vicar," George explained. "Physically male no doubt, but spiritually the complete old maid."

"Never mind that," Bell said. "I want that pistol, please."

"There isn't one," George told him. "The dear vicar couldn't tell a pistol from a feeding bottle."

"It was a gas lighter," Rhoda explained. "One of those they sold before the war, shaped like a pistol. I was trying to get it going again."

"They won't believe that, you know," George said jeeringly. "They'll be sure now it was you bumped off the poor devil they've found. They'll have you in the dock before you know it. Police," he said contemptuously.

"You deny the possession of any pistol or other firearm at any time recently?" Bell asked.

"Of course she does," said George.

"Will the young lady answer for herself?" Bell persisted.

"I deny it absolutely," Rhoda said. "You can search the house if you don't believe me."

"No, they can't," snapped George. "I'm not going to have my papers all turned upside down."

"A small automatic pistol is easily disposed of," Bell said. "If you had had one and produced it, we could have made sure it wasn't the one used. Have you had any firearm in your possession since you came here?"

"No," said Rhoda. "None."

"I may have to ask you to make a written statement to that effect, miss," Bell told her.

"Don't forget me," said George in the same jeering voice.

"We won't," promised Bell, who was growing tired of the young man's aggressive manner. "We have received some further information. It is to the effect that there has been quarrelling between you, Mr. Rogers, and this man, Biggs, and that you and he have been seen fighting. Is that true?"

"No, it isn't," growled George, but in a much less confident tone.

"Both stories then, you say, are untrue," Bell remarked. "Both this one and the one about the pistol?"

"I don't go about fighting people," George said resentfully. "Biggs may have been fighting someone but it wasn't me and there's never been any pistol here. I wouldn't have one of the beastly things in the house. I suppose that fatheaded old vicar knew Rhoda had been in the A.T.S., and probably he thinks all the girls went about armed to the teeth, and still do."

"Thank you," Bell said. "I think that's all. Do you think there's anything else we ought to ask, Mr. Owen?"

"I understand Biggs served in Egypt," Bobby said. "Perhaps we might ask Miss Rogers if she knew him there. I think she served in Egypt, too."

There was a silence then, a silence so complete that in it the ticking of a small clock on the mantelpiece became suddenly audible. Rhoda could not well become more pale than she had been before nor could her intent and blazing eyes seem to burn more fiercely. Yet it was as though both these things happened, and the utter stillness and rigidity of her attitude appeared a mere camouflage of intense inner awareness. George's scornful and superior manner left him too, as a roof may leave a house when a bomb bursts near. With an effort, in a shaken voice, he said:

"You've no right to badger us with a lot of pointless questions. Till them you won't answer any more, Rhoda."

"That is your right," Bobby said. "But is it wise? Inquiries can be made in other quarters. We have information that a court martial took place in Egypt and there seems to have been an idea that there was something behind that didn't come out at the time. I expect that could be inquired into."

"Damn you," said George furiously.

"By all means," said Bobby cheerfully, "but wouldn't it be better to tell us all about it now? You'll have to in the end and it might be better if Mr. Bell heard your version first. Of course, you can take time to think it over. Or you can consult your solicitor. But I warn you. Secrets can't be kept. That's my experience. Things are bound to come out in the end."

"Oh, all right," Rhoda said. "We lived together in Cairo."

"Now you've got your bit of dirt," said George. "Hope you're satisfied."

"It's not dirt," Rhoda flashed, turning on him in a fresh and fiercer blaze of anger.

"They'll make it sound so," George retorted. "To the dirty mind, all is dirt."

"Shut up," Rhoda said. She turned to the two detectives. "We met out there," she said. "We couldn't marry. He was a private. I was an officer. That's what upset them at their court martial. If I had been living with an officer, that would have been all right, that would have been normal and proper, provided you didn't do it openly. Most likely all the court martial lot were doing it. Men officers could with other ranks in the women's services, but not the other way round. That was outside the rules. Not that a word about it was said at the court martial, not a word or a wink. We all knew about each other but we never said. Only a spiteful old fool did once. I gave her the scare of her life. That's what the court martial was about. I wish I had done what they said. Tried to shoot her, I mean. I fired miles over her head, and she squawked like the old hen she was. I could have shot the pips off her shoulder if I had tried, but I didn't. They said they let me off lightly because of the state of my nerves. What they meant was they made it as bad as they could because they weren't going to have officers living with privates. An insult to His Majesty's commission. My nerves are all right. If you want to know, Fred and I are getting married soon."

"More fool you," said George.

"No one asked your opinion," Rhoda retorted.

"Fred is Mr. Biggs?" Bobby asked.

"Yes."

"Thank you," said Bobby. "One thing more. You are acquainted with Miss Bellamy?"

"Miss Bellamy? Yes. Why?"

"Do you know on what terms Miss Bellamy was with Mr. Biggs?"

"On what terms? I don't know what you mean."

"They think they've dug up something else," George interrupted. "Go on. Tell us what it is."

"I should like Miss Rogers's answer first," Bobby said.

"I don't know anything about it," Rhoda answered.

"Our information," Bobby explained, "is that he has been seen visiting Miss Bellamy's cottage late at night."

Rhoda only stared. She shook her head and said with some contempt:

"Is this some sort of trap? It's all nonsense. Of course, he was acting as Mr. Fielding's chauffeur and Mr. Fielding and Miss Bellamy are very friendly. I believe in the village it's expected they'll get married soon. I suppose Fred might have been taking a message."

"It might be that," Bobby agreed. "I expect Mr. Bell will think it'll have to be inquired into. Very unpleasant but things have to be sorted out."

"The trouble is," said Bell sadly, "that Biggs has got to be found before we can ask him anything."

Rhoda said and she spoke slowly and heavily:

"What do you want to find him for? Fred would never murder anyone. You don't think he did, do you?"

"There is not enough to go on yet," Bobby said, "but I think you think perhaps he did."

Rhoda stood looking at him. She changed. All at once she ceased to be the tragic muse she had seemed before and turned into a small and frightened girl. Slowly, disconcertingly, silently, with painful difficulty, she began to cry.

CHAPTER XIV

WEALTHY CHAUFFEUR

'CONSCIENTIOUS OBJECTOR," BELL said unexpectedly as he and Bobby left the bungalow. "Might be a pretty good camouflage."

"Why, yes," agreed Bobby. "I hadn't thought of that. But I don't think so. He has the hallmarks—aggressive and dogmatic."

"What about the pistol?" Bell asked. "I mean about its being really a gas lighter the vicar saw?"

"Struck me as pretty thin," Bobby answered. "The best Miss Rogers could think of probably. Even the most unworldly clergyman should be able to tell the difference between a gas lighter and a pistol. I should guess she has given it to Biggs, or it may have been his originally, and now she is terrified for fear Biggs is the killer and the pistol what he used."

"What made her break down the way she did?" Bell asked thoughtfully. "Does she know her brother and this Biggs bloke and the dead man are all in it together? That smash-and-grab raid of yours must come into it somewhere."

"The opal ring proves that," Bobby agreed again. "Only where?"

"What about lunch?" asked Bell, changing the subject.

"My wife's expecting us," Bobby said. "There won't be much but she'll have fixed up something." This was said with all a husband's easy optimism and then he added, "I don't know about your chaps."

"Oh, they're all right," Bell explained. "The canteen is sending over sandwiches and bread and cheese. I suppose," he added, "the pub will have some beer?"

"Not," Bobby assured him, "not for cops. If the village saw their beer going down the throats of cops there would be a row. Riot probably. Lynching I expect. Your chaps will get no beer here."

"And we are told," Bell said sadly, "that we can always rely upon the co-operation of the public while engaged in the execution of our duty."

"We must make allowance for the weakness of human nature," Bobby pointed out and Bell said gloomily that he didn't see why.

Then he said he thought he must pig in with his men. He could share their sandwiches, their bread and cheese, and their thirst. He felt he mustn't impose upon Mrs. Owen, already no doubt driven distracted by useless efforts to provide for Bobby's enormous and ferocious appetite, satisfying which probably meant that she herself went hungry to bed every night. Bobby, slightly pained, retorted that he ate practically nothing, just pecked at his food so to say, and wasn't there a lot of unnecessary grumbling about the rations? In his view they were ample for anyone for at least three days a week. Anyhow, out of airy nothings and mere unconsidered trifles to concoct a meal was part of every housewife's daily round. Besides, it wasn't fair for senior officers to pig in with their men. What other chance had the men to tell each other how badly the affair was being handled and how much better they could do it themselves?

Bell, admitting the force of this argument, then accepted Bobby's invitation. Olive was in fact expecting them, and, if she had not exactly prepared a meal from airy nothings, had at least done so from materials that in former days would have roused her to hearty laughter. She was not altogether displeased that they disposed of it in a hurry—'gobbled it down' was her own expression—and rushed off immediately, because thus any indigestion they suffered could be blamed upon their haste and not on what they had eaten.

First they visited Miss Cann again. When they entered the little shop and Miss Cann appeared, there followed her from the inner regions a smell so savoury as to set the mouths of both men watering.

"No austerity meal in progress here," Bobby murmured.

"You don't supply lunches as well as teas, Miss Cann, do you ?" Bell asked wistfully.

"No, I don't," said Miss Cann, repulsing wistfulness with firm decision.

The inner door opened again and there emerged a small, square-set man with a square face, incongruously adorned by a round little blob of a nose. He was wiping his mouth as he came in and he said aggressively:

"Our dinner's our affair, isn't it?"

"Of course," agreed Bell.

"If an Englishman's home," Bobby explained gravely, "is his castle his dinner is his keep."

"Eh?" said Cann suspiciously.

"It's an aphorism," Bobby explained.

"We've never had any, have we, aunt?" declared Cann. "We never got a smell of any blessed thing off the rations."

"We only thought what a nice smell it was," Bell told him. "You know a man has been found dead this morning in the grounds of Mr. Fielding's place?"

"Nobody's talking of anything else," Cann answered. "That bloke with the sham jewellery, isn't it? Is it true Biggs did it and you're after him?"

"Biggs seems to have taken himself off," Bell answered. "We would like to question him if we could find him. That doesn't mean he is the murderer."

"Well, I haven't seen him since last night. He was stand-ing at the entrance to Mr. Fielding's as I was passing. We had a bit of a chat and then I came on home and had supper."

"What time was it when you saw Biggs?"

"Ten o'clock. I remember the church clock was just striking. Aunt will tell you the same. Aunt and I sat up a bit talking."

"That's right," said Miss Cann,

"A bit after twelve it was before we got to bed," Cann as-serted.

"What I told them before," said Miss Cann.

"The doctor," said Bell, "seems to think the dead man was shot about twelve. Most people were in bed and asleep. Did you hear anything like a shot?"

They both denied it, but, or so Bobby thought, with unnecessary emphasis. It wasn't likely they would hear anything, Cann pointed out, considering the distance. Both the detectives were inclined to agree, though on a quiet night sounds travel far. In reply to further questions, Cann said he had left his employment with Mr. Fielding because he wanted a change and had heard of another job he thought might suit him better. But he hadn't liked it and so he had thrown it up and come home for a holiday before looking for fresh work. No trouble about that. A man, providing he knew his job, could pick and choose at present. And it certainly wasn't true he owed Biggs a grudge for displacing him at Mr. Fielding's. Nor was it true that he and Biggs had quarrelled. The story about their fighting was just a silly pack of lies. His aunt had told them, hadn't she? that it was that young swank pot, Mr. Rogers, who had had the fight. If you could call it a fight. Young Rogers hadn't stood a chance against Biggs. Biggs was tough. Biggs could whip a dozen like Mr. Rogers with one hand tied behind him. No, you couldn't call it a fight. Biggs had simply turned the young man round and dismissed him with a couple of hearty kicks. Asked how he knew, he replied that Biggs had told him, and Bobby reflected that one story is always good till another is told.

There was nothing more however that apparently Cann knew, or at least was willing to tell, and the two detectives retired, profoundly dissatisfied.

"They're hiding something," Bell said as they went away, and Bobby was in full agreement.

"Something," he said thoughtfully, "that happened about midnight, or why are they so anxious to establish an alibi for then?"

"Have to keep an eye on Cann," said Bell, "only why should he want to do in this salesman bloke?"

"We've no hint as yet," Bobby reminded him, "of any shadow of a motive."

They walked on, still talking, to Middles, where Mr. Fielding was alone, the vicar having left some time before. Bell asked once again a few questions about Cann without learning more than he knew already. Biggs had applied for the job on his own initiative. He said he heard at the London garage, where Mr. Fielding occasionally parked his car, that Mr. Fielding required a new chauffeur, and as he wanted a job, and understood Mr. Fielding was a good employer, he came along. Mr. Fielding engaged him on the spot, only too thankful to get the vacancy filled so quickly. Biggs had shown his discharge papers from the army and with that Mr. Fielding had been satisfied.

"Competent, decent men are hard to get," he said.

With regard to his present disappearance, no news of him had been received. Mr. Fielding said he had been round to the garage once or twice. He couldn't understand it.

"You've got a man there," he remarked. "He wouldn't let me into my own garage."

Bell apologized. A necessary precaution. Would Mr. Fielding accompany them there now? Both he, Bell said, and his colleague, Mr. Owen, thought the time had come to make a closer search. There was a locked cash box they had found during their previous visit. They had decided to open it, and would be glad, when they did so, of the presence of a responsible witness. Mr. Fielding agreed. Not too willingly. He was feeling the strain. A most dreadful business. What he wanted to do was to go away and pretend it had never happened. Bobby remarked that that was a not uncommon wish, and Bell said he didn't suppose any amount of wishing would ever make things better. Worse probably. After this plunge into philosophy they went round to the garage where a bored, hungry and forgotten constable, who had never received his share of the sandwiches and bread and cheese from the canteen at county headquarters, was very pleased to see them. He had nothing to report. No one had been near the place except Mr. Fielding himself to whom, as 'per instructions received' he had refused admittance. Bell said that was all right. Mr. Fielding quite understood; and the constable could cut off now, tell the sergeant to send someone else in his place, and himself collect his share of what was left of the bread and cheese. Respectfully the constable submitted that this would be just exactly 'nil,' and Bell said severely that the constable must learn to look on the bright side of things. So the constable saluted and departed and Bell opened the garage door. Mr. Fielding hung back a moment.

"Hear it?" he asked.

"Hear what?" Bell asked, listening.

"I think it's music," Bobby said. "Music from the cottage down the lane."

"Oh, that," Bell said and went into the garage.

"It sounds like a funeral march," Bobby said, still listening,

Mr. Fielding said nothing, but he seemed even more pale than before as he followed Bell, almost at a run. Bobby followed too, and Mr. Fielding banged the garage door behind them. It was almost as though he wished to shut the music out.

"The thing is," Bobby said, "why should anyone, anyone at all, want to shoot the man'?"

"Perhaps no one did," Mr. Fielding said, as if to himself. He said: "Things happen."

"Or is it that we make them happen?" Bobby asked.

Mr. Fielding did not answer and Bell had not heard. They went on up the stairs to the rooms above. Bobby produced the cash box from its unobtrusive place in the wardrobe. Bell produced some tools they had brought with them. The lock was of cheap construction and gave no trouble. Within were papers, including a list of investments amounting to rather more than £3,000. There was also a cheque book issued by a London branch of the Great Central Bank and a letter from the manager of the branch, giving the credit balance as about £400. There was also a small sum of money in one pound notes but nothing apparently of a personal nature.

"With all that money," Bell said, "what was his idea, taking a three pound a week job? He could have started on his own or bought a share in a business."

"Four pounds a week," said Mr. Fielding. "That's what I was paying. You have to. I had no idea I had such a wealthy chauffeur."

"He may have been just putting in time, looking round and waiting for an opening," Bell suggested.

Bobby, lifting some of the papers left in the cash box, disclosed beneath them two clips of cartridges.

"Look," he said, and the three men regarded them gravely.

"Looks to me like three point two stuff," Bell said. "Same as those we found."

"Yes," said Bobby.

"Does that mean . . .?" began Mr. Fielding and paused. He began again: "Do you think . . .? I don't believe it," he said firmly. "I can't believe I've had a murderer in my employ."

"He wasn't a murderer then," Bobby said.

"That's true," agreed Fielding. "Perhaps he never meant to be."

"Someone playing all right," Bell said, as faint strains of music entered by an open window. "Who is it?"

"I'm inclined to think it was like that," Bobby said. "Biggs was putting in time, looking round, waiting for an opportunity."

"Opportunity for smash-and-grab raids?" Bell asked. "A chauffeur's job might have its uses."

"That music," Mr. Fielding said irritably, and he went across to close the open window.

"For that or for some other reason," Bobby answered Bell.

CHAPTER XV

THEORY AND DOUBT

THE GARAGE WAS left under the care of the newly arrived relief constable; Mr. Fielding returned to the house, still shaking his head over this discovery of ammunition in his chauffeur's possession; Bell went off alone to see how his assistants were getting on; Bobby smoked a meditative cigarette, or rather, took it out to smoke, and then held it unlighted in his hand for so long that he had only just got it going when Bell returned. He had for him an unusually satisfied air.

"They've found a pistol," he said. "In the hedge. Point three two automatic, same as the ammo Biggs had. We'll have to send to Hendon for expert report, but conclusive, eh?" Bobby nodded an assent but Bell began to look less cheerful. "You know," he said with a depressed air, "it's always when things seem conclusive that the snag comes in."

"Too true," agreed Bobby, "and there's a lot to fit in yet. That opal ring, for instance, and why the vicar found it, and about half a hundred other things."

"What about," Bell suggested, "forgetting all the rest of it and just concentrating on Biggs shot the chap, and that's that and all we need."

"Yes, provided that that is that," Bobby said, "but I think you'll find you need the whole picture. Or there'll be too many gaps for the defence to slip through."

"I suppose there might be," Bell agreed, more dispirited than ever. "Good enough to put out a general for Biggs, do you think?"

"Oh, yes," agreed Bobby.

"There's that piano going again," Bell said, listening. "Sounds like she was asking . . . asking like us." He went on: "I've sent our dabs man to see what he can find in the garage. Ought to be plenty. There should be some of Fielding's as well. I said to get them, too. Just as a check up."

"Worth trying," Bobby said, "but no good all the same. As soon as Fielding knew I was a cop he started talking about fingerprints and put his own on a cigarette case by way of illustration. Plenty of people know about fingerprints and like to talk about them. But he wouldn't have done it if his own had been on record."

"It was only an idea," Bell said deprecatingly. "I didn't expect it to get us anywhere. What about having a chat with this musical lady of yours?"

They set off accordingly and as they left Middles they were met by a dispatch rider from county headquarters with a report just received from Scotland Yard. Earlier in the day, almost the first thing done indeed, the dead man's fingerprints had been taken and sent to London where they had at once been identified as those of a man named Myerson who had served two or three terms of imprisonment for unlawful possession and other similar offences, and who was known to be connected with the Burden gang, though never as an active participant. He was more, to adopt a current expression, a 'back room boy,' a kind of general scout, intermediary, and hanger on. The gang itself, known by the name, real or assumed, of its leader, was more than suspected of having been involved in other similar raids, but so far sufficient evidence had not accumulated for effective action. Their speciality lay in producing convincing alibis, and it was in this department that Myerson was said to have been so remarkably efficient.

"Seems to bring the smash-and-grab business to the front again," Bell observed. "Biggs was in it and he and Myerson quarrelled over the share out, so Biggs did Myerson in. Makes it simple."

"So it does," agreed Bobby.

"Leaves out a lot," said Bell.

"So it does," agreed Bobby again.

"Not satisfied, are you?" said Bell. "Some people never are," he complained.

"Well, there's that alibi Fielding gives Biggs," Bobby pointed out.

"Couldn't Fielding be in it, too?"

"Not likely, not the type," Bobby said. "Quiet, respectable and well-to-do. That's Fielding."

"In my view," Bell declared, "we've enough to hang Biggs— or at least enough to make him talk to save his neck, supposing it was really someone else did in Myerson and Biggs has done a bunk because of being scared. Got to find him first, though."

"I'm beginning to think," Bobby said slowly, "that when you do find him it won't be to hang him or even to make him talk."

"Oh, well," Bell replied, "I see what you mean but I do always try to look on the bright side of things."

Bobby left it at that and they went on to the Bellamy cottage, both of them conscious of many confused and troubling thoughts. As they drew near, Bell remarked:

"Thank goodness, the piano isn't going. I'm no hand at music, no time for it, but it sounded funny stuff she was putting over. Reminded me somehow of questioning a suspect."

"I think," Bobby said, "her playing makes you think of what you are already thinking, even if you didn't know it."

"I don't get that," Bell announced after a pause. "Beyond me. I'm not educated like you."

"You mean," said Bobby severely, "that by sheer good luck and no merit of your own, you dodged the dead hand of the tutor and the don. I," he added, a little proudly, "escaped by an innate inability to pass exams. Just a gift," he explained.

"Oh," said Bell puzzled, but there was no time to say more for now they had reached the cottage where Miss Bellamy was busy in the small front garden.

When they paused at the gate she stood up, putting down the trowel she had been using. They entered. She watched them gravely from those dark, deep-set eyes of hers, as if she saw them and yet saw them not, was aware of them but only as on a plane of existence other than her own. An aloof and hidden figure, Bobby thought her, and he wondered what experience it was that seemed to have cut her off so completely from everyday humanity. Motionless she waited as they entered and Bell raised his hat and said:

"I think it is Miss Bellamy, isn't it? I hope you'll excuse our troubling you like this—"

"Is there anything fresh?" she asked, cutting him short, but with no air of interrupting him, more as if she had not even known he was speaking.

Bell said he didn't think so. Not what you could call fresh. But it was important, necessary, to gather every possible piece of information. People didn't always understand that. They complained of unnecessary questioning. He hoped Miss Bellamy wouldn't feel that way. There were one or two little things perhaps Miss Bellamy could tell him about, if she wouldn't mind. Miss Bellamy said they had better come inside if they wanted to talk and led the way into the cottage, into that front room which the big grand piano at one end made seem even smaller than it was. She sat down before it and pointed to two chairs. Bell asked if he might see her identity card and asked also a few preliminary and unimportant questions. She answered indifferently, and then he said:

"Can you tell us anything about Mr. Biggs?"

"Mr. Fielding's chauffeur? Is it true he can't be found?"

"No one seems to know what can have become of him," Bell answered.

"Isn't Mr. Fielding the person to ask?" she suggested.

"We're asking everybody," Bell said.

She remained silent, staring at them, but still with that odd effect of seeing not so much what her eyes were so intent on but something quite other. The two men waited but she made no effort to speak and her silence seemed to them to be full of meanings they could not understand. She was sitting on the stool before the piano, her back to the instrument. She swung round suddenly, as if to ask from it counsel and guidance, and Bell was afraid for the moment that she was about to play. But she turned back and said:

"What do you think there is that I can tell you?"

"Well, ma'am," Bell answered, "that's what we're asking. Is there anything you know about Biggs, or have noticed about him, or have heard even?"

"No," she said. "Why do you come to me? Mr. Fielding was his employer. Ask him."

"Why do you say 'was'?" Bobby asked.

"I understood that he had gone away," she answered. Then she said abruptly: "I like your wife."

"Oh, yes," Bobby said, slightly taken aback. He nearly said 'So do I,' but thought the remark sounded superfluous. He said instead, rather feebly: "I'm very glad."

"But I think there is much cruelty in you," Miss Bellamy said.

"I hope not," Bobby said, "but I do what must be done."

"That's what I mean," she told him.

Bell, who was beginning to have a puzzled air, intervened.

"When did you see Biggs last?" he asked.

"I think I saw the car go by yesterday morning, was it?" Miss Bellamy answered. "I often do. I think Mr. Fielding was inside and Biggs was driving. I didn't notice. The car often passes. Mr. Fielding doesn't drive himself as a rule. He says why keep a dog and bark yourself. Mr. Fielding likes making little jokes like that."

"Does he?" said Bell, vaguely aware that it was a little joke Miss Bellamy had not much liked herself. But then Miss Bellamy did not impress him as being very fond of jokes at any time— either little jokes or big ones. He went on: "Can you tell us the last time you spoke to Biggs?"

"I'm not sure. Perhaps it was when he brought me some flowers from Mr. Fielding. That was two or three days ago. I'm not sure. Mr. Fielding has been very kind, sending me flowers from his garden. Fruit, too. He says it's only payment for my playing. He is trying to help me with it."

"From what I've heard of your playing, Miss Bellamy," Bobby said. "I don't think you need much help. I'm no great judge, I suppose, but at least I know how it makes me feel."

"How does it make you feel?" she asked.

"Well," Bobby answered doubtfully. "I . . . I don't know. I think I could only tell you by music like your own playing."

"You have never heard me really playing," she told him, and now there seemed more of human warmth and feeling in her voice than ever he had heard before. "All you've heard is when I'm strumming to amuse myself, to pass the time, like talking to yourself when you've nothing else to do." With a gesture she seemed to abolish her 'strumming.' "I'm working on an opera," she explained. "An opera of Peace and War."

"Coming back to Biggs," Bell interposed, thinking there had been enough of this irrelevant interlude about music. "Please understand, Miss Bellamy, that what I'm repeating is merely what we've been told. Information received. In a case like this when a man has been killed we can't ignore any gossip, however ill-natured or spiteful or unfounded. We have to ask."

"Why don't you?" Miss Bellamy said.

"Don't we?" Bell repeated, puzzled for the moment.

"Ask," she said.

"Oh, yes," he said, slightly disconcerted. "Yes. Well, our information is that Biggs has several times been seen visiting your cottage late at night."

"Who told you that?" Miss Bellamy asked, aloof and indifferent as before.

"Is it true?"

"If it were, you would expect me to deny it," she replied. "I don't admit it, if that's what you mean. I might even think it was my own business and nothing to do with anyone else. I'll give you a formal denial if you like. Who was it told you?"

"We never give names," Bell said.

"It would be Rhoda, I expect," Miss Bellamy remarked. "Rhoda Rogers, wasn't it?"

"No, it wasn't," Bell said hastily. "I'm not going to say who else it wasn't but it definitely wasn't Miss Rogers."

She gave him a hard smile.

"A formal denial," she said. "It doesn't matter. I'll ask her myself."

"I hope you won't," Bell protested. "It would only make bad blood and it wasn't Miss Rogers, I do assure you."

With a faint gesture she both accepted and repudiated his denial.

"It's by way of being a coincidence," Bobby remarked, "that a man I thought at the time strongly resembled Biggs vanished near here. You remember?"

"I remember," she agreed. "You thought he might have got inside and be hiding in one of the rooms. I didn't know why you thought so but I was very glad you came to look. I should have been dreadfully frightened if I had found a strange man hiding here—even though it wasn't late at night."

CHAPTER XVI

DOUBTFUL FOUNDATIONS

SINCE IT SEEMED that Miss Bellamy was either unwilling or unable to say more, the two police officers took their leave.

"I expect she'll start off playing again now," Bell said gloomily as they walked away. "Telling that piano of hers all she wouldn't tell us."

But that didn't happen. The silence remained unbroken, and if to both men it seemed a pregnant silence, full of the tale of things that were yet to come, that was probably only because of the impression her sombre and remote personality had made upon them. When they reached the Fern Cottage gate, Bell said again:

"Gets on your nerves, doesn't it? I mean, that playing of hers. I've never heard anything like it."

"I haven't either," Bobby said.

They parted then. Bobby was due to deliver a lecture that evening to newly joined C.I.D. men, and he knew, too, there would certainly be correspondence waiting for him and needing attention. Rather to his own surprise, he was finding his lectures very successful, and in considerable demand. Still more to his surprise, for he had always regarded speaking in public as the worst form of torture known to man, he had also developed both aptitude and liking for the job. But then, of course, there was considerable difference between talking to your own people about a job you knew through and through, and talking to strangers on some subject concerning which you were almost certainly ill-informed.

"When I'm talking to our own chaps," Bobby used to say with quiet satisfaction, "the poor devils daren't yawn, daren't go to sleep, or walk out of the room or anything. I've got 'em and they know it and that's a great help."

Olive said it sounded more like taking a mean advantage and Bobby was hurt, and asked what was the good of being senior if you couldn't take mean advantages when you wanted to? Now he got out the car and started for town, while Bell went to see how the investigations was getting on and to attend to all the innumerable details requiring the decision of the officer in charge. One confession had already been received, and valuable time and energy had had to be expended in ascertaining beyond doubt that the half-wit who had made it could not possibly be guilty. He had merely been caught up in the prevailing excitement and had been unable to resist the impulse somehow to thrust himself into it. It is a psychological phenomenon familiar in murder cases. Not till late was Bell able to feel that he had done all that for the time was possible.

Not till later still did Bobby return to partake of the light supper that, not without difficulty, Olive had been able to get ready.

"And then," she said briskly, "the sooner you're in bed the better."

But Bobby shook his head.

"All the time I was talking," he said, "all this business was going round and round in my head. The odd thing is the lecture came out all right all the same. I had a sort of feeling it was Biggs and Myerson, and the motor cyclist who perhaps was Biggs and perhaps he wasn't, Mr. Fielding and Cann, Miss Bellamy and Miss Cann, the Rogers brother and sister, even the vicar with his opal ring, I was really talking to, and yet I don't think any of the fellows noticed it and they asked just the same questions as usual."

"What you want," Olive declared, "is bed. As soon as ever you've finished your supper."

"What I want," Bobby said, "is to get things sorted out so they'll stop buzzing. Take the beginning of it all."

"The smash-and-grab raid?" Olive asked.

"Oh, no, that's a thing apart, complete in itself," Bobby answered. "No, our getting this house just when we wanted it so badly."

"Bobby," said Olive in a panic, "don't you dare go bringing this lovely house into it. I just simply couldn't bear it if you did."

"I won't," Bobby promised. "Not unless it's there already. But did we get it because by pure chance Mr. Fielding picked your letter out of a pile of others, or because it was necessary for some reason either that I should be here or else that I should not be somewhere else? And, if so, which?"

"I suppose," admitted Olive, "perhaps to get you here. There wasn't any reason why we should be somewhere else rather than anywhere else, if you see what I mean." She went on bravely: "It might have been just luck. Why shouldn't we have a little bit of luck sometimes?"

Bobby agreed that anyhow they deserved it. But the question was, had they had it?

"Take them all in order," he said.

"Must we to-night?" asked Olive, wistful now.

"Against," Bobby went on, "the background of physical fact that, thank goodness, is just simply fact. The raid, the opal ring, and my chase that led me here and only ended at Miss Bellamy's cottage. She was still playing when I drove past just now."

"She has been playing all evening," Olive said. She went to the window and opened it. The strains of distant music floated in. "The queerest stuff," Olive said. "It makes you feel—oh, I don't know."

Bobby came to her side and they listened together for a time. Abruptly, in the middle of a chord, as if the player's hands had dropped even as they hovered over the keys, the music ceased.

"Now why was that?" Bobby said, and then he laughed angrily. "I'm letting it get on my mind," he said. "What made her stop like that?"

"I think it sounded as if it was the end," Olive said. "I think she knew it was no longer any good going on."

Bobby remained for a moment or two standing at the window, listening to the enormous silence that now as it were enveloped all things. He shut the window and went back to his chair.

"Oh, well, I don't know," he said. "What's playing the piano got to do with murder? Let's begin again. Facts first. Raid. Opal ring. Motor cyclist, who looked like Biggs but can't have been because Fielding gives him an alibi. Or could he?"

"Could he what?"

"Be Biggs. Anyhow, there's the foundation."

"I don't call it a foundation," Olive said. "I call it quick-sands."

"Well, a background," Bobby conceded. "Take the people who come into it, Mr. Fielding, for instance. Call him 'A'." Bobby had paper and pencil now and was jotting down disconnected and mostly illegible notes. "What do we know? Respectable, middle-aged, well-off; long established in the village, well thought-of. Typical bourgeois pillar of society. Very last man to be mixed up in smash-and-grab raids. Sort of semi-retired, apparently—that is, has stopped being a go-getter, but if any promising deal comes his way doesn't re-fuse it. Was a sort of freelance of business. No record.

"Very good so far.

"Queries.

"Was it by pure luck or was it by design that he let us have this house? If it was luck, why is luck taking a hand in it all and why does it all begin to happen as soon as we get here? If on purpose—well, what purpose? Why should any-one want a cop for a neighbour?"

"Why indeed?" echoed Olive with some feeling, "Why should anyone be a cop? Oh, Bobby, why can't we have a shop and stand like gods behind the counter, telling people what they can't have?"

"Yes, I know," said Bobby yearningly. "Saying to one 'Go' and she goeth in tears and to another 'Come' and she cometh—if she's waited long enough in the queue. Oh, well, too late now. Let's get on. Everyone in the village seems to think Fielding is in love with Miss Bellamy and is going to marry her."

"I don't know about being in love with her," Olive said. "I told you. I thought—well, not afraid exactly. A sort of fascination, resignation, waiting."

"Waiting?" Bobby repeated. "What for?"

"For something to happen and you know it has to. Like hearing a flying bomb coming and waiting for it to cut out. Only more as if it were one you had started off yourself."

"I don't know where you get all that from," Bobby said.

"From watching her watching him watching her," Olive explained. "I think he attracts her, I think she is sorry for him. But all that's not going to make any difference any more than it makes any difference being sorry for the worms you cut in half when you're in the garden. You go on all the same because what's sown has to be reaped. That's what her playing has been saying to me."

"That's not the sort of stuff you can put into a police report," Bobby commented.

"Repulsion creates attraction and attraction repulsion again. A sort of dialecticism. An affect of opposites. That's how I see their relationship," Olive told him. "It's all in her playing."

"Strikes me it's what you got out of those lectures you went to," Bobby said accusingly. "No good taking lectures seriously. I hope no one takes mine like that. What it all comes to is that there's something between them and we don't know what, and they won't tell. So we'll have to try to find out.

"Take the next.

"Cann, for instance, Call him 'B'.

"B.

"Queries.

"Why did he leave when he did and why did he come back when he did? Why do he and his aunt want to establish an alibi for twelve o'clock which is just about the time the doctor thinks Myerson was killed? And is that nice savoury smell in the Cann kitchen in any way relevant?"

"Good gracious," Olive protested, "you're not going to bring what the Canns had for dinner into it, are you?"

"I'm fairly sure it's one of the items that has to be fitted in," Bobby said. "Don't you see why? Well, you ought to, and you a housewife."

"Oh, well," admitted Olive. "If you put it like that . . ."

"I do," said Bobby. "Quite clear. Another query. Does he or does he not bear a grudge against Biggs for displacing him at Fielding's? Yet it seems clear he left of his own accord so why should he? Not reasonable, but then so few of us ever are. But the possibility does seem to bring him into touch with the missing Biggs on one hand and Rogers on the other. We'll have to return to him when we get to them. Take his aunt next.

"Miss Cann and call her 'C'.

"C.

"Queries.

"Is she telling the truth about Biggs visiting Miss Bellamy late at night? If it's a lie, what's the object? Another point we'll have to come back to when we get to Biggs. It was she who told us the story about the fight being between Rogers and Biggs, not between Cann and Biggs. There is some corroboration there fortunately to support her version."

"What?" asked Olive.

"Cushion," said Bobby. "I mean—pillow."

"Oh yes, of course," agreed Olive.

"On the other hand the village seems to think it was Cann and Biggs who fought and the village generally knows, but not always. How about its being all three? Cann sore about Biggs having his job and Rogers joining in because no pacifist or conscientious objector can help joining in a scrap, provided it's not his concern or his duty."

"Bobby," said Olive rebukingly, "you're very unfair and prejudiced."

"Not me," protested Bobby. "I love the whole lot of 'em, the little dears. We needs must love the highest when we see it, you know, and we know they're the highest because they always tell us so themselves. And who are we to doubt or question?

"Well, take 'D' next.

"D.

"Biggs.

"Query.

"What's become of him?"

The 'phone rang and Bobby went to answer it.

CHAPTER XVII

THE PASSER BY

THE MESSAGE WAS from Bell at county police headquarters. He had sent Sergeant Shaw, his fingerprint expert, to London, with the dabs obtained in Mr. Fielding's garage. Shaw had now ascertained, as Bobby had felt certain would be the case, that those of neither Fielding himself nor of Biggs were to be found in the Yard files.

"Something else," Bell went on. "I rang up the City blokes re the financial angle. They generally know all there is to know about that side to it. They got on to the manager of the branch of the London and Central Bank where Biggs had his account. It's a new account, what the banks call a 'de-mob' account, and they know nothing about any investments. He made none through them, he has never paid in any divi. warrants, and they have nothing of his in their care. And Biggs's name isn't in any list of shareholders or in any recent transfers. What do you make of that? Why no trace of any of the securities on his list?"

"Plenty of possible explanations," Bobby answered. "Trustee, nominee, bought in another name, anything you like."

Bell said he didn't like anything about it. It only made it all more difficult, and Bobby said perhaps it made it easier, and Bell said he was glad Bobby thought so and rang off. Bobby went back to Olive and told her.

"Another little bit of information to fit in," he said. "It all helps. Let's see. We had got to Biggs in the catalogue, hadn't we? Call him:

"D.

"Queries.

"First and most important, what's become of him?"

"Run away?" Olive asked.

"I hope so," Bobby answered. "Next, is he identical with the motor cyclist I followed till he disappeared in a way to suggest he knew all about the vanishing lady stunt? If he is the same man, what about the alibi Fielding gave him? Rather suggests they are pals, but are they?"

"No," said Olive.

"Agreed," said Bobby.

"They watch each other," said Olive.

"Agreed," repeated Bobby. "Then there's the way Biggs does seem to have wished himself on Fielding. But if they aren't pals, why the alibi Fielding offered at once?"

"It may be true," Olive pointed out. "Or it might be that Mr. Fielding didn't like the idea of his chauffeur being mixed up in a smash-and-grab raid. You called him the perfect type of bourgeois respectability. Bourgeois respectability doesn't like the idea of a gangster chauffeur."

"Possible," agreed Bobby. "We've got to remember, too, that Biggs certainly knew me as soon as he saw me. Though it's true more know the police than police ever know. Well. Next. And important. What is his exact relationship with the Bellamy woman and with the Rogers girl? I'm assuming, of course, that the story about his visiting Miss Bellamy late at night is true, and not merely Miss Cann's invention. Miss Bellamy denies it but the evidence seems fairly strong. And we have only Miss Rogers's version of her connection with Biggs. Until we find him, we can't know if he had the same idea about marrying. It might be there's a clue there," he added slowly.

"Where?" Olive asked.

"We'll come to it later when we come to her," Bobby said with an expression even more worried than before. "Leave it for the moment. Next, why, with a capital of £3,000 in hand, if he had it, that is—"

"It's all 'if' and 'if' and nothing but 'if'," interrupted Olive impatiently.

"You're telling me," said Bobby, who always liked to keep up with the latest verbal development in literary circles. "If he didn't have those investments, why the list? Nostalgia for lost gilt-edged? It was a gilt-edged list all right. And if he still has them, why isn't his name to be found?"

"Because Biggs isn't his real name," Olive said promptly.

"Exactly," said Bobby. "So what is? Bellamy?"

"Oh-h," said Olive. "Oh-h, do you mean they're married?"

"Only a guess," said Bobby. "Probably a bad one. She's a good deal older."

"Haven't you seen his identity card?"

"No. It hasn't turned up. Probably in his pocket wherever he is. Identity cards don't mean much anyhow. They are three a penny—if you know where. Biggs must have been the name on his army discharge papers. Not that that goes for much either. Also he was in possession of ammo which seems to fit the automatic used to kill Myerson. That is going to take some explanation. I think that's all we know about Biggs, but not all we need to know, not by a long chalk. Well, Miss Bellamy next. Call her.

"E.

"Queries."

But then he became silent and remained silent so long that Olive said:

"Yes. Miss Bellamy?"

"Her playing," Bobby said.

"I know," Olive said. She repeated: "I know. It makes you feel—"

She was silent in her turn. Bobby said:

"It makes me feel it's all there. And there," he added, "it's likely to stay as far as I'm concerned. You can't put piano playing into a report to the public prosecutor." He went on: "With her, it's all one long query. What's she doing here? What has she to do with Fielding? If he is afraid of her, why? Is it just the impact of a rather tremendous personality on a grubby little business man, who never knew before that there were such things as art and music and emotion? Is he afraid because she has opened new worlds to him and he doesn't know where he is in them, or is it because she is reminding him of a world he had hoped to forget forever? Which?"

"I think," Olive said, though without answering this directly, "she rather makes me afraid, too."

"Leave her," Bobby said impatiently. "She is all one query all to herself. She may be in the centre of it all or she may have nothing to do with it. Miss Cann's tale may be merely a malicious invention and very likely the motor cyclist's vanishing act happening so near her cottage was only accidental, not her fault. Or was it?"

"You went over her cottage, didn't you?" Olive asked. "I thought you made certain he wasn't there."

"I thought so at the time," Bobby agreed, "but I thought she was helping, wanting to make sure, too. I wasn't thinking then she might be in it, and I wasn't looking out for prepared hiding places—trap doors, loose floor boards, that sort of thing."

"I don't see how that's possible," Olive said. "Not in that cottage. It's so tiny."

"No," agreed Bobby. "No. I don't think so either. No. I think we can rule out prepared secret hiding places. Give her up and go on to the other. Miss Rogers. Call her:

"F.

"Queries.

"What does she know that makes her so afraid Biggs may be the murderer?"

"Is she?" Olive asked, startled.

"It's why she lied about the pistol the vicar says he saw her cleaning," Bobby asserted. "Does she know about the visits Biggs is said to have made at Miss Bellamy's cottage? We don't know why Biggs wanted to be here, in this neighbourhood. But did she know? And is that what is worrying her? jealousy? Or something else? Jealousy is a strong motive. You can't help remembering that she has killed twice already."

"Oh, Bobby, no," Olive cried. "You can't mean that? Myerson was killed, not the other."

"I don't know what I mean," Bobby said. "But I must consider everything." He said slowly: "There is in this business a tangle of human relationships that we've got to understand before we can even begin to get at the truth. Well, leave her as another unsolved enigma and go on to her brother.

"George Rogers.

"G.

"Query.

"First, the reported quarrel and fight between him and Biggs. Did it take place and, if so, what was it about? Why did he and his sister come to this particular village to live? They were here before Biggs. How does that fit in? If they had followed Biggs, it would have been easier to understand."

"Why couldn't Biggs have followed them or her rather?" Olive asked. "He may have wanted to be near her and she may have told him about Cann leaving?"

"It's an idea," Bobby agreed, "but why, when he was well-off for money, had he to wait to get a job before he came? Unnecessary, one would think. Besides, that seems to leave Fielding out of it altogether. Perhaps he is, for that matter. Next, we come to the vicar. Call him:

"H.

"Query.

"Why did he find the opal ring?"

"Because he did, I suppose," Olive said, puzzled. "It just happened to be lying there and he saw it."

"There's one thing in all this that is quite certain, one thing and only one," Bobby told her, "and that is that nothing in it just happens. We've got to do with a long prepared, careful plan—and if I'm wrong in that, may bread rationing go on forever."

"Oh, Bobby," cried Olive, terrified, "don't. I don't know how you can say such awful things."

"To impress you," Bobby explained. "What I mean is that I don't think the ring was dropped there by accident. I think it was there to be found, and it had to be found by someone who could be trusted to take it at once to the police and tell them when and where. The idea might be that the vicar could be trusted but that anyone else might pocket it and say nothing."

"Yes, but," Olive asked, "why should they want the police to know about it?"

"Perhaps to lay a false trail," Bobby suggested. "If the inquiry into the smash-and-grab affair could be canalized here, instead of where it ought to be, there would be a good chance of its failing to get anywhere. In every inquiry, time is of the essence of the contract. Delay means safety for the criminal. There may be some quite different explanation. But there has certainly been a deliberate attempt to get the inquiry started here—true scent or false scent and with what object, is just something else to puzzle out. Continue with the motor cyclist and call him:

"J

"Query.

"Is he Biggs or someone else? Simple and solitary question re him, as Bell would say, but what's the answer?"

"Could it have been Myerson?" Olive suggested.

"No. Myerson never rode like that. Whoever he was, Biggs or another, he knew how to handle his machine. Myerson wasn't the man to take the risks that chap took. Finally: Myerson himself. Call him:

"K.

"Query.

"Why was it necessary to kill him?

"He was only a kind of office boy of the underworld and you don't kill office boys—even though you do feel like it often enough.

"The opal ring is direct evidence of connection with the smash-and-grab raid and the sham stuff was probably there for proof of dewey-eyed innocence in case of arrest. One ring is easily disposed of."

"So far as I can see," Bobby concluded, looking dispiritedly at his notes and wondering if he would ever be able to reduce them to order or even to read them, "that about covers the ground."

"I don't call asking a lot of questions and getting no answers," Olive remarked, "covering the ground or anything else."

"If you ask the right questions," Bobby told her, "you are well on the way to get the right answers.

"I take the fundamental right questions to be:

"Why did Biggs want to get taken on as Fielding's chauffeur?

"What was the relationship between Biggs and the two women, Miss Bellamy and Miss Rogers, and between Fielding and Miss Bellamy?

"Why was the smash-and-grab raid inquiry led here?

"What does Miss Bellamy's music tell?

"Why has Biggs disappeared?"

"You've forgotten the most important of all," Olive reminded him. "Why was poor Mr. Myerson killed? Why was it necessary, you said just now."

"Oh, I think that is only by the way, so to speak. It grew out of what happened. No part, I think, of the original intention. What we have to resolve is first of all what I've called the tangle of human relationships you seem to glimpse behind all this. I don't take what's happened here to be any ordinary crime of violence or passion or greed, there is something strange and purposed and complicated behind it all; and until we dig that something up, we shall go on scrambling about in the dark." He paused and looked again at his notes. "I do wish," he said, "I could read them." He selected one sheet of paper, the last he had used. "Can you make that part out at the top?" he asked Olive anxiously.

"Good gracious, no, no one could," Olive answered, and when she saw how disappointed he looked she relented a little and said: "I'll try in the morning, but come to bed now."

"All right," said Bobby. "I think it is writing," he added, "or was I only doodling?"

Leaving this question, too, unanswered, they went upstairs. Olive opened the window. She said:

"Miss Bellamy is playing again. Listen."

"It's nearly one," Bobby said, glancing at his watch. "What can have started her off again at this time of night? What is it she's playing?"

"I don't know," Olive said. "I think it is a lament for someone about to die." She shivered slightly. "Don't let's listen any more," she said.

Bobby said:

"There is someone coming, hurrying up the road—a woman."

"It's not Miss Bellamy," Olive said. "That's her still playing."

"I must go out," Bobby said. "I must see who it is and why."

CHAPTER XVIII

NOCTURNAL TRYST

THE NIGHT WAS clear and very quiet, its stillness only disturbed by those faint undertones of sound which tell at such
times how the small creatures of field and wood, those who
need the protection of the kindly night, are out and about
their business.

Hurry as he might, by the time Bobby had changed his
slippers for outdoor shoes, opened the locked and bolted
front door, hurried down the garden path to the open lane,
there was no sign or trace of the figure, he thought a
woman's, he had seen pass by so silently, so swiftly, as
though upon some errand in which delay would be disas-
trous.

He followed in the same direction. At the entrance to
Middles he stopped. The drive gate was shut. Nothing to
show that anyone had entered there, nor had he heard any
sound of the heavy five-barred gate being opened or closed.
To avoid making any such sound himself, he vaulted over it,
and walked a little way up the drive. The house was in darkness. Nothing to show that any stirred within and no dog
barked. He went back and down the lane once more. There
was a pasture field between Fern Cottage and the trees that
here formed the boundary of the Middles domain. Across the
field ran a path joining farther on another path where that
entered the spinney or small wood in which Bobby, on the
day of the escape of the motor cyclist, had lost sight of him.

As Bobby knew, this first path, following rising ground
and skirting the Middles gardens, gave a clear view of the
rear of the house. He wondered if the woman he had seen
had gone this way. He followed the path some distance,

about half way to the small wood farther on, and assured
himself that there was no more sign of life or movement at
the back than there had been in the front. But what then had
become of that strange figure he had seen flitting so swiftly,
so silently by, and what the errand?

His first idea that a nocturnal visit was being paid to Mr.
Fielding seemed mistaken, unless indeed most careful pre-
cautions were being taken. And that did not seem likely. But
if the woman's destination had not been Middles, what had it
been? There was no other house that way for a mile or two.
A secret midnight tryst, perhaps?

Bobby retraced his steps till he came to the fence that,
beneath the trees, divided the pasture field from the Middles
domain. As he had half-expected, he found a gap that
showed signs of occasional use. Possibly it was used by Mr.
Fielding if he wished to visit Miss Bellamy unobserved, or
by others of his household wishing to reach the spinney and
the path that connected Steep Lane with that other lane
where the escaping motor cyclist had abandoned his machine—since claimed, by the way, by the aggrieved owner
from whom it had been seized when he left it a moment un-
attended.

Through this gap Bobby penetrated. He was not sure, for
he had no great skill in woodcraft, but he thought he could
detect in a freshly broken twig, in disturbed foliage and trod-
den grass, signs that someone had recently passed that way.
He walked on softly, picking his steps with care. Now he
was between the house and the orchard, the one as still and
dark and silent as the other. As quietly as possible he made
his way through the trees of the orchard; and as he came
nearer to the site of the air raid shelter, now nearly demolished, he was aware, most strongly aware, of the presence of
one who listened, who waited in a very extremity of expectation, waited dreadfully, in such a tension as was near to the
limit of endurance.

How he knew, felt, this with such poignant certainty, he
could not tell. It was as though the still calm night was vibrant with an emotion so strong it set up actual physical

waves in the air. Perhaps that was in fact the case, such invisible impalpable waves as we know the air is full of but than are insensible to us till we provide an instrument to translate them into speech or music. The feeling came to him that he must end this strain of expectation, terror, whatever it was, before it became so intolerable it could be borne no longer, and worse happen. He moved forward quickly, taking no care now to move with precaution. He called out:

"Who is there?"

No answer came; but when he flashed his torch he had not used till now, he saw a huddled figure crouched beneath a nearby tree, close to where lay the half-demolished walls and mass of rubble that once had been the air raid shelter. He spoke again; but still there was no answer though it seemed to him that the huddled figure beneath the trees was slowly, very slowly, relaxing into a more natural position. He said:

"I think it is Miss Rogers, isn't it? Why are you here?"

She was still silent. A long shuddering sigh escaped her and then another. Carefully, with difficulty, she seemed to lift herself. She got to her feet, supporting herself against the trunk of the tree under which she had been crouched. She said in a low, unsteady, indeed unnatural voice:

"It's you . . . I thought . . . at least I think I thought . . . "

"What?" he asked when she paused. "What was your thought that made you so afraid when you heard me coming?"

"Was I?" she said, as if surprised. "Was I afraid? I think I was too terrified to be afraid." She said abruptly: "Well, it's you." She moved away from the tree and sat down heavily on an overturned wheelbarrow that had been used during the pulling down of the air raid shelter. "How cold it is, cold," she said, and Bobby could hear her teeth chattering and could see how she was shivering.

He always carried in his pocket a small flask of brandy. He poured out a little and told her to drink. Obediently she did so. It set her coughing but it did her good. Her voice was steadier and more natural as she thanked him.

"Why are you here at this time of night?" he asked once more.

"I could not sleep," she answered. "How did you know?"

"I saw you pass our house," he told her. "Are you here to meet anyone?"

"Oh, no," she answered. "No."

"If not, why were you afraid? I think you expected someone, waited for someone? Who? Why were you frightened?"

"I expected no one, I wasn't waiting for anyone," she answered in low tones. "But I think I thought there might be someone. . . ." She paused. "It was only you," she said. He noticed that she was looking not at him but at the air raid shelter where Myerson's dead body had lain. "I could not sleep," she said once more. "I couldn't sleep or rest. I felt I must get up, go out."

"Where is your brother?"

"George? Asleep in bed, I suppose. He didn't come with me if that's what you mean. I don't suppose he heard me."

"Was it Miss Bellamy you wanted to see?"

"No. Why should I? She was up, though. I expect she couldn't sleep either. She began to play as I passed her cottage. She may have heard me. There was no light. It was strange to hear her begin to play so suddenly, to hear all that music coming out of her cottage just as I was there. It was all so dark and silent before. She must have been playing in the dark. How could she without seeing the keys? But she must have been. She must have been waiting there. Did she know?"

"Know what?"

"Know that I was coming. She must have been sitting there all ready. As soon as I came to her garden gate, she began to play. It was as if she were telling me what I must do and then I knew I had to."

"Knew what? How do you mean, you knew?"

"It was in what she was playing."

"In what way?"

"It was just there," she answered vaguely. "That's all."

"You mean what she was playing made you feel you had to come here? Well, why? How could it?"

The only answer she made to this was to shake her head. Abruptly and surprisingly, she said:

"Have you ever seen a dead man?"

"I saw one here yesterday," he reminded her.

"I have seen two," she said. "Two dead men and I killed them both," and there was that in her voice as she spoke which moved him strangely. She said: "I always knew they would catch up some day."

"It is permitted to kill in self-defence," Bobby said gently. "Sometimes it is very meet right and proper to kill in the defence of others."

"It is still killing," she answered. "Blood calls . . . always. That is the law."

"I am an officer of the law," Bobby said, speaking slowly and very gravely, "and I tell you again—the law permits it for a cause and for a cause it, too, may kill."

"I don't mean your law," she told him. "Your law is only what old men put down in books. Redemption is by blood. That's a law older than your law. I think I must go now." She made an effort to rise but it seemed too much for her and she sat down again. "Oh, well, now then," she said as if surprised.

"Were you afraid when you heard me coming," he asked, "because you thought it might be Biggs and you thought it was he who murdered Myerson?"

"Oh, no, no, I never thought that," she protested. "He would never have done that. Never. He had seen enough of killing." Then she said, almost inaudibly: "I did think at first he might be coming back to me."

"Tell me what you know of him?"

"We loved each other," she answered and was silent.

"What was his real name?"

"He never told me and I never asked. When they sent me back to England he told me I was to come here and wait. He said there was something he had to do before we could be married, but I think I always knew we never would be. When you are a woman, you must give life, not take it. If you take life, then you won't be allowed to give it. I think that may be the law—not your law. The Law."

"You are letting yourself think too much about past things, about what is over and done with," Bobby told her, as gently as before.

"It is not past," she answered, "it is not and it never will be."

"Tell me this, then," Bobby asked. "If you did not think he might be the murderer, what did you think?"

"I thought perhaps he had been murdered, too," she answered.

"But a moment ago you said you thought when you heard me that he might be coming back to you?"

"Yes," she answered simply, and then he understood that she had indeed believed for a moment that his footsteps she had heard were in fact those of her dead lover returning to her. Then she said:

"There is someone else coming," and Bobby turned quickly, for he, too, had caught the sound of slow approaching footsteps.

CHAPTER XIX

A HANDKERCHIEF

SLOWLY, DOUBTFULLY, THOSE faint and hesitating steps drew nearer. Even Bobby, in the stillness of that quiet night, became aware that somewhere, lurking in the background of his mind, was the thought or belief or fear or what you will, ancestral memory perhaps, that in truth the dead do at times return, more especially those who had died by violence, unexpectedly and unprepared, while the full tide and strong impulse of life was yet unimpaired.

He thrust the thought, the fear, aside. Born of the night, he supposed, and of what Rhoda had said and felt, what perhaps she was feeling still. Fear is catching, he knew, nothing more so, and her terror of expectation had been both strong and genuine. He began to move in the direction whence had come those sounds they had thought they heard but that now had ceased entirely. He flashed around the light from the torch he carried. A low voice said:

"Oh, it's you. Is there anyone here? Have you seen anyone?"

"Miss Bellamy?" Bobby said, recognizing her voice. She came forward from behind the apple tree that had been sheltering her. He said: "Why are you here at this time of night?"

"Have you seen anyone?" she asked, without answering his question directly. "I thought I heard someone. I wondered who it was."

"Why are you here?" Bobby repeated. "What brought you?"

"I thought perhaps it was Rhoda," she said now. She was looking past him to where Rhoda had remained, seated on the overturned wheelbarrow. "I think it is Rhoda, isn't it?"

she said. She went past Bobby and said to Rhoda, stopping in front of her: "I thought it might be you. I thought you might be here."

"It was because of your playing," Rhoda said.

"My playing?" Miss Bellamy repeated and seemed puzzled. "Oh, but why?"

Rhoda did not answer.

"It was late to be playing the piano," Bobby said. "What were you playing?"

"I was just playing," she answered. "That's all."

"Miss Rogers found a meaning in it," Bobby said.

"There is always a meaning in what she plays," Rhoda said.

"Some hear more in my playing than I ever knew was there," Miss Bellamy said. "I think it was there already in their minds and all my music did was to make it plain."

"No," Rhoda said. "No," she repeated and said again and more loudly: "No."

"When you listened," Miss Bellamy insisted, "it might be then you remembered what you wanted to do."

"And when you heard Miss Rogers go by, you remembered—what?" Bobby asked. But Miss Bellamy was silent and Bobby went on: "Miss Rogers is afraid Biggs has been murdered, too."

"I have thought that," Miss Bellamy said. "But I do not know."

"You know what is being said in the village?" Bobby asked. "You know what it is natural to think if one man is killed and another vanishes?"

"It isn't true," Rhoda said. "He didn't do it. He knows what it is to kill and he never would again."

But Miss Bellamy was silent.

Bobby said after a pause:

"If it is the fact that he has been murdered, who killed him and why?" When neither of them spoke, Bobby went on: "I think you could both help if you would. I think you both know more than you have said. Do you want the murderer, whoever he is, to go scot-free?"

"Murderers never do, they can't," Rhoda said. Then she said: "I know."

Miss Bellamy said:

"If I knew I should not tell." Then she said: "There are other ways."

"What do you mean by that?" Bobby asked sharply—and uneasily.

Ignoring his question Miss Bellamy said to Rhoda:

"Come home with me. It's no good staying here."

Rhoda got to her feet like an obedient child.

"You won't play any more, will you?" she asked.

"Why are you both keeping things back?" Bobby asked. "It is a serious responsibility. Miss Bellamy, you have denied that Biggs visited you late at night, but I think it is true and that he did."

"Did he?" Rhoda asked. "He never told me."

Bobby said:

"I warn you both. You will both be called at the inquest. You will be on oath. You will have to tell what you know."

"We can't tell what we don't know," Miss Bellamy answered. "Come, Rhoda."

They went away together and Bobby watched them go. He would have liked to forbid any association between them but that he had neither the right nor the power to do. His feeling was that Miss Bellamy was much the stronger personality, that she knew more of the hidden springs of recent action than did Rhoda, and that her influence on Rhoda was likely to be in the direction of secrecy. Whatever she knew or suspected, she meant to remain hidden. No use anyhow trying to question them further. All he could do was to inform Superintendent Bell of his strange midnight interview and let him make of it what he could. Just as well, Bobby told himself bad-temperedly, that he was not concerned officially in the investigation, for it seemed to him it was heading straight for failure. One of those cases, undecided though not unsolved, of which all police records are full. His reputation, such as it was, would have suffered if his had been the official responsibility. A mean reflection, he supposed, and just luck that not he but Superintendent Bell had to carry the baby.

He had seated himself on the overturned wheelbarrow while these thoughts chased each other through his mind, for he had determined to stay till daylight. There might be more visitors. Now he flashed his torch among the trees and called:

"Is that you, Mr. Fielding?"

Fielding came forward. He was only half-dressed, pyjamas showing beneath his trouser ends, his bare feet in slippers. He was wearing the same old raincoat, a handkerchief still dangling from one pocket, he had had on when Bobby had seen him at the time of the discovery of Myerson's body. Apparently he had been in bed and had hastily thrown on the clothing nearest to hand.

"Thank God it's you," he said. "I felt I had to see. I believe I was scared but I had to come and see."

"Why were you scared?" Bobby asked. "What of?"

"Well, they do say murderers return to the scene, don't they?" Fielding said. "I thought that might be it. I don't know if it's true. Is it?"

"I don't know," Bobby answered thoughtfully. "It might be. I haven't come across it myself and I don't think there is any record of it in police work or in criminology. Just as well to keep it in mind though. It might happen. Or perhaps reading the newspapers does instead. A sort of sublimation of the primitive urge. That's what the psycho-analysts would say most likely. I don't know."

"I was scared, dead scared," Fielding repeated. "Silly, I suppose. But I had to see. I felt I had to know. Silly, but that's how it was. It was a big relief when I saw it was you."

"Instead of Biggs?" Bobby asked.

"For God's sake," Mr. Fielding muttered. "Saying things like that. Oh, well, I suppose I'm nervy. If Biggs did it, I suppose he might another. Why not?"

"There is always a danger that if a man has murdered once, he may again," Bobby agreed. "More especially to make himself safe."

"I suppose so," Mr. Fielding said and laughed suddenly and harshly, a discordant sound in that dark stillness. "Safety first, eh?" he said.

"Safety first," Bobby repeated. "Were you awake?" he asked.

"Hurt my hand," Fielding explained. "Blister burst. A bit painful. My window overlooks the orchard and I saw lights. I wondered if your men were there, watching. And then I thought it might be the murderer come back. I remembered it's said they always do. I got the wind up then. Scared. But I had to be sure." He was talking quickly and a little at random. Bobby could see he was only keeping himself under control by a strong effort of will. He repeated: "I had to come. I couldn't help."

"Suppose you had found Biggs here?" Bobby asked.

Fielding did not reply for a moment or two. When he did he seemed to have himself under better control.

"I should have had the scare of my life," he said. "I don't suppose I should have stopped running yet. It was a big relief to see it was you."

"It has been put to us," Bobby said, "that possibly Biggs can't be found because he has been murdered, too."

"Well, you know," Fielding said confidentially, "that has occurred to me once or twice, but I didn't like to say anything. Nothing to go on. I believe in the village they are talking like that. The thing is, why should anyone want to murder Biggs? A very steady, reliable man I always thought him. Told myself I was lucky to have him. Plenty of people I know would have been glad to get him. You have to jump at men to-day you wouldn't have looked at twice before the war. Myerson now. Easy to see what happened there. Clearly he had something to do with that smash-and-grab raid and what's happened is the result of some gang feud or another."

"Are you quite sure about that alibi you gave Biggs?" Bobby asked. "I suppose it isn't possible someone else could have personated him? By the way, could you give me the name of your friend in Reading you went to see?"

"Well, now, that's rather awkward," Mr. Fielding said. "You see I promised I wouldn't—gave my word. And I like keeping my word. You have to in business. Your word's your bond and if people know it's like that, come what may, well, it's an asset apart from any other consideration. The thing is, the chap's not out of the wood yet and there's the devil of a lot of money at stake. If it got about I had been to see him—well, people might get talking and some of 'em might make a good guess. They would guess he had asked me for help and whether he got it or not—no one could tell that or if so on what terms—it would mean he was in difficulties and the whole pack would be on him at once. It might start a minor panic, men ruined, suicides, all that sort of thing. That's why we arranged to meet in Reading so as to avoid being seen in each other's offices. No, I'm afraid I can't tell you the name at present. When the crisis is over, and it very much isn't over at present, then of course you can have it. Not that I can see how it would help. But I can't risk it at present. Starting even the smallest panic in the city just now is like putting a match to dry tinder. Lord, it might be the beginning of another depression like the one in the 'thirties."

"Unfortunate," Bobby said. "We do like to check everything. People make the oddest mistakes over times and dates, even about the day of the week."

"Oh, there's no mistake of that sort," Mr. Fielding said and laughed. "But I will say one thing, even if it does make me look a bit of a fool. You asked me if I was sure it was Biggs. Well, now, that's a question. I was sitting in the back of the car and I was very much occupied with calculations I was making and papers I was busy with. After all, there was a lot involved. I know it may sound far-fetched but it is possible someone else could have taken Biggs's place, someone about his size and height and in the same chauffeur's uniform, and I might never have noticed it. Sounds a bit wild, I suppose?"

"Oh, the truth often does," Bobby answered. "Did you speak to the chap at all?"

"Well, you see, when Biggs put me down at the office that morning I told him I might have to go to Reading and he was to have the car waiting outside the office at a certain time and I gave him a note of the address in Reading I wanted and how to find it. The car was there all right at the time I said and I got in and we went off—I don't think I said more than 'Reading, Biggs', or something like that, and I don't suppose I looked at him twice. And coming back it was much the same. I was more than a bit preoccupied still. I don't suppose I said more than 'Office, Biggs,' and I daresay I never even looked. Took the chap for granted. You see what I mean?"

"Oh, yes," agreed Bobby. "Very interesting. It suggests possibilities."

"It will take a lot," Fielding said, "to make me believe Biggs was the smash-and-grab sort—a most decent civil competent man. I suppose there might be something in his past—blackmail, something like that?"

"You never know," Bobby agreed. He seemed to be rooting about rather aimlessly in the rubble and debris of the now nearly levelled air raid shelter. "You never know," he repeated and gave a sudden sharp exclamation. "My thumb," he said and put it into his mouth, a little like a hurt child. He began to feel in his pocket. "Bother," he said, "I've left my handkerchief at home. May I borrow yours?" He put out his hand, took Fielding's from that somewhat surprised gentleman and began to apply it carefully to his thumb. "I'll let you have it back," he promised. "Cost coupons, don't they? and coupons count."

"They do," agreed Fielding. "I'm glad you were here," he went on. "I had the wind up all right." He laughed nervously. "Not a very nice idea—the murderer back at the scene of the murder and me meeting him there."

"Just as well it wasn't like that," Bobby said. "It's getting chilly," Fielding said. "I'll get back to bed now I know it's all right. What about coming along for a drop of something warm?"

"Thank you, no," Bobby said. "I must wait here till someone else can take over. The murderer might still re-turn—but not now, I think."

Fielding said he supposed Mr. Owen had to think of eve-rything and of course duty was always first. He went back to the house and Bobby resumed his solitary watch.

CHAPTER XX

MURDER AGAIN

FIRST LIGHT HAD not yet shown in the east, though one or two lusty challenges had come from the village poultry yards, when at last Bobby heard the sounds he had been waiting for and expecting—that of an approaching car. He was cold, stiff and more than sleepy. With mingled hope and fear, for this might be another car on another errand, he flashed his torch. There came at once an answering signal, and soon he heard steps drawing near.

"That you, Bell?" he called.

"That's right," came the prompt reply. "You been having a night out? Your missis rang up to say you had gone off in a hurry and not come back, so she thought you must be on something." He gave Bobby a reproachful look of which the effect was somewhat spoilt by a simultaneous and colossal yawn. "My best sleep," he said, "and no proper breakfast."

An attendant and even sleepier sergeant came up and joined them. Bobby turned back to the half-demolished air raid shelter where he had kept his long and tedious vigil. He said:

"Ever hear that murderers always return to the scene of the murder? Think there is anything in it?"

"No such luck," Bell answered. "Make it too easy if all you had to do was to sit and wait for the bloke to show again." He stopped to yawn once more. "Why?" he asked.

"Because three have been here to-night," Bobby answered.

"Was one of them the murderer?"

"Three?" Bell repeated. "Makes it difficult—still got to sort the right one out. Did they say anything? What three were they?"

"Miss Rogers and Miss Bellamy—Miss Rogers first and then the other. They went away together. And then Fielding."

"What did they say? Anything?"

"The Rogers girl was the first. About midnight. She said she couldn't sleep and she got up and came out. Then she heard Miss Bellamy playing and so she came here and she seemed to think it was the music sent her."

"That woman's playing," said Bell thoughtfully, "can account for a lot. Why was she playing? At that time of night. What about her?"

"She says she heard Miss Rogers go by and so she went to see and followed her here."

Bell grunted, looking both puzzled and unsatisfied.

"Fielding?" he asked. "What about him?"

"He saw lights and wondered what was happening. I had been using my torch. It was Fielding who began talking about that idea of the return of the murderer. He thought it might be Biggs here and he was getting ready to run if it was. So was Miss Rogers."

"So was Miss Rogers what?"

"Scared it might be Biggs coming when she heard me—badly scared."

"Thinks he is the murderer, does she? Or does she know?"

"It's not that," Bobby explained. "She seems to believe he has been murdered himself."

"Well, then, he couldn't very well be coming back, could he?" retorted Bell. Bobby did not answer this, for he remembered those strange fears he himself had known for a moment or two as he waited there alone in the night. Bell said: "If it's that way, where's the body?"

"There's that," agreed Bobby. "How about asking your sergeant to go back to my place and have a look in the tool shed at the back of the house? It's not locked. There's a spade inside and if he'll bring it along, we might have a try."

Bell looked thoughtfully at Bobby and still more thoughtfully at the air raid shelter site. Then he nodded to the sergeant who had been listening intently to all this. The sergeant went off on his errand and Bell stifled another yawn.

"I suppose you may be on something," he said, "but why had it got to be in the middle of the night? It's always the way," he added resignedly.

The sergeant came back with the spade. They set to work. At times it was easier to remove the fallen bricks with their hands rather than with the spade. After a time indeed they put the spade aside and used their hands alone, lifting each brick separately and the dust and rubble in handfuls. It was not long before they had uncovered the body of a man in chauffeur's uniform. The head was badly injured but there was no doubt of the dead man's identity.

"Biggs," the sergeant said, the first to pronounce the name. "That is why we couldn't find him."

"Now we have two murders on our hands," Bell said gloomily and then he looked more cheerful. "Got to look on the bright side of things," he said. "Two may be easier than one."

"If it was Myerson did in this chap," remarked the sergeant, "there is still who did in Myerson."

Bell sent him off to ring up their headquarters to ask for help to be sent and for a doctor.

"The doctor had better see the body before we touch it," he remarked. "Looks to me as if the poor devil had been put out by a blow on the head—a brick probably. Lots about."

The light was growing stronger now, but within the air raid shelter, that had been turned into a grave, the night still lingered, dark and heavy. Bobby, using his torch, said:

"Might have been done after death. When the murderer was shoving in the bricks and rubble. There's what looks like a bullet wound just over the heart. You can see where it entered. I should say Biggs was most likely standing there when he was shot. Myerson, too. We've not been able to find any bloodstains or any sign of struggle anywhere else. It would be easy to think up some excuse to get your intended victim to stand where you want him, inside the shelter. Then when he falls, it's in a ready-made grave."

"Cold blooded," Bell said with distaste.

"Murder often is," Bobby remarked. "And generally impossible to hide a dead body. Awkward things to dispose of, dead bodies. A perennial difficulty in murder. A half-demolished air raid shelter must have looked like the perfect answer. Takes time to dig a grave and digging can't be done without leaving plain traces. But here all that was necessary was to push down walls already half down, shovel in a bit more of the bricks and rubble, and that was that. Unsuspecting workmen would finish the job for you, and nothing to make even the nosiest cop look twice. Then the surface would be turfed over and everything as snug as you like."

"What about Myerson?" Bell asked. "It wasn't that way with him."

"Not even the luckiest murderer could expect a ready-made grave every time," Bobby said. "But it all worked in. Myerson's body there and no Biggs to be found. The conclusion obvious. No reason for cops to go looking for a dead Biggs when they were all busy trying to find a live Biggs on the run. There's a description out for him already, isn't there? The perfect red herring to follow up the perfect answer to how to dispose of the body. Our murderer is damnably lucky—or damnably clever."

"Damnably is the right word either way," Bell said. "I suppose you've made up your mind same as me?" Bobby nodded for answer. Bell said: "Well, how are we going to prove it?"

"Don't know," said Bobby. "That's your job, not mine. I'm not in the picture."

"That's a nice, helpful thing to say," complained Bell.

"You've got to work out a theory to cover the whole thing," Bobby told him. "Now and then I do seem to get a glimpse of what it's all about—a hint of the underlying pattern, so to say. I haven't been able to work it out properly but

I'll have another go. There's the dickens of a lot to get in though if all the bits are to fit and if they don't—well, it never takes defending counsel long to spot the loose ends, even if you manage to get them past the public prosecutor's office. Which isn't likely."

"What those blokes want," said Bell bitterly, "is a signed and sworn affidavit by at least three independent eye-witnesses of the crime. And then they would probably grumble that there was no proof their eyesight was perfect. There's nothing," said Bell with great firmness, "you can tell me about that lot."

"And nothing," agreed Bobby wholeheartedly, "you can tell me," and for a moment they both forgot all else in memories of a bitter past. "Oh, well," Bobby said, trying to be tolerant, "you have to think of them as a part of experience—like toothache and the morning after."

"Motive!" Bell reflected, "that's going to be the big snag. They tell you you have only to prove the fact and motive doesn't matter. But that isn't the way the jury looks at it."

"If we can work out a reasonable scheme of things," Bobby said slowly, "then the motive will show itself soon enough. At the moment there are too many unresolved complications. If it's true Biggs was visiting Miss Bellamy late at night, and at the same time promising Miss Rogers marriage, jealousy comes in at once. And jealousy can do anything with a woman."

"Or a man," interposed Bell.

"You mean Fielding?"

"If it's right he wants to marry Miss Bellamy."

"That means three suspects under the jealousy motive," Bobby said. "We've got to remember both the women are strange, passionate types. And one of them has a history of killing behind her. I don't think it has left her quite normal in all respects."

"If you've killed once, you may again," Bell agreed.

"Miss Bellamy, too," Bobby went on. "Is she quite the ordinary, normal woman you see standing in a queue?"

"No woman is," Bell answered with conviction. He added with even greater conviction. "Her playing isn't, anyway."

"Then there's Miss Rogers's brother," Bobby continued. "If there's any truth in all that about the fight between him and Biggs, was it because he resented Biggs's connection with his sister? jealousy of another sort. Might be strong enough. You never know. Defending a sister's honour. That sort of thing. Old-fashioned it may be but strong enough still—especially after being turned round and well kicked, if that's what happened to our George. That makes four under the jealousy heading. I don't like it."

"Conscientious objector, too," Bell remarked. "A prickly lot. You never know where you are with conscientious objectors. They can kid themselves anything's right that suits them. The salt of the earth and ought to be taken as such."

"Prickly," agreed Bobby, "especially no doubt after the kick incident if it ever happened, as I think it did on the strength of that pillow Rogers seemed to find it more comfy to sit on. He may have felt bad about being kicked where it ought to have done most good but probably didn't. And he had access to a pistol, remember. He may have taken it with him another time as a safeguard against more kicks—and used it."

"Yes, but," said Bell earnestly, "we mustn't let ourselves be prejudiced against conscientious objectors."

"I'm not," protested Bobby indignantly. "I take them as I find them."

"That's what I mean," said Bell.

"Then there's Cann, Fielding's old chauffeur," Bobby went on. "We know he's been telling lies. Doesn't prove he is the murderer but you have to take it into account, and both he and his aunt were very keen on trying to put up an alibi for midnight —the time when Myerson was killed. He had worked at Middles so he would know all about the air raid shelter and its possibilities in the way of a ready-made grave, and he may have quarrelled with Biggs over losing his job with Fielding."

"Doesn't seem much in that," Bell objected, "Anyone can get any job anywhere to-day."

"All the same, why did he start telling lies and why were he and his aunt so keen on the alibi for midnight?"

"Don't forget that nice smell from their kitchen," Bell remarked.

"Well, there's that," Bobby admitted. "But there's also the village idea that the supposed fight was between him and Biggs and there's the fact that he has turned up again just now—left for no apparent reason and returned for the same. No good pulling anyone in with defending counsel able to show that others had equally strong or stronger motives— and equal opportunity. Fielding is clearly a centre of it all, but passive or active? conscious or unconscious? and where does the smash-and-grab business come in? And was our letter asking about Fern Cottage picked out by chance or design?"

"Well, of course, a lot hangs on that," Bell admitted.

CHAPTER XXI

ON SPECIAL LEAVE

BOBBY WENT BACK home and to bed, once more deeply thankful that he was not in charge, and could now rest a little. For on Superintendent Bell lay the responsibility for seeing that the general routine of such an investigation was being properly carried out. But first he rang up the Yard to explain his absence, to promise that he would be there to give his lecture, arranged for three that afternoon, to the members of the Double X division C.I.D., and to ask further that any other matters needing attention should be handled by his secretary.

"I must have a bit of a snooze," he explained over the 'phone, "or I might drop off in the middle of talking."

"Yes, I see," agreed a thoughtful voice at the other end of the line. "Good idea. It wouldn't look well if your talk sent the lecturer to sleep as well as most of his hearers," and therewith hung up before Bobby had time to get in a single one of the many brilliant and devastating retorts which occurred to him as he was preparing for bed. Once there, after giving Olive strict instructions not to let him lie one moment longer than two o'clock, he was instantly asleep.

When he woke it was half-past four. One glance at his watch and he was out of bed with a leap that shook the house. Olive heard him. She called from below:

"The water's hot if you want a bath."

"Bath?" Bobby panted as he began feverishly to dress. "Bath? Do you know what the time is? I told you not a minute later than two."

"Oh, that's all right," Olive answered calmly. "I rang up to cancel the lecture."

"You did what?" Bobby wailed as he paused in his search for a wandering stud. "My name will be mud with the Double X people for ever more."

"Oh, no," Olive explained, "you've five days special leave from this morning. Mr. Bell got his chief to ring up the Yard and say about you helping and it's such a difficult case. Mr. Bell said it would be all right because his chief and the Yard gang—"

"Yard what?" interrupted Bobby wildly, thinking he could not have heard aright. "Yard what?"

"Gang," repeated Olive. "Mr. Bell says they all went to the same school or nearly, so they all 'old boy' each other and that makes everything all right. All the same I think they were a bit stuffy about it."

"So I should think," grumbled Bobby, who was not altogether used to having things arranged for him like this.

"You see," Olive explained, "if you were just an inspector or someone like that they could lend you and make a good fat charge—'pay and expenses for the period required'," quoted Olive, who had not read official forms for nothing. "But now you're whatever you are, and goodness only knows what that is. I don't."

"Not being goodness, I suppose," interposed Bobby, but Olive ignored the rude interruption, and went on:

"Whatever it is, it's too important for you to be on loan, so all they can do is to give you extra leave and you can do what you like with it—in theory."

"In theory," echoed Bobby wistfully.

"Mr. Bell's awfully tickled about it," Olive added, "I mean about getting you free, gratis, and for nothing. I saw him smile," she said in a slightly awed voice.

Bobby grumbled that he didn't see why things should be settled over his head and how would Olive like it if he settled about dinner for her? Olive said yearningly that she only wished he would and when would he like to begin? So Bobby broke off the conversation and went to get his bath, secretly grateful for the chance and for being able to dress and shave in comfort. He discovered, too, that he was ex-

tremely hungry, and even if there wasn't much for a combined breakfast, lunch, and tea—he was able to check with
some sternness Olive's surreptitious attempt to give him her
share of the bacon ration in the very natural expectation that
he wouldn't notice the almost negligible addition—at any
rate, there was something. He had scarcely finished, if you
can call it finished when it was so little begun, when there
was a knock at the front door. Olive answered it and came
back to tell him that Mr. Fielding was there and wanted to
know if he could see Bobby. He promised he would not de-
tain Bobby long.

"The whole village is most awfully excited, and it's
buzzing with newspaper men," Olive said, "but Mr. Fielding
went to town early and only heard about it when he got back.
He's in the lounge."

Bobby went to find him there. Fielding was standing by
the window and seemed pale and excited—not unnaturally
so, perhaps.

"This is terrible, Mr. Owen," he greeted Bobby. "Most
terrible. Poor Biggs. I must admit I suspected him. And
now;" Mr. Fielding paused and shook his head gravely. "I
don't like to remember," he said, "that I had such thoughts
when now it turns out the poor fellow was himself a victim.
Have you any clue, any hope?"

"Oh, yes," Bobby answered at once, "I believe Superintendent Bell hopes to make an arrest very soon," and thought
to himself that after all it is always permissible to hope.

"That's good hearing," Fielding said warmly. "You do
understand don't you? that what with it happening on my
land and one of the victims being my own chauffeur, a most
respectable decent hard-working man—well, that I do feel
rather strongly. If offering a substantial reward—really substantial, I mean, if you think that would help . . . ?"

"I don't think so," Bobby answered. "We don't find re-
wards very helpful as a rule. It's apt to encourage irresponsi-
ble interference—even the manufacture of false clues at
times. No, I think we would rather you didn't do that at pre-

sent. But I'll convey your offer to headquarters and it will be kept in mind."

"Well, any time you say so," Mr. Fielding said. "I suppose," he added with some hesitation, "it's not allowed to ask any questions?"

"Questions are always allowed," Bobby assured him. "But not always answered."

"I know, I know, quite right," Mr. Fielding agreed. "Same thing when you're putting through a business deal. Poor chap. Poor chap. A great shock to me. I do hope it doesn't mean Biggs was mixed up in that smash-and-grab business. Such a thoroughly quiet, respectable man he always seemed. There's that opal ring, too. Oh, well, I expect with your experience and reputation you'll soon get to the bottom of it, I don't feel I shall sleep easy in my bed till I know it's all cleared up. You'll excuse me talking like this? It's all been such a terrible shock. It was in the evening paper. I saw it just as I was starting home. Then, of course, I knew why you were there last night."

"Yes," said Bobby, a non-committal remark.

"I met George Rogers just outside the village," Fielding went on. "I asked him if it was true. Of course I knew it was but I simply couldn't believe it. Not Biggs, not my own chauffeur. Rogers wanted to know if I had seen his sister."

"Oh, why?" Bobby asked, a little startled. "Has she gone away?"

"I don't know. He didn't say so. He seemed worried about her. I gathered some of your people had been asking her questions. She was there last night, too, wasn't she?"

Bobby did not answer this question, for he had a strong suspicion that Fielding had been there unseen for some time, watching and listening perhaps. Voices, even low voices, carry far in the silence of the night. But he wondered if Bell knew of this new development. If not, he ought to be informed at once. It might mean no more than that the girl wished to be alone for a time, till she had got over the first shock of the certainty of her lover's death. Or it might mean a good deal more. There were other possible explanations, too, explanations on which Bobby did not care to let his mind dwell before necessity arose. Fielding still seemed inclined to linger, but Bobby explained that he must start out again, and Fielding said he supposed this fresh tragic discovery would mean a great deal more work and worry. Bobby agreed and Fielding, as he was going, turned back to say that it seemed almost providential, didn't it?

"I mean," he explained when Bobby looked puzzled, "the mere chance of my happening to pick out your letter from all the pile I had about Fern Cottage. It meant your being on the spot when all these terrible things began to happen. Providential," he repeated.

"I'm not in charge," Bobby reminded him. "Mr. Bell is the responsible officer."

"Yes, yes, of course," Fielding agreed, "but you were on the spot." At the front door, he said: "When I sent off that advertisement, when by pure chance I picked out your letter, I little dreamed—my God," he said with a sudden violent surprising outbreak of feeling, "how little I dreamed." He paused abruptly and began to walk away but once more turned before Bobby closed the door and said: "Could Miss Rogers be with Miss Bellamy, do you think? Or have you people been asking her questions, too?"

"I don't know," Bobby answered. "I've been asleep most of the day. I've no idea what Mr. Bell has been doing. Why?"

"I've just been to her cottage," Fielding answered. "I couldn't get any reply. I thought Miss Rogers might be there. I couldn't make anyone hear."

"Most likely she was out," Bobby said. "Or asleep," he suggested.

"Yes," Fielding said. "Yes. She wasn't playing," he said and went away.

Bobby waited till he was out of sight. Then he followed, intending to find Bell and ask him if he knew of Miss Rogers's reported disappearance. As he was passing Miss Bellamy's cottage the door opened and Miss Bellamy came out. She came to the garden gate and at first did not speak or seem to notice him, indifferent to or unregardful of her surroundings as she so often appeared to be. But Bobby at least often thought that she was also at the same time, in some strange way of her own, acutely aware of them. Perhaps with another and more remote part of her deeper self. Bobby lifted his hat and spoke a word or two of greeting as he passed. He had gone two or three yards before she called him back, saying:

"George Rogers was here, asking about his sister. Do you know where she is?"

"I've been asleep all day till now," Bobby said. "I don't know anything about what's been going on."

"Have you told her Biggs was sometimes here late at night?"

"Why do you ask?"

"Does that mean you did tell her?"

"It means that in a case like this, police ask questions but do not answer them. Why did you ask that question?" When she still made no answer, he said: "Was it in your mind that if she heard any such story, it might have led to a quarrel? And did you think that quarrels sometimes have tragic endings?"

Again she was silent, again she seemed to have sunk into that part of herself which appeared at once so remote from, and yet so aware of, her environment. He waited, and he had an odd feeling that he was matching the force of his personality against that of hers. At last she spoke, but all she said was:

"If you will not answer my questions, why should I answer yours?"

"Because I am an officer of the law," Bobby answered. "Because it is my duty to ask and yours to answer."

"The law," she repeated, very quietly, but with a small gesture of one half-lifted hand that seemed to sweep the law out of recognition. To Bobby came the thought that it was because of the force, even violence, of her personality that she felt in herself the strength to choose for herself, to follow her own path, and he had the thought also that this would lead to disaster, since there are none so strong as that, nor can be.

"Except for the law," he said, "what can there be but chaos and old night?"

But she was still staring at him in the same way, and he knew that his words meant nothing to her, that they passed her by as though he had not spoken.

"A foolish, man-made thing, your law," she said at last. "That's all. What is it to me?"

"You may find—much," he told her, but felt the utter futility of attempting to persuade her. He said; "Mr. Fielding was here a few minutes ago. He knocked, I think."

"I know, I heard him," she said. "I think I did. I knew it was him." And Bobby did not know whether it was fancy or not, but it did seem to him that as she spoke there came into her expression something more normal, more human even. He wondered if it was a gleam of tenderness? or pity, was it? or something stronger still? He did not know and now she was saying: "I meant to play to him if he had waited but he didn't."

Abruptly she turned and went back indoors and Bobby continued on his way.

CHAPTER XXII

RHODA'S DENIAL

SUPERINTENDENT BELL HAD established his headquarters in the cottage that served both as the residence of the village policeman and also as the local police station. He looked up as Bobby entered and said amiably:

"Hullo, had a nice sleep? I've been working."

"Well, you must expect to do some work sometimes," Bobby pointed out. "How are things going?"

"Badly," declared Bell, not without a certain relish in despondency. "Dead end—several dead ends, all of them as dead as each other."

"Oh, well, early days yet," Bobby said encouragingly.

"You may think you know," said Bell, still more despondently. "But what's the good of that if you've no proof?"

"It's often that way," Bobby consoled him.

"Besides," added Bell, apparently now on the verge of tears, "what's the good of knowing when all the time you know you may be knowing wrong?"

"Have to think that one out," Bobby remarked reflectively.

"You know very well what I mean," snapped Bell. "Things keep turning up," he complained. "Look at this." Bobby looked at it. It was a piece of paper carefully preserved between glass. There was writing on it, still fairly legible, though the paper was badly crumpled, torn, and stained. It read:

Meet me at the shelter at twelve to-night. George is being difficult. He suspects, he is threatening what he will do. R.R.

" 'R.R.' " repeated Bobby. "That means Rhoda Rogers, I suppose. Where did you find it?"

"It was in the poor devil's pocket—the breast pocket of his coat," Bell answered. "What do you make of it?"

"No date," commented Bobby.

"No," agreed Bell, "but needs a bit of explanation. If they met there one night, they might another—that night. The young lady will have to be asked a few more questions."

"I saw Fielding just now," Bobby said. "He says he met her brother looking for her. Has she cleared out?"

"No, that's the brother," Bell answered. "I put a man to keep an eye on the bungalow. There was no answer when we knocked but I've just had word that the girl's back. The brother isn't. Where did Fielding meet him?"

"Somewhere on the London road. Going London way. Cycling. He asked Fielding if he had seen his sister. Fielding hadn't."

"I hope Rogers isn't doing a bunk," Bell said. "I don't much like all that about suspects and threatenings."

"No," agreed Bobby thoughtfully. "No." He said: "You never know in a job like this how things are going to turn out."

"The pistol Biggs was shot with was lying under the body," Bell went on. "The doctor says the time of death was approximately the same as Myerson's. Did he shoot Biggs and then some third person shoot him? Nothing to identify the pistol by. One of those Belgian automatics they used a lot during the war. We can try to trace it but not much chance. The only pistol we can hear of is the one Miss Rogers had and says she hadn't. There's the ammo we found in Biggs's room. It would fit the pistol Myerson was shot with but then so it would any other pistol the same make and calibre. And how much farther forward does all that take us?"

"Not too good," agreed Bobby. "What about this five days' leave someone has had the cheek and impudence to wangle over my head?"

"Aren't you the world's white-headed boy?" asked Bell enviously. "Five days' leave and nothing to do but sit around and think up what might have happened if it was that way, while poor devils like me swot around and do the real, hard back-breaking stuff. How about coming along and seeing what Miss Rogers has to say for herself?"

Accordingly they started off together. The constable on duty near the bungalow told them Miss Rogers was still there and when they knocked she came at once to the door.

"I knew you would be here again," she said. "I knew you would never leave me alone though there is nothing more I can tell you."

She went back into the sitting-room and they followed her. She stood facing them, her thin eager attractive face now white and small and strained, those bright passionate eyes of hers that had been her most notable feature now bloodshot and dull. The intense dynamic vitality which had struck Bobby so forcibly the first time they met seemed to have left her, gone so entirely that no trace of it remained. To his fancy she stood there, empty and drained, a mere simulacrum of her former vivid self. She swayed slightly as she stood and Bobby said;

"Hadn't you better sit down? We do understand how you must be feeling all this."

She gave him a look that was half-hostile and half-grateful, but all suspicion. She did as he suggested. In a high, uncertain voice that seemed as though it might break into a scream at any moment, she said:

"I thought perhaps he had done it but he was killed first himself, wasn't he?" By an effort she controlled herself and in a more normal tone, she said: "Who killed him?"

"Could it have been your brother, miss?" Bell asked, and though she spoke no word in answer it was plain from the way she shrank into herself that it was no new fear to her.

After a long pause she said:

"No. Why should he?"

"Your brother had used threats, hadn't he?"

"No," she answered at once. "No. Never," and she took out her handkerchief and put it to her lips and bit on it.

Bell had brought with him in his dispatch case that piece of paper, preserved between glass, he had previously shown Bobby. He took it out now. He showed it her and said:

"You recognize this, miss? It is your writing and your initials."

"Where did you get it?" she asked.

"That's neither here nor there," Bell answered on the general police principle that it is their business to receive information, not to give it.

"It is something I wrote a long time ago—a week, more," she told him and Bobby had the impression that to her, after what had happened, this was almost the same as saying a year ago—more.

"What threats was he using? What was it he suspected?" Bell insisted. "I am sorry to have to press you, miss, but we've got to know."

"He suspected about me and—and Fred." She pronounced the name with an effort. "He began to threaten what he would do."

"What did he say?"

"He was only being silly. He was very angry and upset. I told him we had lived together in Egypt and that was really why they wanted to get rid of me. Bad for discipline. Living with another rank. George always thinks he's tremendously enlightened and advanced and all that but really he has all the old ideas—at least he has for me. He talked about Fred being a chauffeur as if that mattered. I told him to shut up and mind his own business and he said I was his business. He is my trustee under my father's will and he says he can stop me having my money if I marry without his consent before I'm twenty-five. I told him he was the perfect Victorian father."

"Has your brother such rights under the will?" Bobby asked.

"I've no idea. He says so. It doesn't matter."

But both her listeners were looking very grave as they listened. The implications were only too plain.

"You say this note was written more than a week ago," Bell said, taking up the questioning again. "Can you show us any proof of that?"

"I can't make you believe me if you don't want to," she answered indifferently.

"An envelope with the postmark for instance," Bell persisted. "Or did anyone post it for you? Was it sent through the post?"

"We never used the post," she told him wearily. "If you know anything about villages you would understand why. If we had, everyone would have known at once. There's a woman delivers the letters and the post office is kept by a woman. Between them they know all about it—who gets the letters and who sends them and where they are from and everything."

"How did you manage then?"

"We left messages in the shelter for each other. It is easy to get to it from the footpath across the field. Fred said he didn't want anyone to know there was anything between us and he thought Mr. Fielding's housekeeper was watching."

"Why didn't he want people to know?"

"He said there was something he had to do and he didn't want me mixed up in it."

"Did you never ask him what it was?"

"I expect so. Yes. He wouldn't say."

"Surely if you were going to be married, you had a right to know."

"What good was that?" she asked with a rather bitter smile. "I couldn't make him if he didn't want to. I expect I was afraid to ask too often."

"Afraid? Why?"

"Afraid it meant he was growing tired of me. Perhaps he was."

Bobby knew this questioning had to go on. It was necessary. As he himself had said once before: 'What had to be, must be.' None the less he felt there was something brutal, almost indecent in this slow unveiling of a woman's most secret hopes and fears. Perhaps Bell felt the same for he said now with a clumsy effort at gallantry:

"I can't imagine that's likely, not at all likely." She took no notice. Bell went on: "I'm sorry, miss. But there it is. There's two men been killed and—"

"I know," she interrupted. "Once before two men were killed. In Egypt. Now it's happened again. Here. Is there anything else you want to ask?"

"Did your brother know about your leaving notes for each other in the shelter and your meeting there?"

"Not till I told him. I told him that, too, when I told him about Fred and me."

"When was your last meeting there?"

"With Fred? I don't remember exactly. It was after I left him that note you found—when I told Fred about George being troublesome. Fred didn't seem to mind much. He said I wasn't to worry. I never saw him again."

"We have reason to believe," Bell went on, "that some sort of scuffle or fight took place between your brother and Biggs. What can you tell us about that?"

She was silent for a moment or two. Then she said with deliberation:

"I will tell you anything you like about Fred or me, anything at all. It won't hurt either of us now. He is dead and I think perhaps I am, too. But I won't say anything about anyone else."

"Does that mean you think your brother shot him?"

"He didn't. He never did, he couldn't," she cried with such sudden and such startled vehemence that both her listeners wondered if that was the dreadful fear lurking in her mind. Or was there perhaps an even more dreadful explanation?

CHAPTER XXIII

SIMPLE TEST

IT WAS BELL who first broke the silence as the two men walked away from the bungalow. He said:

"Is it good enough?"

"For action?" Bobby asked. "My own idea is that she's afraid it may have been her brother."

"Yes, I know," Bell said, "but I wondered if perhaps she was just trying to put that across."

It was the same idea that had occurred to Bobby. He said nothing. They walked on in silence. Presently Bell said:

"Well, what next?"

"Better try to find young Rogers," Bobby suggested. "You will have to ask him to make a statement."

"Provided he hasn't done a bunk," Bell said gloomily. "I shouldn't wonder if that wasn't what he was up to when Fielding saw him. Very likely the girl knows and that's what's upsetting her. Confession of guilt if it's that way."

"Only confession of panic sometimes," Bobby said. "Anyhow, he hasn't, for there he is, on that cycle, coming towards us."

In effect, George Rogers had just appeared round a turn of the road. They stood waiting for him. He showed no inclination to stop when he saw them but Bell stepped into the road, holding up a hand. George scowled, but dismounted.

"Been looking for Miss Rogers?" Bell asked. "She is back home now."

"Well, what about it?" George demanded. "I knew she was. I rang up and she answered. Have you been worrying her again? Can't leave anyone in peace, I suppose?"

"Everyone's got to be questioned," Bell told him; "everyone who has had any connection with it whatever. You're an educated man, Mr. Rogers, you ought to understand that without being told. There are some things we've got to ask you as well."

"Go ahead. I don't mind. Waste of time of course. There's one thing I'll tell you without being asked. Do you know why I was worried about Rhoda? Why when she didn't turn up for lunch I went to see if I could find her? Because you had bullied her into such a state of nerves I was half afraid of suicide. She was talking wildly enough, God knows."

"Was she?" Bell asked. "What did she say?" but George did not answer.

Bobby said:

"Was what you call her state of nerves because of our bullying or because of what has happened and of what she knows and will not tell?"

"She doesn't know anything more than anyone else," George asserted. "I don't either for that matter."

"Well, that's what we have to be sure of and at present we aren't," Bobby told him. "We do know Miss Rogers used to meet Biggs at the shelter and that is where these two murders took place. Did she that night, too?"

"No, she didn't," George answered at once and with emphasis. "Rhoda was in bed and fast asleep when I got back, and that was just about twelve."

"Got back from where?" Bobby asked swiftly; and George looked very disconcerted, as if only then did he realize the significance of the words he had left slip.

"I mean when I went to bed myself," he said, lamely enough.

"That won't do," Bobby said firmly. He repeated: "Got back from where?"

George made no answer. He looked more disconcerted and sullen than ever and he pressed his lips together tightly as if to make sure no more indiscreet words slipped out. Bell said:

"Had you been there?"

"Where?"

"At the shelter? The shelter at midnight? Is that where you got back from?"

George had become very pale now. His uneasiness was apparent. He said, and not too steadily:

"Are you going to try to make out it was me?"

"Well, was it?" Bell asked.

"What's the use of my saying anything?" George retorted sullenly. "It wasn't, but a fat lot you care as long as you can pick on someone."

"But you have said something already, Mr. Rogers," Bobby reminded him. "You said you got back from somewhere that night but you haven't told us where that somewhere was."

"It was only a slip of the tongue," George mumbled.

"Mr. Rogers," Bobby said sternly, "for a gentleman who claims a conscience and a sensibility greater than those of most of us, you seem inclined to be much less frank—"

"That's right," George interrupted angrily. "That's what it is. It's always that way. That's what you're after. If you could get me convicted of murder or something, then you could discredit the whole great pacifist movement and that would please your bosses, wouldn't it? That's the game, and you can't deny it."

"We'll leave the whole great pacifist movement out of it, if you don't mind," Bobby retorted with some impatience. "We are asking you to be frank. So far you haven't given that impression."

But George only closed his mouth more tightly than ever, thrust his hands more deeply into his pockets, and stared at them defiantly. Plainly he was challenging them to do their utmost to make him speak, and telling them all their efforts would be useless. No good your trying to make me talk when I don't choose to, his whole attitude was saying. Bobby made up his mind to try a manœuvre he had known used with success in other cases. He said:

"Suppose—I'm not saying it is so, but let's suppose— there is a reliable, trustworthy witness who saw you that night and can say exactly when and where. What then?"

It was a simple test. A man whose conscience was entirely clear would remain unaffected, for he would know that no such witness could possibly be produced. One whose conscience was less clear would hesitate, prevaricate, be doubtful, would want to try to get to know more before giving a direct reply. Sometimes they betrayed themselves even more effectively, as did George now, when he muttered:

"I suppose you mean Miss Bellamy? I didn't know she saw me. I don't see how she could. She was playing that beastly music of hers."

"Don't you think you had better tell us all about it now?" Bobby suggested. "Wisest in the long run, I think."

George began to fumble with a cigarette. He looked very unhappy and was plainly hesitating. The other two waited, watching him silently. Presently he seemed to make up his mind. He threw away the unlighted cigarette and said, unexpectedly:

"If you want to know what I think, it was Miss Bellamy."

"Miss Bellamy what?" Bobby asked, though he felt he knew.

"Killed him," George said. "They quarrelled about Rhoda. It's in her playing. Killing, I mean. You can always hear it."

"Never mind that now," Bobby said. "Tell us about that night and why you think she may have seen you."

"Well, if she told you, she must have," George said. "I knew Rhoda went out sometimes to meet Biggs and I meant to stop it and I knew there were stories about Biggs visiting Miss Bellamy late at night. It wouldn't have done any good telling Rhoda. She would have said it was only gossip. I made up my mind to see for myself. Keep a look out. So I did and I heard Miss Bellamy at her piano."

"What was the time?"

"About ten. I had an idea that when she played at that time it was to let Biggs know she wanted him. That's why I went that night."

"Did you see him?"

"No. She stopped playing and I hung around. I thought I would wait and see if he came and if he did I meant to wait till he was inside and then I would knock and have him out and then Rhoda would have to believe. I didn't mean my sister to throw herself away on a man like that, a chauffeur working for a neighbour. Bad character, too."

"Why do you say 'bad character'? Do you know anything?"

"He was mixed up in that smash-and-grab raid affair, wasn't he? And then I saw him once talking to a man I recognized. I've done time." He smiled, a little proudly. "Probably you knew? I expect that settles it as far as you're concerned. I did a month before it was agreed I should take a job with a farmer. I stood out at first that none of what I helped to produce was to go to the army, but I had to admit it would be hard to manage so I agreed to do what I could to help. The man I saw talking to Biggs was there. In prison, I mean. Of course, nearly all of them were just victims of society—fundamentally the same as anyone else. Merely wanted sympathetic treatment. This man was different in a way. He was at open war with society. You can't wonder. But he did boast of what he had done and what he meant to do. Violence had corroded him. He was most offensive to me. He boasted they couldn't prove anything against him. I suppose he was right about that because they had to let him go."

"He is the man you saw talking to Biggs?"

"Yes."

"Did he recognize you?"

"I don't think so. As soon as I saw who it was I turned back. I have every sympathy with the unhappy victims of society, of course. But this man—not his fault but he did show himself inclined to be violent and offensive even when you were trying to understand him."

"I don't wonder," interposed Bell, very emphatically.

"No, of course," agreed George, pleased with a remark of which it is to be feared he had not quite grasped the exact meaning.

"Can you describe him?" Bobby asked.

George gave a general description that would have applied to at least half the male population of the country, but insisted all the same that he had an excellent memory for faces and had certainly made no mistake. Indeed it is true that some people can keep the memory of a face once seen quite clearly in their memory, and yet be utterly incapable of giving any recognizable description in words.

"You ought to have told us all this before," Bell said severely.

"Why? What's it got to do with it?"

"It may have a lot to do with it," Bell retorted. "How long were you watching Miss Bellamy's cottage?"

"I don't know exactly. It was just about twelve when I got in. I told you. I made sure Rhoda was in her room, asleep."

Bell said slowly:

"Had you been first to the shelter to see if she was there and did you find Biggs instead? For indeed it seems to me that that is very much what your story comes to."

CHAPTER XXIV

PSYCHOLOGICAL STUFF

THAT ENDED THE interview, for it seemed there was nothing more to be learnt, at any rate for the time, and there was much more to be done. The two detectives departed therefore, leaving behind them a young man considerably less perky and self-confident than usual. Bell said in his depressed and worried way:

"Isn't there a story about a donkey starving to death because it couldn't make up its mind which bundle of hay to start in on?"

"Buridan's ass, you mean," Bobby said, searching his mind for memories of old college lectures. "In Aristotle somewhere, I think—or is it Plato?"

"I've heard of them," Bell remarked a little proudly. "On the Brains Trust—Plato," he repeated. "That's the name Dr. Joad writes under, isn't it?"

"I shouldn't be a bit surprised," Bobby agreed. "Where does the ass and the hay come in?"

"It's the way I feel," Bell explained. "Like a prize champion donkey for one thing, and such a good case re both the Rogers girl and the Rogers boy that I don't know which of 'em to pinch. One thing, they may be both in it together," he added with a more hopeful air than he often permitted himself to show.

Bobby shook his head.

"I can't think it's that way," he declared. "I don't believe those two would ever work together. Each one of them might kill —and that's true of most of us—but not in collusion. What's the next move?"

"Better have a go at Miss Bellamy, see if we can get anything out of her," Bell suggested. As they walked along, he
said; "What about Rogers's idea that it's her we want? Anything in it or just him trying to put us wrong to save himself?"

"I don't somehow think it's like that," Bobby answered,
though with some hesitation. "He's an odd type. Confused.
Like most of the rest of us these days, for that matter. A mass
of contradictions. I think one trouble with him is that he
wants to walk by himself, like Kipling's cat, but doesn't
know where to—or how. All dressed up mentally, so to say,
but nowhere to go."

"Do you think he would kill?—and him a conscientious
objector?"

"Oh, yes. Goes with it. They are all like that. Pacifism
nine times in ten is a result of an inner tendency to violence.
There's a subconscious awareness of that, and so there's a
feeling, too, that it must be kept down at all costs. That's
why the pacifists are always so ready for a fight and to defend violence when it's on their own side. It was a well-
known conscientious objector who tried to find excuses for
the King David hotel murders in Jerusalem. Remember what
Rogers said about Miss Bellamy's playing being all about
war and killing?"

"I thought he was just talking through his hat," Bell said.
"It struck me as more muddled up like—rather the way I feel
in all this business."

"The first time my wife and I heard it," Bobby said, "we
both thought it was a kind of warning of trouble to come.
That was because we were both a bit uneasy without knowing it, over our getting Fern Cottage. Too good to be true,
Olive said. I think that's the way with Miss Bellamy's playing. What you hear in it is what is already in your mind."

"Psychological stuff," Bell complained. "Gets you nowhere. No more evidence than what the soldier said."

"Psychological stuff," Bobby retorted, "means character
and in a case like this character means everything." He went
on, ignoring Bell's violently shaken head: "It shouldn't be

difficult to trace the man Rogers says he knew in gaol and saw in Biggs's company. We can look up the records and see who was doing time with Rogers. Most likely we shall find there was one of the smash-and-grab lot we know about but can't pull in yet. If so, there's just a chance some of them may know something about Biggs and be willing to talk."

"Not likely, no such luck," Bell declared. "It's never so easy as that. Afraid of being implicated."

"There's that," Bobby agreed. "Anyhow it's the first hint we've had of Biggs's past and it is a definite link between him and the smash-and-grab business. It may prove important—very important. The lead we want."

"I don't see how," protested Bell in his gloomiest tone. "Ten to one, only another dead end."

They had reached the Bellamy cottage now. When they knocked Miss Bellamy came at once to the door. She showed no surprise, little interest. She stood aside to let them enter, and, but for that gesture, it might well have been that she was not even aware of their presence. As soon as they entered they were in the large front room—large that is by comparison with the other rooms in this tiny cottage. Miss Bellamy crossed slowly the floor and seated herself before the grand piano, her back to the instrument. Bell stood by the fireplace, Bobby by the window. Bell spoke very loudly, as if he wished or hoped by mere effect of emphasis or noise, to recall her from that infinite distance to which it seemed she had again receded.

"Very sorry, miss," he began in this new loud voice of his, "to have to trouble you again, but we've got to. Our duty, ma'am. Necessary. You'll have heard about this new development?"

"Murder," she said. "Murder," she repeated. "Is that what you call a new development?" To Bobby, she said: "You found his body in the shelter where you and I and Rhoda were last night. Did you know while we were watching?"

"No," said Bobby. "One does one's best to draw conclusions and sometimes they are right and sometimes they are wrong. After you had left, Mr. Fielding came."

"Yes," she said, and then she said again: "Yes." Then she said: "'That made four."

"Did you know?" Bobby asked.

She did not answer. It was growing quickly dark now, for all this had taken time and it was late. The shadows were heaviest where she sat at one end of the room and it was out of the gloom that she spoke now—and was it only fancy that made it seem as though her eyes glowed there in the increasing dark as though lit by strange inner light? She said, and her words dropped slowly into the shadow filled room:

"Was he there when you found the body?"

"Why do you ask?" Bobby said, but again she did not answer, and again she seemed to have withdrawn herself into a remote and distant contemplation—or was it memory?

Bell said with some irritation:

"Ma'am, you'll be called at the inquest and you'll have to give evidence." When she was still silent, still, as it were, withdrawn, he said: "You'll be asked what you know about Biggs and you'll have to answer."

"I shall say—nothing," she replied, and they did not know whether she meant she would say nothing or that she knew nothing.

"You still deny that he was in the habit of visiting you at night?" Bell asked.

She took no notice. She was cupping her chin in her hand and seemed again withdrawn into the intensity of her own thoughts. Even when Bell repeated his question she remained silent, but not so much as refusing to answer as ignoring the chatter of a child to which even the child itself expected no answer. Bobby interposed. He said:

"I don't think you often played late at night. When you did, was it a signal to Biggs to tell him to come?"

That startled her. For the first time the armour of her remote indifference was pierced. There was a kind of dark high anger, or even alarm, in the glance she directed at him. She said:

"That's the gossip you've been listening to. I told you before he came occasionally. It may have been late sometimes.

I daresay it was. Mr. Fielding sent me flowers now and then. Sometimes he got things for me in town and Biggs would bring them me. Or a message to ask if I would go for a drive or could he take me to town if I wanted to do some shopping or any business." She paused; and there was a certain soft-ness, a kind of reluctant and hesitating tenderness in her voice as she added: "Mr. Fielding has always been kind and thoughtful and I have not met so many who are that." After another long pause, she said: "I think he meant it." She went on: "I expect that's what started the gossip. I knew people from the village hung about outside. Sometimes I played to them. They said my music was indecent but it wasn't my music, it was their own minds. Peeping Toms, you call them."

"Did that often happen?" Bell asked. "Was Biggs one of them, do you think?"

For the first time in their knowledge of her, she nearly laughed. At any rate there was something like the semblance of a smile that for a moment seemed to touch the corners of her mouth. But it vanished at once, as though alarmed at finding itself where none like it had been for so long. Still, there did remain a touch of something more closely resem-bling ordinary human emotion in her voice as she said:

"Oh, no. No. No, he was never one of them. Anyhow, he was never like that."

"Did he come to see you the night he was killed?" She shook her head. "Did anyone? Or did you hear anyone out-side?"

"I thought I heard something," she admitted, "but when I went to look there was no one there. The man who used to be Mr. Fielding's chauffeur, Alf Cann, was coming up the lane. There was another man with him. I'm not sure, but I think now the other man was the man who was killed, Myerson—wasn't that his name?"

"Myerson? With Cann that night? Why didn't you say so before?" Bell was both startled and angry and he spoke with emphasis. "It's the last time he was seen alive, it may be most important. Ma'am, don't you know it's a most serious offence to withhold information?"

"I didn't know I was," she answered, unmoved. "It was dark. I didn't take much notice and I couldn't see either of them very clearly. It only struck me to-night that it might be the same man. The woman who does my washing for me was here and she was talking all the time about what's happened. No one is talking of anything else. You can't wonder. She had seen the man you call Myerson and it's what she said about him made me think it might be the same man. But I'm not sure, it was dark. I did wonder a little."

"Are you sure it was this man, Cann, you saw?" Bell asked.

"You're not going to suspect him now, are you?" she demanded scornfully.

"I tell you plainly, ma'am," retorted Bell, "there's some we are suspecting, but not so much Mr. Cann, at least, not yet, not so much as others I could name."

"You mean you are suspecting me, you think it might have been me?" she asked, but with complete indifference. "It wasn't. Or was it? But not in the way you mean."

"In what way do you mean?" Bobby asked, interrupting suddenly.

Miss Bellamy turned her attention once more to him, her generally remote and far-off gaze now grave, intent, inquiring.

"In no way you would understand," she said presently. "Or any policeman." She was still watching him gravely, doubtfully. "If you are a policeman," she added presently, as if not quite sure.

"I am certainly a policeman," Bobby told her, "and it is part of a policeman's duty to understand many things. I will ask you again: In what way do you mean?"

"I killed neither of those two poor men," she said, without answering him directly. "I think if I ever killed anyone I should kill myself too. And I do not know who did kill either of them, though I may think that I could—guess. Even if I knew I do not think I should say. When a thing is over and done with, isn't it better to let it stay so lest worse comes?"

"Nothing is ever over and done with," Bobby said. "It goes on."

CHAPTER XXV

DIFFERING INTERPRETATIONS

"AND NOW," SAID Bell gloomily as they walked away, "there's four bundles of hay for the donkey that's me. First, this Cann bloke we've never thought of before—at least, I haven't, not in any serious way, I mean, just in the margin, so to say, and her as well. Because, blessed if I don't think it might just as well be her as not. She's holding back on us all right."

"We've got to find out what and why." Bobby said.

"I know," agreed Bell with a hopeless sort of gesture. "Only how? And then this Cann business. What was he doing and why was he with Myerson, if he was? How about this? He knew Myerson had some good stuff as well as the costume stuff that was just a cover. Well, he wanted it, and he got it all right—up there by the air raid shelter. What do you say?"

"It's an entirely new line," Bobby said, and he sounded very worried. "You'll have to follow it up, of course. If it's that way, it cuts out a lot."

"Too much?"

"You can't tell yet," Bobby answered, and he still sounded very worried indeed. "It would simplify everything enormously. Everything we've been working on there all right, but all quite irrelevant, because Cann cuts in, and it turns out to be a chance murder for money—or for money's worth, jewellery. But how could Cann know Myerson had anything as valuable as all that with him? There's been no suggestion of any previous connection between them. Again, would a man like Cann—quiet, peaceful, respectable, in steady work, no record as far as we know—is it credible he would become so sudden and so desperate at a moment's notice?"

"Anything's credible about anyone," asserted Bell, "especially if it's something bad. And we're all respectable till we're found out. Besides, remember that first time we went to see him?"

"You mean the very agreeable smell in the kitchen?" Bobby said, and he was on the point of rubbing the end of his nose in perplexity when he remembered in time that was a gesture wifely authority did not permit, so he stopped. "There is that," he admitted. "It might be important. You'll have to follow that up, too."

"Easier said than done," grumbled Bell. "How do we know Miss Bellamy is telling the truth? Invented the yarn to put us off as like as not. It might just as well be her as any one. Jealousy. Jealousy accounts for a lot. Always does. Much more reasonable to my mind than Cann thinking Myerson, whom he's never seen before and knows nothing about, might have worthwhile stuff in his pocket, so knock him off and that's that. A bit of a stretch, don't you think? Now, take it Miss Bellamy was carrying on with Biggs and she found out about him and Miss Rogers having been together in Egypt and perhaps were still. How about that?"

"Good working theory," agreed Bobby, "only it works just as well the other way round—Miss Rogers finding out about Miss Bellamy."

"Yes, I know," Bell said in tones of the deepest despondency. "The fourth bundle of hay and me, the donkey, not knowing which to start nibbling at." They had been standing still as they talked and now Bell looked at his wrist watch. "Not too late," he decided, "to pay Cann a visit and check up. Most likely he'll trot out something entirely new he's only just thought of and it turns·everything upside down again. It's what's generally happened so far. Every time we think we really are on something at last."

"It all helps to getting a complete picture in the end," Bobby told him, but this was a cheerful view that Bell could not feel was in any way tenable.

He was indeed just about to voice a protest as they started to walk on, when he paused suddenly.

"Listen," he said, and from the cottage they had just left there came pouring out into the night a flood of melody. "She's at it again," he said in a voice full of resentment.

They stood still, listening almost against their will. The music seemed to envelop them, to flood the whole earth as it were till it was almost as though nothing existed in all the universe save these passionate, possessive strains. To Bobby the impression came that some other mind was striving to enter into his mind and control it. Bell was trying to light a cigarette, but he kept forgetting, letting the match burn out and then striking another. They heard slow footsteps approaching. The night was not so dark but that soon they were able to recognize Mr. Fielding. He recognized them, too. He said:

"That's her playing. I must go." But he did not stir. The music continued and they remained standing there, listening, as it flowed around them, like the slow rising of deep water. Fielding said in a loud, accusing voice: "You've been asking her questions."

"So we have and we'll have to ask her more," Bell answered, he, too, speaking more loudly than usual and even angrily, giving indeed an odd impression of defying the music that now was not nearly so loud but equally insistent. Then it ceased, broken off in the middle of a strain. "Well, now then," Bell said, and this time there was relief in his voice.

"I'll go back home," Fielding said, and Bobby thought there was relief in his voice, too, as if with the cessation of the music the compulsion it had laid upon him ceased also.

"I've never heard anyone play like her before," Bobby said, and was not sure that he did not to some degree share in the relief his two companions so evidently experienced.

Fielding had turned and was in the act of moving away as Bobby spoke, but now he said, over his shoulder:

"You've never known a woman like her before."

"One moment," Bobby said as Fielding began again to move away. "One moment, please. There's a question I think we must ask you. You may think it impertinent. It isn't. It's necessary. In the village they seem to think there is some probability of you and Miss Bellamy getting married. What they say is that you are courting her. Is that true?"

Fielding was silent; and yet, in spite of the darkness that made it impossible to see his features clearly, Bobby felt that the question affected him profoundly. Twice he began to speak and twice he stopped. At last he broke out in a queer, half-strangled voice:

"We should have met before."

"Are you in love with her?" Bobby asked.

"My God, there's a question," Fielding said.

"Well, are you?" Bell interposed.

"There it is again," Fielding said; and once more that strange music poured out into the air, passionate, enigmatic, questioning. "I'm going home," he muttered, but still he made no effort to stir, and still the three of them stood and listened as all around them flowed that dark, compelling music.

When presently it stopped, and how long this time it had lasted none of them had much idea, Fielding said for the third time: "I'm going back home." Then he said: "I can't stand any more."

"Is she wanting you? expecting you?" Bobby asked.

"What do you mean? why should she?" Fielding retorted; and this time Bobby was not sure whether there was more of fear, of anger, or of surprise in his voice, but something, Bobby was sure, of all three.

"Well, why?" he asked again.

"She'll have to talk at the inquest," Bell said. "So will you, Mr. Fielding. You'll be called, too."

"I'll be getting back," Fielding said, taking no notice of this, as if indeed he had not even heard it. "It'll begin again if I don't."

He hurried away, almost running at times. He vanished in the darkness. When even the sound of his footsteps had died away, Bell said:

"Well, now then, what are you to make of all that? Is he going home, do you think?"

"If he does, I don't think he will stop there," Bobby said. "He is certainly under some strong nervous strain."

"Well, two murders on his doorstep nearly. A bit upsetting," Bell said tolerantly. "Do you think he is really in love with her?"

"I am sure there is a very strong emotional connection of some sort or another," Bobby said. "The difficulty is to relate it to the murders—if there is any relation. Possibly there isn't. It might be one of them knows the other is guilty—or thinks it. My own feeling is that my wife was right when she said she thought on Miss Bellamy's side it was a kind of pity, a kind of remorseless pity, the pity an airman may feel for the town on which it is his duty to drop bombs. And on his side a sort of fascination like that you experience when you look down from a great height and feel as if you've got to jump. But where what you can call love comes into it, goodness knows. Or what the two murders have to do with it, either."

"I don't know about all that," Bell said doubtfully. "It's this education, I suppose. There's times I'm glad I never had any. Confuses you. You see double, like having had a drop too much."

"Well, you know," Bobby agreed, "there's a lot in that."

"It beats me," Bell went on complainingly. "This music of hers, I mean. I wonder what it was. It wasn't anything I've ever heard before, and I listen in to the B.B.C, every chance I get. Soothes you somehow."

"So it does, doesn't it?" Bobby agreed again. "I don't much expect you ever have heard it before or anyone else for that matter. I think she improvises when she plays like that."

"You mean she makes it up out of her head as she goes along?" Bell asked in a slightly awed tone. Then he rallied a little: "Of course," he said, "that might be why at the end it sounded all sort of bits and pieces, muddled like, same as I am."

"To me," Bobby said, "it sounded more like a sort of general protest—as if she were crying out against fate and God and all mankind and herself as well and what she had to do. There are moments when I feel like that myself when I have to bring to justice some wretched man or woman only half to blame for what they've done." He paused and then in a surprised voice, he said: "I didn't know before I ever felt like that,"

"If it sounded different like to you and me," Bell said, "how did it sound to Fielding?"

But Bobby had no answer to make to that question. They had been walking on as they talked and now were back in the village, near Miss Cann's shop. When Bell knocked at the side door Miss Cann appeared but showed small pleasure on seeing who it was.

"You again," she grumbled. "What is it this time?"

"Your nephew in?" Bell asked. "If he is, we would like a few minutes' chat with him, if he doesn't mind. We've received some fresh information we should like to check up with him."

"He is having his supper," Miss Cann said. "I suppose you've got to see him if you want to."

She went back into the kitchen. Cann was sitting at the table before a simple meal of bread and cold sausage. This time no agreeable, appetizing smell was there to cause to water the mouths of visitors.

"No rabbit stew this evening, Mr. Cann," Bobby remarked cheerfully.

"What about it?" demanded Cann, anything but cheerfully. "What are you getting at?"

"Only remembering," Bobby explained, "how nice it smelt the other night we were here."

"No law against rabbit stew, is there?" Cann asked defiantly.

"Of course not," declared Bobby. "Why, we've had it once or twice lately. My wife says it's a lot easier to get rabbits in the country. Pays a whole lot better to sell on the spot at full controlled price than sending them to town for sale at dealer's wholesale price. Not to mention the rabbits that pop out of the fields straight into the kitchen and very nice, too."

"Not here," declared Miss Cann firmly, "and me that's always kept respectable and no one can say different."

"Think you're being funny, don't you?" snarled Cann. "Cops being funny, that's a good one, that is."

"No, there's nothing funny about murder," Bobby said with a sudden and startling change of voice.

"Well, then," said Cann, and nervously helped himself to all that remained of the cold sausages.

"There's no more where they came from," Miss Cann warned him.

"Mr. Cann," Bobby said in the same hard tones, "we have received information that you were seen in the company of one of the murdered men shortly before he was killed."

"That's a lie," shouted Cann. He thumped on the table for emphasis, but he was very pale. "Who told you? No one ever did. It's a lie."

"Is it?" Bobby said. "That remains to be seen. I am afraid we can't merely take your word for it. Because we know you have lied to us before, and so perhaps you have again."

CHAPTER XXVI

SOUND ALIBI?

CANN WAS ON his feet now. He gesticulated, began to shout, his eyes were on the door as though he contemplated flight. Bobby told him roughly to sit down and keep quiet.

"That sort of thing is doing you no good," he said. "If you have anything to say, any explanation to offer, we are here to listen to it."

"Don't say a word, Alf," Miss Cann interposed. "He ain't treating you fair. He hasn't given you any warning, same as he did ought. It's not legal."

"We only warn people," Bobby explained, "when we have decided to make a charge. That is for Mr. Bell to decide, but at present I don't expect he has it in mind. It all depends on our information, and what we want to know now is why Mr. Cann lied when we saw him last?"

"I never did," Cann said sulkily. "You've no right to go saying as I did."

"They're scandalizing us, so they are," protested Miss Cann. "They did ought to be ashamed. First it's rabbits and then it's lies and us as always kept ourselves respectable."

"Let us hope," Bobby said, "it will stop with rabbits and lies, and the way to stop it is to tell the truth this time. When we were here before, Mr. Cann, you stated that you had seen and spoken to one of the dead men, Fred Biggs, at ten o'clock on the night of his murder and that you then came straight home but stayed up talking till midnight when you went to bed."

"Well, what about it?"

"Just this," Bobby answered. "That it's not true. At ten o'clock that night Biggs was with some other men outside the Much Middles Arms. They were talking about a darts match. I know because I happened to be passing and I both saw him and heard what he was saying. I advise you, Mr. Cann, to tell us the truth. Much better than having it dragged out of you under cross-examination by King's Counsel at the inquest."

This suggestion of possible cross-examination by a K.C. at the inquest made its impression—and not least upon Bell. For to Bell a K.C. meant the payment of a fee about which a Joint Standing Committee examining police accounts would ask indignant and startled questions. To Miss Cann and her nephew it meant a formidable figure in a wig, a pointing finger, a voice of doom, all kinds indeed of known and unknown terrors.

"You had better tell it 'em all," Miss Cann said tremulously. "We shouldn't never be able to hold up our heads again and you been cross-examined in police court."

But Cann wasn't beaten yet.

"Maybe it was later," he said. "I thought it was ten but it might have been later. I don't know as I noticed so particular as all that."

"You said you did," Bobby reminded him. "You said you heard the church clock strike."

"It might have been eleven," Cann suggested, fighting to the last. "I might easy have been mistook."

"That won't do either," Bobby told him. "You said you came straight back here. That would make it about a quarter past when you got in. Then you said you stopped up talking till midnight. If you noticed the time when you thought it was striking ten, and the time at twelve when you went to bed, you must have noticed, too, that you had missed an hour. You can't have thought you and Miss Cann had been talking nearly two hours when in fact it was only somewhere about forty minutes."

Cann did not answer at once. He was still standing by the table, still casting furtive glances at the door, still looking sullen and afraid. Miss Cann was sitting by the fire. She muttered something to herself about being respectable and to ask vicar or the neighbours. Bobby, getting no answer, resumed. He said;

"Another thing. The two of you were at some trouble to tell us that it was twelve or a little after when you went to bed. You both stressed that. Why? The perfect alibi, of course, if we can accept it. The medical evidence gives twelve as about the time when Biggs was killed and if you were in bed at twelve—but were you?—then you couldn't have been shooting Biggs by the air raid shelter at the same time. Is that what you were thinking?"

"No, it wasn't," interposed Miss Cann. "How could it when we didn't know anything about it's being twelve when it happened. It could have been any time for all we knew."

"That's right," Cann said, looking relieved. "We didn't know, how could we? No idea we hadn't."

"Shall I tell you what I think?" Bobby asked. "It will most likely be the lines you'll be cross-examined on." He paused to let this sink in, for he had noticed that the expression 'cross-examined' produced its effect—as words often do by reason of the strange magic that is in them. "Cross-examined," he repeated, "on what I'm going to suggest really happened. Probably it was eleven you heard striking and very possibly you did see Biggs about that time. I don't expect you spoke. I don't think you much wanted to be seen, either by him or by anyone else. I put it to you that you were about your own business and that that business was—rabbits. A spot of poaching. Rabbits have their value in these days and even if you don't want to sell them, they make a nice addition to the rations—a nice change for dinner. Shall I go on to tell you why you were both so keen on trying to tell us you were in bed by twelve or thereabouts?"

"I suppose Sammy Potter's been talking," Cann said. "I had to cut and run for it, only I didn't think he could spot it was me. I don't see how he could, too dark. He nearly got me though, only lucky for me he came a cropper. Caught his foot or something. I heard him go flop into Singles brook." Cann allowed himself a faint smile at the memory. "Mind you," he added, "it wasn't rabbits, nothing to do with rabbits or such like. I was just having a stroll round, breath of fresh air before bed, and I missed my way in the dark. Only you know yourself what a bullying, suspicious lot game-keeper blokes are. As soon as they see you, sure it's rabbits and all that you're after, and you as innocent as the babe unborn."

"Don't talk nonsense," Bobby snapped irritably.

"It's gospel truth," began Cann, and then paused as he saw how Bobby glared. "Well, you can't prove anything," he said sulkily. "Sammy Potter would swear to anything but he can't deny it was pitch dark under them trees."

"Alf wouldn't ever murder anyone," Miss Cann interposed anxiously, and still more anxiously, more pleadingly, she said: "You don't think he did it, do you?"

"I only think at present," Bobby told her in a sudden burst of temper, "that he's about the biggest kind of fool I've come across for a long time."

"Oh, well, if that's all," said Miss Cann contentedly, "I could have told you that much long ago."

"All very well for you to talk," grumbled Cann. "Nobody wasn't after you on a hanging job."

"You've only yourself to thank for it if you came under suspicion," Bobby pointed out. "If you had told the truth at first you would have saved a lot of trouble. Now I want to know something else and try not to tell any lies this time. Why did you give up your job with Mr. Fielding and why have you come back now?"

"That was Biggs," Cann explained. He was still sulky but all the same he was showing manifest relief at the turn things were taking. "Biggs offered me twenty quid and said where I could get another job. He had applied for it himself and he had an answer but he said they wouldn't care who it was so long as they got someone. He told me his girl lived about here and he wanted to be near. I didn't mind making a change to oblige, and twenty quid—well, it's twenty quid."

"Did he say who the girl was?"

"No, and I didn't ask. I'm not nosey."

"Aren't you? I am," Bobby said. "Why did you return?"

"She told me," Cann said and jerked a thumb at his aunt.

"It's handy to have a man around, even if it's only Alf." Miss Cann explained. "He wrote he wasn't finding his new job all it could be. Real tip-top swells they were, and that hard up they hadn't hardly a penny to bless themselves with. I knew there was likely to be a dust-up soon what with Mr. Fielding courting Miss Bellamy and Biggs hanging round her place late at night—and if you ask me, it's him done it—Mr. Fielding, I mean. He found out they were carrying on together and so he shot him, same as you read in the papers."

"Mr. Fielding she means," Cann explained. "But what I say is why should he? All he had to do was to give Biggs the sack. Let alone it's not likely she was Biggs's girl. Twice his age she is or thereabouts, and Mr. Fielding was buzzing round her long before Biggs came. What's more, even if he was courting her, it wasn't that way. Not the sort to lose his head, Mr. Fielding isn't, not over any woman. It's Mr. Fielding first, last, and all the time with him. If he wanted a woman it would be polite and peaceable like, reasonable if you see what I mean."

"Quite the psychologist, aren't you?" Bobby remarked, slightly amused. "But I'm not sure you're right. When it's a man and a woman together, you can never be sure of anything."

"Except that they're likely to make fools of themselves," interposed Miss Cann.

"Except that, of course," agreed Bobby.

"If it had been him done in," commented Cann, "Mr. Fielding, I mean, I would have said it was likely her all right, seeing what I know, but then it wasn't him, so there you are."

"What do you know?" Bobby asked.

CHAPTER XXVII

PURSUING MUSIC

CANN HAD SEEMED inclined to be more communicative now he knew that he was not under immediate suspicion. But at this question he hesitated, evidently reluctant to reply. He glanced at his aunt, and she, having made up her mind that frankness was the best policy, said briskly:

"Frightened! That's what Alf said. Frightened. As soon almost as she took that cottage of hers Alf said as his guv'nor seemed scared like she had something on him. Frightened fit to die, Alf said." As if the last word sounded ominous now, she added defensively: "That's what he said and I said not to talk so silly, but he stuck to it."

"What made you think that?" Bobby asked Cann.

"What he said," Cann answered. "The way he looked, too. In my job you got to know your guv'nor pretty well. You have to. They have their fads and fancies you've got to play up to, unless you want the sack and no reference. And the guv'nor was frightened all right. Not at first. It sort of came on slow like. First he didn't take much notice. It was just 'Good morning, Miss Bellamy. Nice day.' and that was all. But I noticed she looked at him a bit hard like, and then I noticed he was beginning to keep out of her way. When we were starting out he would tell me to drive fast down the lane. Sometimes he would take the wheel himself though he's not so keen on driving, and a good thing, too. I never saw a worse. But when he did he would go past her cottage like hell, with her at the piano as often as not, and her music following us down the road, like it was pursuing us. It's gospel truth I've seen him fair sweating as he heard her at it, playing away for all she was worth. I said to him one day that it was funny stuff and I'd never heard the like, not on the wireless or anywhere and he said if ever he was found with a bullet through his head, I would know. Only it isn't him or her either that's been found that way, so it don't come in."

"Did he say anything else? Did you say anything?" Bobby asked.

"I was a bit shook up but I didn't know how to take it, and the guv passed it off as a joke like. Only joking he said. But that wasn't the way it sounded to me. Next thing he was making up to her, only in a funny scared sort of way—like petting a dog you aren't sure isn't going to bite. Seemed somehow as if he couldn't keep away. I've known her at her playing at night and him sneaking out as if he had to, and then sort of hiding in the hedge near, as if he didn't dare go on. Sometimes when they were together you could see her watching him as if she were sorry for him, only all the same it couldn't be helped. Because what must be, must be."

"Fancy talk," commented Miss Cann disapprovingly. "No sense to it. What I say is she meant to marry him and he didn't want and was scared like, only he couldn't make up his mind. Men are a poor weak lot," she explained, "and if you make up your mind to it, you can always get the one you want—and bitter sorry for it afterwards most like."

"You wouldn't call it fancy talk if you had seen them like I have," Cann retorted, "or the way it took him when she started playing. She can make that piano of hers talk like a Christian."

"Talk perhaps—but hardly like a Christian," Bobby remarked. "What you've told us has been very interesting though it's hard to see what it all adds up to."

"You won't want to have Alf cross-examined now, will you?" Miss Cann asked anxiously.

"That's for Mr. Bell to say," Bobby answered, turning to Bell, who had been listening to all this with close attention. "Shall you call Mr. Cann at the inquests, do you think?"

"Not as far as I can tell at present," Bell answered. "Even if I wanted to, I don't think the coroner would agree. He would be liable to say Mr. Cann's evidence wasn't relevant."

Cann looked extremely relieved at this, but much less so when Bell added: "Now tell us what you and Myerson were doing in Steep Lane the night of the murders."

"I don't know anything about Myerson," Cann protested. "I bumped up against a bloke at the foot of Steep Lane but I hadn't an earthly who he was. He said good night and I answered civil like and went on. But I didn't like it when he followed. I got the idea it might be one of Potter's snoopers. You can never trust a gamekeeper, and it would be just like one of their tricks to get in a stranger to do their dirty work. I hung back a bit to let him join me and I started talking, trying to pump him, see? But it wasn't any good. Kept his mouth shut except for yes or no, or such like. So I said I must hurry or else my girl I was going to meet would give me fits for keeping her waiting, and I pushed on, and when I got near Middles, Biggs was hanging over the gate. It was striking the hour, same as I said, only eleven, not ten. I saw him plain. He was lighting a cigarette and the match showed him up. I wasn't keen on being seen, in case of questions being asked, so I dodged into the field opposite behind the hedge to get by, and I don't reckon he saw me. And it's gospel I haven't a notion, then or now, whether it was this Myerson chap I saw or some other bloke, or what Biggs was doing. I wasn't thinking of anything but not being seen myself. There's not a thing more I can say, so it's no good asking,"

"Why didn't you tell us all this before?" Bell asked severely, "We don't like people who only talk when they're cornered. They may be keeping something more back for all we know."

"I'm not, why should I now Potter's been putting you wise?" Cann asked, sulky again. "All I wanted was not to be mixed up in it and be asked what was I doing there that time of night, and Potter swearing it was me he saw, and a lie if ever there was one. It was pitch dark nearly, and I heard him coming and I cleared off long before he was near enough to be sure. Just guessing, that's all, but ready to swear to it all the same, perjury being nothing to a keeper, if he thinks he can make a case. And what's more," Cann added in a burst of candour, "I wouldn't have said a word now if it hadn't been for Potter's lies, saying it was me and him never nearer than twenty yards on as dark a night as ever you saw," and Cann sounded very hurt and indignant, as though the keeper, in recognizing him, had not been playing fair.

As however it did seem that he had told all he knew, the two detectives departed. When they were a little distance away, Bell said, and in his voice there was just a touch of doubt and mistrust.

"Was it from this man Cann talked about—Potter, wasn't it? —you got all that from? You never said."

"I never heard of him till to-night," Bobby answered promptly. "A game-keeper about here evidently, but that's all I know. I suppose you'll get on to him? If he confirms Cann's story, if he did come across some poacher that night about twelve, and if he did in fact trip and come a cropper while in pursuit, as Cann said, I take it Cann will have to be considered cleared."

"Well, where did you get it from?" Bell asked. "You didn't build the whole thing up merely because there was a nice smell of cooking in the kitchen that first time we were there, did you?"

"Oh, well, not entirely," Bobby answered, a little amused at the note of incredulity he had seemed to detect in the other's voice. "There was that, of course, but chiefly one or two other things I noticed. It wasn't difficult. If you put two and two together, it's bound to make four, isn't it?"

"It is," agreed Bell. "I've noticed that much all by myself. Only there is getting hold of the two to add to the other two."

"Oh, well," Bobby explained, "I happened to remember Fielding's saying something about keepers having less work and more rabbits now Cann had left. It seemed suggestive, though at the time I only thought it might explain why Cann had taken another job, if he thought the local game-keepers were getting after him. And I knew he was lying when he said he had been talking to Biggs at ten o'clock that night, because I saw Biggs myself at that time and Cann wasn't

with him. I suppose Cann wanted to explain why he was sure
of the time. He heard the clock striking when he saw Biggs
at Middles, so all he had to do was to say ten instead of
eleven and make it sound convincing. Detail is always convincing, but then, for another thing, the times didn't fit. Neither that nor the nice smell of cooking in the kitchen that almost shouted rabbits or some sort of game, would have
counted for much alone, but taken together I thought it was
good enough. As it was, because if you show you know a
good deal, then an uneasy conscience always thinks you
must know the rest as well. As you'll have noticed yourself."

"Oh, yes," Bell agreed. "That's right—only you have to
be sure you've got the right two to add to the proper two to
make the correct four. What about Cann's story of Fielding
being scared of Miss Bellamy? Are we to take it as meaning
something? or was the old lady right when she said it was
only the way any bachelor is scared when he knows a
woman is on his trail?"

"More to it than that I think," Bobby said, "though it's
hard to say what."

"If there is," Bell asked in his depressed way, "what's it
mean? where does it come in? How about adding that two
and two together and telling me what sort of a four it
makes?"

"I'll have a try," Bobby promised. He glanced at his
wrist watch. "Time for bed," he suggested.

"That's right," Bell agreed, quite cheerfully for him, "and
me that's been hard at it since all hours, and not, like some I
could name, snoozing comfortably away all day in bed."

Bobby, unable to think of an appropriate reply, contented
himself with a mild threat to ring up Bell at the very beginning of his beauty sleep to inform him of some fresh difficulty.

"Lots of 'em for that matter," he added, as gloomily as
Bell at his gloomiest, and then they parted, Bell to find his
car and drive home and Bobby to seek supper and bed, both
equally welcome in spite of the long daytime sleep.

Supper was there all right, and Olive waited till her man was fed before she said:

"Miss Bellamy has been playing again. It sounded so strange. I went down the lane to listen. Do you know, Mr. Fielding was there, listening."

"At the cottage, you mean?"

"Yes, not inside, in the lane, huddled up against the hedge opposite, almost as if he were hiding. I shouldn't have seen him, only Miss Bellamy stopped playing and he moved. It gave me such a start. Do you know . . .?"

"Know what?" Bobby asked when she paused.

"It sounds impossible, I know," she said, "but really and truly, it was almost as if—well, as if he was hiding. Do you know . . .?"

"Go ahead," said Bobby. "Everything seems impossible in this affair."

"It was exactly as though he was most awfully relieved to see me. He seemed to think my being there was a kind of protection. He said, thank God you've come, and I said, Why? He said to get away quick. He took hold of my arm and it was just like a child wanting to hold your hand in the dark. All the way back up the lane he was talking at random and laughing in a silly nervous way. I asked him what was the matter but he didn't say anything. He just went on talking. I thought at first he had been drinking, but it wasn't that. Why was he glad to see me and why was he crouching there in the hedge, outside her cottage, as if he were hiding or waiting or whatever it was?"

"I'll have to ask him," Bobby said. "To-morrow morning," he added, glancing at the clock. "Or Miss Bellamy," he said.

"She started playing again," Olive said. "All the way up the lane we could hear her. It was almost as if the music were pursuing us."

"That's the second time I've heard that said to-night," Bobby remarked, and he looked grave and thoughtful.

CHAPTER XXVIII

IDENTIFICATION

ONE OF THE most valuable gifts Nature had bestowed upon
Bobby was that of being able to put all doubts and worries
out of his mind and sleep untroubled through the night, no
matter how deep in perplexity and apprehension his thoughts
had been during the day.

Ungratefully enough, he was apt to complain that the
soundest sleep never provided him with any solution to his
problems. Not for him, as he had read it often was with others, to wake up with a clear answer to his difficulties; handed
to him as it were on a plate by his unconscious mind, hard at
it during bodily slumber. Olive's occasionally proffered explanation that this was because he hadn't got an unconscious
mind, he tended to regard with some suspicion since he was
not altogether sure of the spirit in which it was put forward.
However, if his unconscious fell down on the job as usual,
there arrived, during breakfast, by special messenger, a note
from Bell to say that his inquiries showed that during George
Rogers's so brief sojourn in gaol, there had been another in-
mate, on the verge of release, a man named Burden, known
now as the leader of the gang which was rather more than
suspected of responsibility for that smash-and-grab raid hovering so curiously and in so puzzling a manner on the pe-
rimeter, so to speak, of these events. Also there were included seven or eight photographs together with one of the
Mr. Burden in question. These were to be shown to George
to see if he could pick out that of the man he had noticed
talking to Biggs. In addition there was a photograph of an
elderly man with a short white beard. It was that of a man
named Frank Bardsell about to be released on ticket of leave

but who had committed suicide during Rogers's stay in the prison. Bell thought it might be useful. Bobby thought so, too. Olive asked why but Bobby wouldn't tell her.

"You ought to know," he said severely. "A long shot, of course, but it may come off." He added: "Bell doesn't say anything about the handkerchief."

"What handkerchief?" Olive asked, at a loss for the moment.

"The one I borrowed from Fielding," Bobby reminded her. "It's been sent up for examination."

"Oh, yes, of course," Olive said. "I know. Of course, if that stunt of yours comes off—"

"It isn't a stunt," Bobby interrupted indignantly.

"Well, tour de force," Olive corrected herself.

"That," agreed Bobby, placated, "is much better." He added: "I made sure it was fresh from the laundry. It had to be. Fielding had none left before the laundry came."

Olive asked for no explanation of these last somewhat cryptic remarks. For the moment her mind was much occupied by an incredible rumour that had reached her to the effect that just possibly oranges might be on sale some time during the day. So, as breakfast was now over, she departed as on a search for lost El Dorado, and Bobby went to show the snapshots to Rogers to see if he could make the hoped for identification.

Rogers, untidy, unshaved, unwashed, in a worse temper even than usual, was still at breakfast—the meal consisting chiefly, to all appearance, of burnt and lumpy porridge. An old newspaper was doing duty for a tablecloth and the room had an untidy, unkempt, unswept appearance that reminded Bobby of his own bachelor existence when once he and a friend had tried to run their own small flat for themselves. Before he showed the other photographs he had brought with him, Bobby produced that of the unfortunate elderly man who had committed suicide in the prison. George had a vague memory of having heard of the occurrence, but knew nothing about it and had never seen the victim or known anything of him or the circumstances. So Bobby put it away, while George made a few remarks on how this suicide showed up the brutality of the prison system and the inhumanity with which it was administered. It could, in George's opinion, give points to the Spanish Inquisition at its worst and as for the comparatively mild Nazi concentration camps—

However, Bobby cut this tirade short by spreading out the other photographs he had brought with him and Rogers picked out that of Burden at once.

"That's the man," he said. "What a crew," he added, and indeed they were an ill-looking lot. "What are they? Some of Mosley's fascists?"

An ill-looking lot they had, of course, to be, for such was Mr. Burden, or even more so, and had they been markedly different the identification would have been valueless.

"Burglars. Habitual criminals. That sort," Bobby explained. He let his hand hover lightly over the row of photographs and then he indicated carelessly two of the worst and most repulsive. "Conscientious objectors," he observed.

This statement was entirely without foundation and no excuse can be offered for it. It is good to be able to report that when he told Olive later, expecting approval, he was suitably and severely rebuked. Rogers received the untruthful information with a scowl. He went back to his breakfast, filled his cup from the teapot, and looked surprised.

"Damn," he said, and for once sounded quite human. "I must have forgotten to put in the tea."

"Put the kettle on again," Bobby suggested helpfully.

"There isn't any kettle any more," said Rogers, surveying sadly a cup full of clear and limpid water. "I forgot to take the thing off after I had filled the teapot, and now it hasn't any bottom."

"Hard luck," said Bobby, sniffing at the porridge.

"Things burn," Rogers explained, not without indignation.

"Nasty trick they have," agreed Bobby.

"It's all there is," Rogers said, sniffing in his turn. "I can't even find the toasting fork and where Rhoda's managed to hide the tin-opener, goodness only knows."

"Miss Rogers away?" Bobby asked.

"At Miss Bellamy's," Rogers said resentfully. "Spent the night there. God knows why. And left everything in a muddle and not even the supper things washed up."

"Too bad," Bobby said, and for the moment the two men forgot all else, united in a common bond of masculine martyrdom.

Bobby began to gather up the photographs. Rogers continued to gaze disconsolately at the breakfast table. Bobby, his preparations for departure completed, remarked casually:

"You wouldn't care to make any further statement, would you? The inquests will be held in a day or two. Superintendent Bell may ask for an adjournment. I expect you may be called."

"What for? I know nothing about it," Rogers retorted. "All I can say is, I don't know, and that's all I shall say." He paused, hesitated, and then blurted out, with less self-assurance this time: "I suppose you still want to think it might be me—or Rhoda?"

"Oh, yes. That's obvious."

"Jolly for us."

"It would help if you would try to be a bit more candid and tell us the whole story. I mean, that is, if you are both innocent. Of course, if you are guilty—one of you . . ."

Bobby left the sentence unfinished, but he could see plainly that now there was unease, fear, in the young man's eyes. Not surprising, Bobby told himself. Few, innocent or not, could hear with equanimity that they were under suspicion of complicity in murder. But Rogers remained silent. He might be uneasy or afraid, but he was still obstinate. Bobby nodded, said good morning, and moved towards the door. Rogers watched with relief. At the door Bobby turned and asked:

"Seen the papers this morning?"

"No. Haven't had time. Why?"

"There's a very good photograph of the pistol used to shoot Myerson. First class reproduction. It was found near by, the pistol I mean. I expect you heard?"

"How do you know it's the same pistol?"

"Oh, that's easy. The ballistics expert can prove that easily enough. Same basic idea as finger-prints. Markings made by different pistols never the same. Nature is always unique. What the books call the inherent individuality of the real. No finger-prints, though. Wiped off probably. Or rubber gloves. You go in for photography, Mr. Rogers, I think? I wonder if you use them— rubber gloves, I mean. Some photographers do, I believe."

"I don't," Rogers snarled. "I know what you mean. I know what you're trying to hint."

"Just this," Bobby told him, "that it would be a lot more sensible and save a lot of trouble and worse perhaps, if you would tell the whole truth instead of making us dig it out by degrees."

But that appeal, too, went unheeded. Bobby again turned to the door, reflecting that an obstinate man must go his own way. He was on the threshold when Rogers called after him.

"No one can identify a pistol from a photograph," he said.

"Oh, well, you have a look at it," Bobby answered. "There's a mark on the butt that shows up rather well. It's quite plain. The ballistics experts think that most likely some time or another a bullet grazed it. Must have been a narrow squeak if it was like that. It might have got talked about, might be remembered. If so, someone may come forward to tell us. That will give a starting point and then it may be possible to trace the possession of the pistol. Only a chance, of course, but detective work is like that. If the idea does work, it may be very important. We may be able to trace the pistol and identify the last owner. Then he'll have something to explain. Think it over, Mr. Rogers, and do try to believe me when I say again that it's best in the long run to tell the truth. Bound to come out in the end."

Rogers still made no attempt to reply. It seemed better to leave him to think over what had been said. Bobby closed the bungalow door behind him and walked on. But he had gone only a few yards when he heard Rogers call. He looked back. Rogers had come to the door of the bungalow and was standing there. He called something Bobby did not hear distinctly and went back inside, leaving the door open. After a moment's hesitation Bobby returned. If this meant Rogers had changed his mind and was willing at last to talk, it would be better to hear what he had to say. Rogers was sitting at his writing table, his head in his hands. When Bobby came in, Rogers began to talk in a low, rapid voice, without looking up. He said:

"I expect it's our pistol all right. Rhoda had it when she found those Egyptian spies at the safe in her office. One of them fired at her and the shot hit her pistol and knocked it out of her hand. That's when she grabbed a tommy gun and turned it on them. Everyone out there knew the story. I expect dozens of them will be wanting to tell you all about it."

"Well, I'm glad you've told me first," Bobby remarked, "though I wish you had before. Superintendent Bell will want you to make a statement. Will you go at once to find him and do that?"

"Oh, all right, I suppose I had better," Rogers grumbled.

"Much better," Bobby agreed. "Have you any explanation of how the pistol got where it was found?"

"No. I had no idea it was Rhoda's, not till now. The last I saw of it was when Biggs had it."

"Biggs?" repeated Bobby, surprised and doubtful. "How was that?"

"Biggs was trying to get hold of Rhoda. At least, that's what I thought. I had no idea that they had been together in Egypt. Rhoda only told afterwards. I felt I had to warn Biggs to keep off. Hang it, a man's got to protect his sister and I didn't want her mixed up with a man like Biggs, a surly brute at the best, a chauffeur in private employ. He had been exceedingly rude to me as well. What sort of a future could he have offered her? Wanted to get hold of her money most likely, I thought. And then I knew there was gossip about him and Miss Bellamy. I made up my mind I had to take steps in her interest, but I knew he was a violent ruffian and he had already used threats towards me—punching my head, vulgarities of that sort. So I think it was perfectly natural for me to slip Rhoda's pistol into my pocket. You agree?"

"Go on," said Bobby.

"Of course, I had no intention of using it. I merely intended a precaution, a warning to keep his distance. I did not even know it was loaded."

"Go on," Bobby said again.

"There was a kind of scuffle, an undignified—scuffle," Rogers explained reluctantly. "I was entirely unprepared, taken unawares. I unfortunately slipped and fell. Biggs took the opportunity to—to—"

"Administer a kick or two," suggested Bobby without sympathy.

"They might have inflicted serious injury," Rogers said. "I suffered great pain and inconvenience for some days."

"And the pistol?" Bobby asked.

"Biggs put it in his pocket. That was the last time I saw it. He said he would give it back to Rhoda but he must have kept it."

Bobby listened to all this with close attention and some discomfort. Did Rogers understand, realize, the full implications of these last words of his? For they seemed to suggest that Rhoda herself was the last person in possession of the weapon with which murder had been committed. Could the young man's story be accepted? It was a question to which Bobby felt he could give no very confident reply. It might all be a clever invention, an ingenious mixture of truth and falsehood designed to clear Rogers himself of suspicion. Even that casual remark about Biggs's promise to give the pistol back to Rhoda might be merely an attempt on Rogers's part to save his own skin. Bobby was not willing to believe that, but it would have to be taken into consideration. Was it possible that George knew his sister was guilty and had deliberately mentioned Biggs's promise in order to put the police on the right track? Or did Rhoda know that it was her brother who had killed her lover? Was that why she had left home and sought refuge with Miss Bellamy? A tragic supposition. Had she perhaps threatened to denounce him and was that why he in his turn had directed suspicion towards her? Or had the remark slipped out inadvertently and without intention? Bobby felt himself in such a sea of doubt as he had not often known. He said at last:

"Have you any proof of what you've told me, any evidence to confirm it?"

"What's the good of my saying anything if you don't believe it when I do?" Rogers demanded as with a sort of desperation he helped himself to the burnt porridge in an attempt to satisfy with it his matutinal hunger.

"I didn't say I didn't believe it," Bobby pointed out. "I asked if you had any supporting evidence."

"I wrote a full account in my diary that night, if that's any good," Rogers answered, apparently deciding as he put down his untasted spoonful of porridge that hunger was a far, far better thing.

"That would certainly be a considerable help," Bobby said. "May I have it?"

"The diary?" Rogers exclaimed, quite startled. "Oh, no. I could copy out an extract for you, if you like, but I don't intend the diary itself to be seen until it is published and that will only be after my death."

"I'm afraid that wouldn't be much help at present," Bobby pointed out. "But why not?"

"It is," explained Rogers, "in all probability the most ruthless and penetrating analysis of human motive and character that has ever been made. In it I explain what lies behind the behaviour of all I meet, including myself. I tear away the veil and show the hidden motive."

"Dear me," said Bobby, interested in spite of all the other thoughts and doubts that filled his mind. "What are they generally?"

"Startling," Rogers told him. "Startling in their revelation of the essential bestiality of the subconscious mind. What often appears the most innocent action can be shown quite clearly to have its origin in the sexual urge, the merely brutal, the wish to dominate, to possess and to enjoy regardless of anything but the gratification of the ego."

"All according to Freud?" asked Bobby. "By the way, is that the way to pronounce it? I think G. K. Chesterton said it ought to be pronounced as if spelt—f r a u d."

"Oh, no," Rogers answered, unfortunately missing the point. "The way you said it is correct," he added graciously.

CHAPTER XXIX

POUSSINS AU HENRI QUATRE

LEAVING ROGERS STRUGGLING to open a tin of pilchards by the aid of hammer and chisel, Bobby went on to Miss Bellamy's cottage. Necessary now, he decided, to question Rhoda, now that her brother, intentionally or otherwise, had directed suspicion once more towards her.

There was no immediate answer when Bobby knocked. Not till he had knocked again, and more loudly, did Miss Bellamy come to the door. She was wearing a large cooking apron and her gaze seemed as ever to wander away into far off and remote regions as she waited for him to speak.

"Sorry to bother you so early," he began, "but I believe Miss Rhoda Rogers is here."

"I thought you were the chickens," Miss Bellamy said, as if with difficulty recalling her attention from whatever distant lands it had seemed to escape to and be lost.

"Chickens?" Bobby repeated.

"I ordered two," she explained. "They should have come last night. I hope they won't be long. I only got them as a great favour, but they are paid for and they were promised for first thing. You see," she explained, as if realizing, probably because Bobby was looking rather bewildered, that some explanation was needed, "Mr. Fielding is coming to dinner to-night, and so I am going to give him poussins au Henri Quatre. That needs two at least, you know. And preparation. Luckily I've got the mushrooms. And cream and sherry, too."

Bobby didn't know, and didn't care, whether it needed two chickens or a dozen, or any, or no, preparation. Miss

Bellamy went back into the cottage but left the door open as if expecting him to follow. He did so and said:

"Will you please tell Miss Rogers I should like to speak to her if I may."

"I must have something special to-night," Miss Bellamy said. She was returning towards the kitchen as she spoke. She explained: "That's why I thought of poussins au Henri Quatre. I know most people would say it was too difficult in a little place like this. Nothing you really need, just a case of make-do. I should think it rather silly if anyone else tried, but then no one else would—ever. I think I can manage, though."

She was back in the kitchen now, as if she had entirely forgotten, or had made up her mind to ignore, Bobby's presence. Impatiently, he said:

"Will you please tell Miss Rogers I am here and wish to speak to her?"

"She'll be asleep still," Miss Bellamy told him over her shoulder. "I expect she will be down presently."

"I have no time to spare, I wish to see her immediately," Bobby said with even more impatience than before. "Please tell her I am here and ask her to dress and come down as quickly as possible."

"I don't expect she undressed," Miss Bellamy remarked thoughtfully. "We were talking all night—she was. I listened. She fell asleep when it was nearly light. I got her upstairs to lie down on my bed. She'll be still asleep."

"Haven't you been to bed either?" Bobby asked.

"Well, there's only the one bed and there's so much to do," Miss Bellamy explained. "Mr. Fielding is coming to dinner to-night," she told him again.

If she had been sitting up all night, she showed small sign of it. The dark pallor of her countenance was unchanged, her gaze far off and inscrutable as ever.

"What were you talking about all night?" Bobby asked.

"She thinks it may have been me who shot those two men," Miss Bellamy explained. "So she came to ask."

"What did you say?"

"I said I didn't. I don't know if she believed me. She went on talking. It got rather hysterical at times. It's all been too much for the poor child. It's those two Egyptians she can't forget." After a pause, she added: "To remember too well and too long is worst of all."

"What do you remember?" Bobby asked.

The question seemed both to startle and to disturb. For almost the first time she began to bestow upon him her full attention. Her eyes were no longer distant, inscrutable, but intent and bright and searching. She was almost staring at him as she asked presently:

"What do you mean? Why do you ask?"

"For the only reason why I ever ask a question," Bobby told her. "Because I want to know."

"Well, then," she said, and stared at him more intently still. It was as if only now were she fully persuaded of the reality of his person and his presence. "I shan't tell you," she said. "At least not now, not yet." She went on: "Rhoda thinks if it wasn't me, perhaps it was her brother."

"That her brother killed Biggs? Do you?"

"I have thought so sometimes," she admitted. "They had quarrelled. George Rogers is very old-fashioned in some of his ideas. What makes it worse is that he thinks he is so terribly advanced. He will talk all day about complete sex equality and the rate for the job and so on, and still expect Rhoda to wait on him hand and foot, day and night."

"Could it have been Rhoda herself who shot him?" Bobby asked, neither surprised nor interested to hear that George's theories and his practice had small connection.

"I have thought sometimes it might be her," Miss Bellamy said. She came back into the room and sat down. She said: "When you care for anyone very desperately, then I think sometimes it is more than you can bear. Perhaps when you have killed once, then there's a kind of desperation comes upon you. I don't know. She had lived with him and she never had with anyone till then and now she wasn't sure any longer. I think it may have been like that."

"I take it," Bobby said, "you know that many people in the village think that it was you?"

"Oh, yes," she agreed indifferently. "I can see them looking at me. Very likely you think so, too. I didn't, but I expect I should say so even if I had. I daresay that is what is in your mind."

"What we think doesn't matter," Bobby answered. "What we need is evidence. Of course, we can't just accept denials. Have you any idea yourself who might be guilty?"

She did not answer, only stood and looked at him, and yet now again as if she did not see him, as if indeed she saw nothing that was there, but only her own thoughts, her own memories that she would not tell. When she had been silent some minutes, Bobby said:

"Will you not tell me what you think?"

"Not yet," she answered. "Not now. Never, I think."

"Will you tell me this? Why is it necessary—I think you said 'necessary'—to have something specially good for Mr. Fielding to-night?"

"It may be the last time," she answered, speaking very slowly. "At least, that is what I think."

"The last time?" Bobby repeated. "Why?"

"I think so," she said slowly. "I think it may be that to-night he will ask me to marry him."

"Oh, yes, indeed," Bobby said, surprised, for he had not expected this. "I . . . would it be too impertinent to ask if you mean to accept him?"

"I don't know," she said slowly. She was still seated, and once again she seemed to have withdrawn herself not into herself but as if to regions that as yet did not exist. There was something unearthly, even terrifying, in what seemed so intense a contemplation of the as yet unknown, unseen, unexperienced. It was as though her spirit wandered where none had as yet any right to be. In a voice as remote as her own gaze, she said: "Perhaps there is something else that may be in his mind," and there was a quality in her slow voice that sent through Bobby a chill of apprehension and of fear.

"What do you mean?" he asked sharply.

She did not answer. Perhaps she did not hear, so withdrawn seemed now again her mood. She got to her feet and
went back into the little kitchen. Bobby followed and stood
in the doorway, watching her doubtfully.

"What do you mean?" he asked once more.

"As to that," she began and then paused. "Well, there it
is," she said and turned her attention to her culinary preparations. "It would be the end, wouldn't it?" she said abruptly.

"What would?"

"If he asked me to marry him and I did. It would end it
all," she said again, "and then there wouldn't be anything to
be afraid of any more."

"Are you afraid?" he asked, and he knew very well that
at least he was.

But she shook her head.

"I think he is," she answered and presently she repeated:
"I think he is."

"What of?"

This time it was long before she replied, and then it was
with an almost solemn gesture that she pointed to the grand
piano that filled so much of the other room. But still she did
not speak, and, having made that gesture, she returned to her
work as if she had no other thought in her mind but that of
preparing with care a dish of unusual excellence for a specially welcome guest. But to Bobby it was as though he
watched not a woman busy getting ready a meal but, rather a
priestess of some unknown altar occupied with the solemn
rites of an impending sacrifice. To whom or what, he did not
know. When he spoke again he had to repeat his remark
twice before she seemed to hear what he said, and then she
only answered by a glance that could be taken to mean assent
when he said:

"You mean it is your playing he is afraid of?" Then he
said: "Is that because you put into your playing your memories you refuse to tell me?" She was still silent. He said: "It
may be I can guess them." She seemed a little startled at that,
and she made a slight negative gesture, slight but expressive.
For it indicated very clearly that she held that to be quite im-

possible. He said then: "It would be very much better though, if you would tell me what they are."

"Not yet, not now," she repeated. "Never, I think. You must find out first who killed—and that I think you never will."

"Unless I am very much mistaken," Bobby said gravely, "I know both who and why. We have enough information by this time to feel that what we need now is not to know but proof. It is useless to put forward evidence that the defence could show might conceivably point to some other. The jury would get confused and would naturally prefer to say 'Not guilty.' That could mean a murderer going free and that might well mean more trouble presently. Memory can be a poisonous thing. You've said that yourself or much the same."

"Have I?" she asked. "I didn't know. I think it's true."

"For instance," Bobby went on, "my present information is that the weapon used in one of the murders was last in Miss Rogers's possession. There seems to be direct evidence that Biggs got hold of the weapon and meant to return it to her. That must be cleared up. If it is known to have been in the possession of one of two people at the time of the murder and one is dead and one is left alive, the inference is obvious."

She had now a strangely troubled air and presently she said:

"Does all this mean you think it was Rhoda?"

"It only means she is one of those against whom there is evidence which must be satisfactorily answered. You are one yourself, of course. You realize that?"

"If only I could make up my mind what I think," she said slowly. "But I can't. I know it wasn't me, but it's no good saying so. It's no good any more trying to get it all clear playing. When I do everything only gets more confused— more doubtful and more strange."

Bobby went on:

"If Mr. Fielding is going to suggest marriage to you to-night, then that means he must be what is called in love with you?"

"I don't know," she answered. "I wonder. I don't know. I don't suppose he knows either. He may be. I think—"

But what it was she thought she left unuttered, and Bobby said:

"Or you with him?"

"Oh, no," she exclaimed at once, in a very startled and surprised voice, as if such an idea were as unexpected as unwelcome. "Oh, no," she repeated, but now with a puzzled air. She seemed to be thinking it over. She brought, as it were, that distant gaze of hers back to nearer things, though still she seemed even now but half-conscious of the presence of any other person. All the time it had been much as if she were talking to herself; expressing her own thoughts to herself to clear her own mind and inform herself, rather than with any wish to communicate them to anyone else. Bobby waited. "Am I?" she said at last. "You ask such questions," she complained. "No," she said more loudly. "No. It is only that I have great pity for him—for him and for me and for all of us, for I think we are all caught and trapped in what we never meant."

"A child's excuse," Bobby said. "If you choose a path to follow, it's up to you to know where it leads."

"There's Rhoda," Miss Bellamy said. "I can hear her moving. I expect she heard us talking. She'll be coming down. I'll make some coffee—strong. She'll need it if you are going to ask her questions like you have me."

CHAPTER XXX

THE END IS NOT YET

RHODA CAME SLOWLY down the stairs and into the room. She did not seem much surprised to see Bobby. She said:

"I thought it was you. I heard you talking."

She spoke in a very low voice, not much above a whisper. She showed, far more than did Miss Bellamy, plain traces of the long night's vigil Miss Bellamy had described. Her face was deathly white, her features drawn and tight, beneath her red-rimmed eyes dark circles showed, her dress was so crumpled and untidy Bobby could well believe that she had slept in it, her whole expression was one of extreme weariness and lassitude, as if all vitality in her had drained quite away. Bobby pulled forward a chair and she sat down without speaking again. Miss Bellamy came back into the room and said:

"I'll make some coffee and a little toast."

"Please don't. I don't want anything," Rhoda said.

Without answering this, Miss Bellamy went back into the kitchen, and Bobby said:

"You look tired, Miss Rogers, but I am afraid I shall have to ask you a few questions."

"Are you going to arrest me?" she asked, her voice even more of a whisper than before.

"Why should you think that?" he asked in return.

"I thought you might," she said, and then: "It doesn't matter." Then she said: "How did you know I was here?"

"Your brother told me," Bobby answered. "I have been talking to him. It is because of things he said that I am obliged to ask you a few more questions."

"What's the good?" she asked wearily. "I have done nothing but ask myself questions ever since it happened and there are no answers."

"The weapon used in the murder of the man Myerson," Bobby went on, "has been clearly identified as your property. Further, our information is that it was in your brother's possession when he went out one night, but that during a scuffle Biggs took it from him."

"I know," Rhoda said. "My head's funny but I remember that. He told me. Did he tell you?"

"Is it true, do you think?"

"I suppose so. Yes. Why not?"

"Our information is that Biggs refused to return it to your brother but promised to give it to you instead. Did he do that?"

"I told him to keep it. I said I didn't want it. I said to throw it away or something,"

"What did he say?"

"At first he said he would give it back to George. I said not to and he said perhaps I was right and he had better not. He said it might put ideas into George's head."

"What did he mean by that?"

"You knew they quarrelled. About me. George was trying to interfere. He got a good thrashing. I told him it served him right. It was no business of his. It was then I told him about our having lived together in Egypt. He made a dreadful scene. We often rowed but never before like that. I suppose he was really shocked. I said I hoped he would get another thrashing if he dared say another word. He said if Fred tried that on again, he would know how to protect himself. He said another time he would be ready. I think that was why I didn't want the pistol given back to George. It was really mine, so Fred didn't need."

"What did he do with it finally?"

"At first he said he would keep it and then he said he would give it to Miss Bellamy to keep for me. And he said perhaps she might need it herself. That's what I came to ask her about."

Miss Bellamy was still busy in the kitchen. She had paid no attention to what they were saying. Bobby got up and went to the door of the kitchen. He said to her:

"Miss Bellamy. It seems Biggs intended to hand the pistol to you to keep for Miss Rogers. Did he do so?"

"The coffee's ready now," Miss Bellamy said. She was pouring some out. She put a cup on a tray together with dry toast. She took it to Rhoda and to Bobby she said: "The pistol? He wanted to but I told him I wouldn't have it. Drink your coffee," she added to Rhoda. "It'll do you good."

Rhoda obeyed, and the hot, strong, sweet drink brought a little colour back to her pallid cheeks. Miss Bellamy went back into the kitchen to fill Rhoda's cup again. Rhoda said she had had enough and Miss Bellamy told her to eat the toast. Bobby said to her:

"If Miss Bellamy did in fact have the pistol, do you think she may have used it?"

"I don't know. I daresay," Rhoda answered. "I wondered."

"Or if Biggs after all did return it to your brother, then it may have been your brother used it?"

"I thought that too," Rhoda said.

"Or again if it was given back to you, if you in fact took it when he offered it—"

"Then it might have been me," she agreed. "Because once I killed two men and so I might another. If you dream of two, why not of three?"

"You mustn't dream," Miss Bellamy said loudly. "You must stop it."

"The coffee was very nice," Rhoda said, "even if you did kill poor Fred. We shall never be married now. Perhaps he didn't really want. Sometimes I thought so. It's made me sleepy again—the coffee, I mean."

"Why did he think Miss Bellamy might need a pistol?" Bobby asked.

"He didn't say," Rhoda answered. "I asked him but he didn't say, only that it might be better if she had it by her. I don't know any more," and when Bobby did not speak at once she closed her eyes and fell asleep where she sat.

Miss Bellamy had gone back into the kitchen where she was busy again. Bobby went to the kitchen door and said:

"Did you hear?"

"Hear what?" she asked. "What Rhoda said? "No. What was it?"

"She said Biggs told her he meant to give you the pistol because you might need it. Why did he say that?"

"I very often don't know why I say things myself," she answered. "How can I tell why other people say them?"

"Can you tell me anything at all about the pistol?"

"He said he had taken it from George Rogers. I asked him if it was true they had been fighting. He said it wasn't— he said you couldn't have a fight with anyone like George. He said George hadn't the stuff in him to stand up to a schoolboy, but he took his pistol from him in case he man- aged to hurt himself or someone else. That was all."

"When was this?"

"The day before it all happened."

"Did he want to give it you because he thought you might need it to protect yourself?"

"You asked me that before," she remarked. "It's no good keeping on like that. Asking and asking."

"Refusing to answer a question," Bobby told her, "is of- ten much the same as answering it—and sometimes more likely to be true. This time I think it means you know he did believe you might need to protect yourself. I am asking you another question. Did he in fact give you the pistol he took from George Rogers?"

"I am not answering that either," she retorted, and this time with impatience. "Well, what does it mean this time— that I won't answer?"

"If he gave it you, did you use it?"

"You have to find out first whether he did give it me," she reminded him. "If he did, if he gave it me because he thought I might need it, would I be likely to use it to kill him, if that is what you are thinking? Are you trying to make out that he gave me a pistol to protect myself with against him himself?"

"More likely from someone else," Bobby said. "There is another point I must put to you. Two men have been killed. Myerson was one. We are not sure yet why Myerson was here but it seems certain he had something to do with the smash-and-grab raid. Another man who was mixed up in it, and who was either Biggs or closely resembled him, vanished near this cottage. Then Myerson turns up and, later on, Biggs is killed. Myerson is killed soon afterwards, and with the weapon Biggs may have given to a person he thought might need it. It seems a possible theory that Biggs and Myerson were both concerned in the smash-and-grab raid, that there was a quarrel, as gangsters do quarrel over sharing their plunder, that in the quarrel Biggs was shot by Myerson, and that then Myerson was killed by a friend of Biggs who had been perhaps watching, unknown to Myerson. Have you anything to say to that?"

"No," she answered, "except that it is very ingenious but it isn't true." There came a knock at the door. She went to answer it and came back with two plump chickens ready for cooking. "Aren't they nice?" she said. "Now I can get on. It's very good of them to let me have them. They didn't want to."

"What time are you having dinner to-night?" Bobby asked.

"About half-past seven or eight, I expect," she answered, surprised at the question. "If you don't want to ask anything more, should you mind very much going away? I have to be very busy. When it's poussins au Henri Quatre, everything has to be exactly right and everything ready on the dot, just when you want it."

"Miss Bellamy," Bobby said, his patience giving way for once, "two men have been killed and all you can do is to talk about this wretched what-d'you-call-it stuff."

"Poussins au Henri Quatre," Miss Bellamy interposed tranquilly.

"Yet one of those dead men thought you might need a pistol to protect yourself with?"

"It was silly of him if he did think that," she answered. "So are you if you are thinking it, too. It is not I who need protection but another."

"Who?"

"If you know as much as you pretend," she told him, turning from her work to face him; for the first time, too, showing a flash of anger, "then you should know that already."

"I think perhaps I do," he answered, watching her steadily.

"Then," she said, now speaking slowly, "then you must know, too, that there is nothing for you to do."

"I think there is," he told her. "Please understand that and that it will be done." She shook her head, denying it. A moment's pause. He was looking at the piano. He said: "Is it from your music that the another you spoke of needs protection?"

"If it is, do you think you can stop me playing?" she asked. She left her work in the kitchen and came and stood by his side. Abruptly she laughed but it was no pleasant laugh. "How did you get such a stupid idea into your head?" she asked.

Bobby did not answer that. He was looking at Rhoda, lying back in her chair, her eyes closed, her breathing deep and regular.

"She is sleeping soundly," he said.

"Let her be till she wakes," Miss Bellamy said. "She is worn out and the end is not yet."

"No," agreed Bobby, "not yet. But I do not think it will be long."

Miss Bellamy returned to her busy occupations. She might have been any woman in any kitchen, busy with preparations for a meal meant to be more elaborate than usual. But it was not so that Bobby saw her; and when he had watched her for a little he went away, grave and troubled.

CHAPTER XXXI

FURTHER DOUBTS

FORTUNATELY BY THIS time Superintendent Bell had arrived to continue direction of the various supplementary lines of investigation that were being followed up, and with him Bobby now had a brief consultation.

"What it adds up to," Bell said finally when Bobby had finished his account of these recent developments, "is that you've managed to confirm that the murder weapon was last in possession of one of the three of them—the Rogers', brother and sister, and the Bellamy woman. Only each of them pushes it off on one of the others. Rogers says Biggs was going to give it to his sister. The sister says she wouldn't have it and Biggs told her he would give it to Miss Bellamy who might need it. Miss Bellamy denies having it and says anyhow someone else needed it more, but she won't say who." He ran his fingers despairingly through his hair and said in tones of utter gloom: "And how in thunder are we to know which of 'em is lying and which is telling the truth, if any?"

"Possibly all three," suggested Bobby.

"Telling the truth? When they all contradict each other?"

"Well, Biggs may after all have kept it himself. If he did, and if he still had it when he was killed, then his murderer may have taken it and used it in the second murder, Myerson's."

"Which means," grumbled Bell, "that your fine new theory that Myerson shot Biggs and then was shot himself by a pal of Biggs's—possibly the Bellamy woman—goes down the drain?"

"Well, I should say goes into cold storage," Bobby said. "Together," he added, "with most of the rest of the probabilities and possibilities we've been working on."

"You do like making it difficult," sighed Bell. "Always got a new line for us to follow up your sleeve, haven't you?"

"I don't want anyone following anything up my sleeve," protested Bobby indignantly. "Makes you think of earwigs and spiders and all that sort of thing."

"What about motive?" asked Bell, unheeding this protest. "You must have a motive. I can see it with the others. Rogers didn't like the idea of Biggs messing about with his sister, tried to interfere and got a good thrashing for his pains."

"Matter for murder, there," agreed Bobby.

"Especially," agreed Bell, "when it's a bloke like Rogers who can think up the noblest motives for doing anything that happens to suit him."

"Rationalization is the word," Bobby explained.

"Then there's the sister," Bell went on. "Of course, any woman is always liable to do in any man she is really in love with. Killing and loving are close at times."

"I think," Bobby said, "you've got to the heart of it there."

"Some bit of poetry about it, isn't there?" Bell asked. "Something about how we all kill what we love."

"An overstatement," Bobby said, "but something in it all the same and in this case worth remembering."

"Miss Bellamy," Bell said, "was she in love with Biggs?"

"I've seen nothing to suggest it," Bobby answered, "and I don't believe it. Some connection, some sort of common understanding between them. That's plain. But I don't believe there was any question on either side of their being in love."

"If you rule that out," Bell commented, "then it's being accomplices. That means they were in the smash-and-grab raid together—her doing the planning or scouting as they often get a woman to do. And that might mean Myerson butting in and threatening to turn informer or demanding to go shares and why she needed a pistol for her own protection. I think," said Bell thoughtfully, "we could put that to

the public prosecutor outfit. Only," he added with resignation, "they would turn it down same as they always do unless
we can give them at least a dozen eye-witnesses, all certified
of good character."

"Well, you have to admit," Bobby pointed out, "that
there are at present rather a lot of loose ends. That would be
seen at once. Jam for defending counsel to be able to lead a
jury up half a dozen different garden paths all at once. Confusion means acquittal, and that's bad when it means a killer
let loose on the world all because we haven't done our job
properly."

"All very well," complained Bell, "but when you have
about two dozen different paths to follow all at once—well,
where are you?"

"Oh, it's not so bad as all that," Bobby declared, trying to
cheer him up. "Two dozen is piling it on, and there are one
or two leads that to my mind give a fairly clear line."

"Well, of course, if that handkerchief stunt of yours—"
began Bell, but Bobby interrupted him and very crossly indeed. "It's not a stunt," he protested. "It's a—a tour de
force."

"Is it?" said Bell, suitably impressed. "I didn't know.
Mind you, I'm all for looking on the bright side of things.
That's my line and always has been. It pays. But all the
same, even if that handkerchief idea of yours does come off,
you'll never get it past a jury. Not a hope. Just rosy-fingered
optimism to think you will, like telling us about all the good
things the atom bomb is going to give us some day. No," he
said, and shook his head with great decision. He asked: "Do
you think there is anything in this idea Miss Bellamy is trying to sell us—that Mr. Fielding is going to propose?"

"I don't doubt it for my part," Bobby said, though not
without hesitation. "I am sure she thinks so and I expect
she's right."

"Poussins au Henri Quatre, whatever that is," Bell repeated thoughtfully. "Feed the brute and he pops the question. That the idea?"

"There's more to it than that," Bobby said.

"I suppose there is," agreed Bell. "I suppose there's things behind it's hard to understand. When you join you think police work's just a straightforward job of running in drunks and keeping the traffic straight, and then you run up against this sort of thing. They aren't just in love with each other like anyone else, are they?"

"Certainly not like anyone else," Bobby answered. "So far as I can see it," he went on slowly, "I think a very curious and rather terrible relation has grown up between them—a mutual attraction, a mutual repulsion, each as strong as the other. I don't know. It may be my fancy, but I have sometimes thought that they are bound to each other as man and woman have seldom been. I doubt if there is any emotion they have not felt for each other in measure and degree. But in what measure and degree I don't know, though I am sure there is passion somewhere—and passion in a form not everyone is capable of enduring. All depends on that and it may be it all adds up differently every hour almost."

"There you go," complained Bell. "How can any plain everyday cop like me be expected to deal with a thing that's never the same two minutes together? Where does this poussins and the rest of the stuff come in?"

"That's just one side to it."

"And the music—the piano playing business?"

"That's another side."

"I've heard her," Bell said. "Gives you the willies, listening. Digs deep," he said. "Seems to make you see yourself as you never knew you were. What did she mean when she said there might be something else Fielding had in mind, not proposing but something else?" Bobby sat silent, making no attempt to answer. But Bell seemed to understand. He said uneasily: "If it's like that, what are we to do?"

"I think," Bobby said, "that I had better be there."

"At dinner?" Bell asked. "But . . . well, a bit awkward?"

"I'll try to get there as near the sweet and coffee stage as I can manage," Bobby explained. "I think that will be about right. Bad if it isn't, but I think it should be time enough."

"Why not a bit earlier?" Bell asked. "Safer and you might come in for a share of the what's its name stuff." The words were light but the tone was grave. "Shall I come with you?" he asked.

"I think I shall have a better chance of pulling it off if I go alone," Bobby said. "The important thing is to be there before she gets down to her piano playing."

"Yes, of course, I see that," Bell agreed. "Have it your own way. But there'll have to be someone on hand. Outside. Waiting. Got to be on the safe side. You never know how a thing like this may turn out."

"Thank you," Bobby said. "If you don't mind posting one of your chaps near, it might be as well. I suppose you couldn't spare the time yourself, could you?"

"Well, I might," Bell answered. "I would rather like to be in at the death." He paused and looked uneasy. "That slipped out," he said.

CHAPTER XXXII

AFTER DINNER

BOBBY TIMED HIS arrival well. It was almost at the exact moment when Miss Bellamy returned from the kitchen with the coffee she had just prepared that he knocked at the door. When she opened it and saw him she said simply: "Oh, it's you," and went back into the room.

Bobby followed. Fielding was sitting at the table on which now only the coffee pot and cups stood, the other dishes having been cleared away. It all looked very homely and comfortable and ordinary. Fielding glanced up as Bobby entered and he, too, said "Oh, it's you," but made no other comment. Miss Bellamy was pouring out the coffee. She went back into the kitchen and returned with a third cup. She was beginning to fill it when Bobby said:

"Please. If that's for me, please don't trouble."

"It's good coffee," Mr. Fielding said. "You don't often get it like this. And it's not poisoned."

"I'm sure it isn't," Bobby said. "Poison is not in Miss Bellamy's line." He glanced at the grand piano, standing open behind where Fielding sat and he saw that both the others noticed the direction of his glance. "But I'm here on duty," he explained.

"That's not it," Miss Bellamy said. "You mean you won't eat or drink with suspected murderers."

Her former manner or air Bobby had so often noticed of a remote indifference, of an almost total unawareness of surroundings, had vanished. Now her eyes were quick and alert, her every movement brisk and to the point. One might have said she was displaying now the eager attention of a young child to every detail of a world entirely new, so closely did she seem to focus the full concentration of her thought on each passing moment. It was a change of mood that seemed to Bobby significant and full of meaning and that made him uneasy. It suggested she had come back from the distant realms into which she had apparently so often wandered, come back with her decision taken, her purpose at last determined. But he could not be sure. It might mean her spirit had returned from its wanderings, as for ever baffled and now merely acquiescent.

"Murderers?" Fielding was saying. "Well, that's not us, is it?" he asked comfortably. To Bobby he said: "Well, have a cigar. That's not eating or drinking."

He offered his cigar case as he spoke but Bobby thanked him and begged to be excused.

"I so seldom smoke cigars," he said. "I would really rather not if you don't mind."

"Oh, I don't mind," Fielding said chuckling. "Ten bob each they cost and a favour at that."

"I've some brandy," Miss Bellamy said. She went to get it from a cupboard in a corner of the room. "Would you like a little in your coffee?" she asked Fielding. She added some to her own. "We shall need it," she said, "when he starts asking questions. It's hell when he asks questions."

"That's O.K. by me," Fielding said as he held out his cup for the offered brandy. "I have dined well and fate cannot harm me now. Those poussins au Henri Quatre—marvellous. You ought to have been here a bit earlier," he said to Bobby. "Then you might have had some. Marvellous."

"If there is hell in any question of mine," Bobby said, "it is not I who put it there."

"Perhaps we shan't answer and what the hell then?" asked Fielding, still chuckling. "Hold your tongue, and let anyone who wants make what they like of that." He added, sipping it: "This coffee—it's up to what went before. Marvellous."

"If you don't answer," Miss Bellamy said, "that's as good an answer as any—so he says."

"Bluff," explained Fielding. "You come across it in business. 'You won't show the figures? We know what that means,' the other bloke tells you and expects you to wilt. Well, you don't, and he has to guess. No good guessing. You can't make an estimate on a guess—or a balance sheet, either."

"Very true," Bobby agreed. "A guess is useless. A logical deduction from accounts presented may be different, more reliable. It's that I should like to attempt with your assistance."

"Suppose we refuse our assistance?" Miss Bellamy asked. "What then?"

"Oh, I do hope you won't," Bobby said. "The logical deduction then might be unpleasant, and surely it's better in every way for us to talk it over together now than for you both to have to stand up to cross-examination by a K.C. at the inquests when they take place."

"Ask away," Fielding said, waving his cigar in the air. "It's O.K. by me, though I don't know there's much I can tell you you don't know already. I've told you how that poor devil of a Biggs wished himself on me. Nobody's sorrier than I am for what's happened to him, but I don't see what I could have done. Well, go ahead, if you want to."

"Thank you," Bobby said. "Well, the point we have to arrive at is who killed those two men."

"That's right," Fielding said, shaking his head gravely. "A bad business. You ought to get to the bottom of it."

"I'll try," Bobby promised. "The point we have to start from is how did it happen that Mr. Fielding out of all the replies he received to a very attractive advertisement, picked ours?"

"I told you," Fielding said, looking surprised. "Pure luck. It had to be someone. I simply took the first that came along."

"I have so little faith in pure luck," Bobby said, "especially when purpose seems to appear. There is so little need to advertise a house to let to-day, unless the purpose is to secure the highest rent possible. Every house agent has a long list of waiting applicants. But Mr. Fielding didn't ask a high rent. He quoted a most moderate, reasonable figure. Hardly the figure indeed the keen city man might have been expected to ask."

"Oh, come," Mr. Fielding protested smilingly, "we are not such sharks in the city as all that."

"I wondered," Bobby continued, "if there could be some other, special reason why the house was being offered to us. It might of course have been merely our bit of good luck and in any case at the moment it didn't seem important. Or else getting a decent house at a fair rent seemed to be a whole lot more important. I expect what I thought was that I would wait and see—wait developments. The first development was that a man who took part in a smash-and-grab raid and who bore what struck me as a resemblance to Mr. Fielding's chauffeur—the one who had wished himself on Mr. Fielding, as Mr. Fielding says—was followed to this neighbourhood where he vanished close by this cottage. I had to ask myself if there was any connection between our being given a house here and this vanishing act here. It began to occur to me that possibly suspicion that a gang of criminals was operating, or had their headquarters somewhere near, had induced a good, law-abiding, but possibly nervous citizen to feel he would like extra protection. Such a citizen might not have wished to risk making a fool of himself, and perhaps getting laughed at, by going to the police with an unsupported story and possibly unfounded suspicions. Alternatively he might simply want to avoid being mixed up in any sort of criminal affair. Some people rather like a bit of newspaper publicity and some people dread it like the pestilence. So it did seem possible that our good citizen had thought it would be a bright idea to get hold of a fairly highly placed police official as a neighbour. The idea would be that his presence would soon become known to the possible criminal gang and would act as a kind of disinfectant, so to say. It might get the gang, if it existed, to fade away without fuss or bother, and a good riddance to bad rubbish. It seemed an attractive idea and I very nearly put it straight out to Mr. Fielding. Only one soon learns in police work not to be in too much of a hurry. Hasten slowly has to be the policeman's motto."

"Well, as you put it like that, and very smart of you, too," Mr. Fielding said beamingly, "I don't mind admitting it was rather that way. I was beginning to notice little things. I couldn't even tell what they were. Trifles. Looks. And then this crime wave the papers are full of and the way I found myself with a new chauffeur, though I hardly knew how or why. By pure chance—just that, believe it or not—a man I had a deal on with dined one night with a friend at the hotel where you were staying. You were pointed out to him as a big noise at Scotland Yard, and it struck me that I wanted a responsible tenant for Fern Cottage on a short lease. If it suited you, it suited me, and if you answered the advertisement—well and good. If not, no harm done. I suppose now you'll be telling me all that may be used in evidence."

"Well, yes, now you mention it," Bobby admitted, "I suppose I ought to remind you both that anything you say may be used like that."

"I told you to take care," Miss Bellamy interposed. "He's making you answer his questions already."

"He hasn't asked any," Fielding retorted.

"No, he's just rambling along," Miss Bellamy said. "That's worse."

"Questions or rambling, all one to me," Fielding assured her smilingly. "Besides, I take it I may put forward a humble claim to be a good citizen and as such ought to be willing to help. You, too."

"I never claimed to be a good citizen," she answered. "Or wanted."

"Fire away," Fielding said to Bobby.

CHAPTER XXXIII

SOME SUGGESTIONS

BOBBY TOOK A MOMENT or two to express with much feeling his appreciation of Mr. Fielding's readiness, as a good citizen, to co-operate. He hoped, he said, he would not have to trespass too far upon Mr. Fielding's kindness.

"Though indeed," he concluded, "it's no less than I expected. Or should I say no more than I expected?" He paused to consider this nicety of language and Mr. Fielding smiled in his genial way and Miss Bellamy stared at him even more intently and more challengingly than before. He resumed: "My first idea when the gangster I was after vanished near here was that possibly he might be hiding in this cottage or one of its outbuildings. People in the country do sometimes leave their front doors open or the door key hanging up in some quite conspicuous place. Disturbing idea that a gangster might be hiding in a cottage where a lady lived alone. Suppose she found him under the bed or something like that?" He smiled at Miss Bellamy who did not smile back. He continued: "Besides, I wanted the fellow rather badly. So I got hold of Miss Bellamy and we went through the cottage carefully. No sign of him and no sign of any possible hiding place. It was only later that I remembered how Miss Bellamy had shown—I don't quite know how to put it—a sort of girlish—no, not girlish, decidedly not, considering the modern girl—no, a kind of old-fashioned, old maidenly reluctance to let me into her bedroom. I remembered how she stood in the doorway with her back to the half-open door. Plainly, she didn't like the idea of my going in and there seemed no reason to. I could see the whole room. I could see that nowhere, neither under the small, low iron bed nor in any cupboard, was there any spot where man or boy could be concealed. Later it did occur to me that I hadn't seen behind the door. Miss Bellamy stood with her back to it. There was room there all right for a man to be hidden, and then, too, neither old maidishness nor girlish modesty struck me as very characteristic of Miss Bellamy."

Miss Bellamy showed no sign of wishing to make any comment though Bobby stopped to give her the opportunity. But Mr. Fielding was plainly indignant and was moved to protest.

"Oh, well, come now," he said. "Isn't that all rather far-fetched?"

"Not so much so as two dead men," Bobby answered, "two dead men and music so strange as that Miss Bellamy lets us listen to."

"What on earth," demanded Fielding, "has Miss Bellamy's playing got to do with it? Magnificent, of course, but all the same . . . well, let's keep to the point."

"The next thing," Bobby continued, "was the appearance of the unlucky Myerson with his satchel of jewellery he showed off in the pub., having had too much to drink, apparently. Well, naturally I wondered if that was the genuine loot from the smash-and-grab raid. Apparently it was, for a ring found on Mr. Fielding's drive was easily identified as part of it. The inference seemed obvious. That it had been dropped by Myerson on his way to dispose of the loot to a receiver."

"Me?" said Mr. Fielding, amused. "Did you really think that?" he asked incredulously.

"I began at least to think that that was what I was intended to think," Bobby answered. "You see, I was sure I had been deliberately led here by the gangster I followed but failed to catch. A careful plan and careful preparations were evident. I was equally sure the ring had been deliberately put where it was so that it could he found there and that it was there specially for the vicar to find. I expect the idea was that the vicar could be trusted but that it might have been kept and nothing said if it had been found by, for instance, the

laundry delivery boy who, by a most extraordinarily fortunate coincidence, called only a little before."

"Why fortunate?" asked Miss Bellamy abruptly.

"What on earth—" protested Mr. Fielding. "First music
and then the laundry boy! Really, aren't we rather wasting
time?"

"The connection will appear," Bobby promised, "and all
apologies to the laundry boy who is, I am sure, perfectly
honest. Anyhow, I felt pretty sure there was some deep and
strange business going on. I couldn't for the life of me imagine what, but obviously it was up to me to find out."

"All this seems so very much in the air," Mr. Fielding
remarked. "Theory. Guess work. Oh, ingenious, I admit, but
still—nothing solid to go on. Airy fairy stuff. All in the air."

"It might have remained in the realm of theory," Bobby
said, and now his voice was a little grim, "had not two dead
men intervened. For dead men are matter not of the air but
very much of the earth."

"Earth to earth," Miss Bellamy said and laughed harshly.

"There was the background to whatever was going on,"
Bobby continued. "Miss Bellamy's playing Mr. Fielding
mentioned a moment ago. A disconcerting background. I
heard someone say once in a lecture on music—a very
highbrow lecture—that music tells all. I thought the same of
Miss Bellamy's music, but of course only for those who
knew the language. But that it had a purpose and a meaning
was clear to me and I thought sometimes that it was clear to
Mr. Fielding, too."

"Oh, well," Mr. Fielding said. He turned where he sat
and stared at the grand piano behind him, and for a moment
it seemed he was going to say something. But he turned back
and looked at neither of the other two. "Oh, well," he said
again, and was silent.

"There was an odd contradiction to be faced," Bobby
went on. "For if there were, as it seemed, a plan to direct
suspicion to Mr. Fielding as some sort of criminal—or else
why was I led here and why the opal ring where it was?—
and if there were any truth in it, then why had Mr. Fielding

himself helped to engineer my arrival on his doorstep, so to speak?"

"That's easy," Fielding said. "The gang knew I suspected something wrong, they guessed it was me got you here, and they wanted to get a bit of their own back."

"I did think of that," Bobby said. "But they would have been running a big risk to satisfy a very small grudge. It could have been managed much more easily with much less risk. Besides, I didn't think it likely there would be any very serious resentment felt. These men are oddly reasonable. They don't bear malice against police for instance. They feel we are just doing our job. They quite see the public has a right to look after itself and to be looked after by us. They do object very much to what they call outside interference. But I couldn't feel that getting a policeman on tap, so to say, would call for anything more than a few hearty curses—quite impersonal curses. Certainly not for such elaborate, carefully thought out plans. I turned down that idea."

"I'm not so sure," said Fielding reflectively. "I may have been treading on the toes of a pretty big organization."

"It was plain though," Bobby resumed, "that Biggs had something to do with it, and why had he thought it necessary to become Mr. Fielding's chauffeur? It seemed part of the plan. And what had he to do with Miss Bellamy, for I was getting more and more to think she had deliberately hidden him behind that half-open bedroom door of hers. Another conclusion followed. It was two or three years since Miss Bellamy came here to live and therefore, if she was in it, the plan, whatever it was, must have its roots in the past. Possibly even the distant past."

"All very well, all very pretty," Mr. Fielding said, puffing hard at his cigar. "Quite frankly, I'm a business man. In business these fancy frills don't go. We prefer an ounce of fact to any number of tons of theory. In business, we don't think much of the 'it might be this' or 'it might be that' line of country."

"Then," Bobby continued, "came the murder of the unlucky Myerson, paying the penalty for butting in on what didn't concern him."

"Best not to interfere," said Miss Bellamy. "Best to let things take their own course. They will anyhow. That's bad enough. But keep away."

"Even to keep away means helping to shape how things happen," Bobby said. "While we live, we can't help being in life. Biggs disappeared at the same time as the murder. That naturally pointed to him as the murderer."

"I thought so," Fielding admitted. "I've been sorry about that ever since. Shouldn't jump to conclusions," and he shook a warning head.

"I never thought it," Miss Bellamy said. "I knew better."

"I rather expected you would," Bobby agreed. "The disappearance of Biggs and the natural suspicions caused, made it necessary to search his rooms. We found he had a banking account with a fair sum of money to his credit and we also found a list of investments. Quite a good list and carefully detailed. Odd, we thought, that a man with a good capital should take the trouble to wangle himself a job as chauffeur—even pay a bonus to get it. Another thing. His name didn't appear in the list of shareholders in any of the companies he had down. That could only mean, that is, if his investments weren't an exercise in imagination, which didn't seem likely, that Biggs wasn't his real name. That could mean the actual share certificates were in safe keeping somewhere—with a friend or lawyer perhaps, but also perhaps with a safe deposit concern. It seemed worth trying and a photograph was taken round. It has been recognized now as the photograph of a man who gave the name of Smith when he hired a safe with the Northern Security Company in the city. We haven't got permission yet to open the safe but we hope to soon. That may give us his real name and may help us to find out more about him—and his past. But I'm running ahead. When I first saw Mr. Fielding's shelter I noticed it was being pulled down. I remembered, too, that Mr. Fielding complained that the man from the village doing the job hadn't been for some days. But I could see that much more demolition had been done since I was there first. I noticed the west wall was almost level. I wondered why? Why get on with it instead of waiting for the workman who had been given the job? Obvious, though, what a handy and convenient grave was there, ready-made, so to say, for any murderer's convenience. All you had to do was to dig the grave—no need for it to be deep—in the rubble already half-filling what had been the shelter. Then you fill it in and on top of that throw down more of the shelter walls. There is the job done and nothing to cause any suspicion. Even if a dog started sniffing and scratching, as might inconveniently happen, the explanation was simple—Myerson's death had taken place there."

"Seems," observed Mr. Fielding thoughtfully, "as if whoever thought that one out—and very smart, too, whoever it was—hadn't reckoned with you, Mr. Owen."

"Merely," Bobby explained, "a quite reasonable hope that appearances would be taken at their face value. By the way, Mr. Fielding, I remember your saying that night that your hand was hurting. I think you said it had kept you awake. Rather a bad blister. Wasn't that it?"

Mr. Fielding looked at him blankly.

"Oh, no," he said, "Oh, no. What I said was that that lazy old scamp who had been doing the job had made a blistered hand an excuse to stop away."

CHAPTER XXXIV

ATTRACTION—REPULSION

THERE WAS A SLIGHT pause after Mr. Fielding said this. He took another violent puff at his cigar and put it down. Miss Bellamy said:

"I remember."

But what or how she remembered she did not make clear nor did Bobby ask. Instead he said:

"That reminds me. That was when I borrowed Mr. Fielding's handkerchief, wasn't it?"

"I don't think I ever had it back, had I?" Mr. Fielding asked. He took out his shining cigar case and selected another cigar. He said: "No, I never had it back." He began to busy himself lighting his fresh cigar. He said casually: "Got it still? The handkerchief, I mean."

"Oh, yes," Bobby said. "As a matter of fact, I've got it with me now."

"Oh, it didn't matter, you shouldn't have troubled," Mr. Fielding said amiably. "Damn," he added as he let his cigar slip from his fingers and had to stoop to pick it up. "I beg your pardon," he said to Miss Bellamy as he retrieved it. But she did not seem to have heard. She was staring at Bobby in the same fixed, intent manner that was now hers. She said: "Handkerchief? What's that mean?"

"When we found," Bobby went on without answering this, "that Biggs was himself a victim—the first victim indeed that night—we did think at first that we might be up against a gangster feud. The very fact that gangsters can't appeal to the law for protection or redress does sometimes make them take to violence instead."

"That's what I thought from the very start," Fielding said. "It all points that way." He added, inhaling gently the fragrance of his newly lighted cigar: "These Havanas are worthwhile. Cost real money but value all right."

"Ten bob each, you said," Bobby remarked, "I wish I could afford that price and then leave them only a quarter smoked."

"What's that? What do you mean?" Fielding asked, and then seemed to realize that he had lighted a second cigar, leaving another hardly touched. He gave Bobby a quick look, but his voice was still steady and unconcerned, as he said: "That comes from being so interested in what you're telling us, Mr. Owen."

"Cigars and handkerchiefs," Miss Bellamy said. "He's rambling still, but he's getting nearer. That means mischief."

"I'm not so much getting nearer," Bobby said, "as getting near the end. But as against the gangster feud theory our inquiries also showed there was a lot going on in the neighbourhood that needed explaining. A very important clue, I might almost say a decisive clue, was given us by young Rogers, though he didn't know it. I had already noticed that Biggs seemed to know who I was as soon as he saw me. Nothing much in that. He could easily have been in court—even on the jury—when some case I was connected with came up. But I was more interested when Rogers said he had seen Biggs talking to a man he recognized as someone he had seen in gaol when Rogers himself was serving a term as a conscientious objector. Of course, you see at once that was a tremendous help."

"Why?" asked Fielding. "You knew Biggs had been in the smash-and-grab raid that started all this horrible business."

"Suspected, not knew," Bobby said, "and the raid was no beginning. We are watching a dénouement, not a début—the fifth act, not the opening scene. The question now was how a man, with a certain amount of money, a steady job, a satisfactory army discharge, no criminal record—we knew that because we had his dabs for comparison and they weren't in the files— how he had got in touch with an habitual criminal whom it hadn't been hard to identify from Rogers's description as a very old customer of ours. Of course, by the way, we looked him up immediately. We soon got proof that he had nothing to do with the murders, and that he and the rest of his pals were very much puzzled and worried by Myerson's murder. It had upset the whole lot of them considerably; and while of course none of them would make any admissions, it was clear they would have been willing to help us find the murderer if they could. They were all sure, too, there could have been no reason for any quarrel between Biggs and Myerson over a division of loot. That part of it had all been settled before. So there was an end of the gangster feud theory and one more possibility at least out of the way."

"I wouldn't be so sure of that if I were you," Fielding said. "Those fellows are up to all sorts of tricks."

"Very few in point of fact," Bobby told him. "A hidebound, routine-ridden mind, the gangster's. The problem we had before us then was how Biggs had got in touch with a professional criminal. Not too easy. Professional criminals don't care about casual acquaintances. Too risky. Might be a cop in disguise, they think. Unlikely, though it might happen, I suppose. Well, I went over every possibility I could think of and it occurred to me that there is one place where rogues and honest people may meet on more or less equal terms. As friends, even pals. Visiting day. We know because occasionally the fact that, say, Mrs. X has visited Mr. X serving a term for, shall we say? making mistakes in a balance sheet, or has been there to meet him on his discharge, has been used by others present on much the same sort of errand, for trying a little blackmail. We started inquiries. Inconclusive. You see, we had no names to work on. But a list was made out and we noticed it included the name of an elderly man of the name of Frank Bardsell. What drew our attention at first was the initials, F.B. They are the same as those of Fred Biggs and it's an odd fact that when people change their names they often keep the same initials. Some primitive racial fear of loss of identity perhaps. Anyhow, the initials being the same made us pay special attention to Mr. Bardsell. He had had a high reputation till somehow he had got mixed up in the issue of a fraudulent balance sheet. He got seven years. It was thought rather a lenient sentence. An hour or two before his discharge on ticket of leave, he committed suicide. Apparently he felt he could not face the outside world. Of course, all this happened years ago, before the war. But it was rather clearly remembered at the prison, because it had been their job to tell Mr. Bardsell's daughter what had happened. She had come to meet her father and was actually in the prison at the time. A special favour, of course. Some sort of introduction to the prison governor perhaps, or someone like that. What made it worse was that when the daughter went back and told what had happened, the mother had a heart attack and died the next day. A tragic and unhappy story." Bobby turned to Miss Bellamy. "Was that daughter you?" he asked.

She did not reply in words but in her eyes the answer was clear.

"Where's all this leading if it all happened years ago?" Mr. Fielding asked. He looked with surprise at his cigar which he had allowed to go out. He laid it down very carefully by the side of the other one. "No good lighting a cigar again once it's gone out," he observed. "Flavour all gone. Because," he explained, "of being so interested. Only how's all that helping you to find out who did the killing? Isn't that your job, not rooting round in what's dead and past and done with?"

"What is dead and past and done with, but it never is," Bobby answered, "gives us the background, the atmosphere, the history so to speak. That's what you have to understand before you can understand what's happening now. There was Miss Bellamy's playing. I felt the whole story was there. Her music told all. At least, it did if you could understand. But to understand you had to know the history behind. And that began to make plain the rather terrible attraction-repulsion that seemed to exist between you."

"It didn't take me long," Fielding said, "to know who she was. It wasn't my fault things happened as they did. If Bardsell hadn't been too pig-headed to do as I said, we should both have been in the clear. But when he began to worry about doing what he called the right thing, I saw it was time for me to look after myself. I had to. He said he hadn't understood where it was leading. That was his affair. One has to take risks and if he thought my figures too optimistic, or ill-founded, or anything like that, he ought to have said so. But he just accepted them. The truth is, he didn't want to check them. I could see that and I could see it was time for me to cover up. When I went into the witness box I was complimented on my clear, straightforward evidence. I think the old boy on the bench knew. But nothing he could do, except pass as light a sentence as he dared. It was a great relief to me. The figures were all in Bardsell's writing, he had signed the books, I was only a sort of backroom boy. And I couldn't stop Mrs. Bardsell's giving up everything to the creditors. A drop in the bucket anyway. I would have helped her all I could if she had let me. Why, she even tore up the cheque I sent her. I wanted there to be as little ill-feeling as possible. When Miss Bellamy took the cottage I soon recognized her. And I guessed there were still sore feelings, even after all that time. But I made up my mind to do all I could to help her and to try to smooth things over. Never pays to bear a grudge. Write off losses and bad debts. That's a sound business maxim. It pays. I tried to see what I could do." He paused; and then in a slightly different tone, one more genuine, Bobby thought, less full of an anxious self-justification, he said, and slowly: "If only we could have met before, with nothing between us, just as—as friends."

"When mother died," Miss Bellamy said, "my brother and I were holding her hands and we looked at each other and Frank said: 'That's both of them—father and mother, too.' So I kissed mother and I said to her: 'Tell father when you meet him that we remember.' Only then there was the war and Frank had to join up. That was when he changed his name. The last thing Frank said was not to lose sight of Mr.

Fielding. He said I was to go and live near and find out all I could. So I came here. We both had a little money. Uncle left it us when he died. Soon after I came, Mr. Fielding began to call. It was his cottage, he was the landlord. I didn't know he suspected anything. I wanted to be friendly so as to have more to tell Frank. Then I began to notice that he was growing attentive and all at once I found I was beginning to look forward to his coming. I think in a way it was because of what he had done, because I hated him so much for that, that I was attracted to him. I think it was because of what he knew he had done to us that he was attracted to me. Hate drew us and hate made us one with each other. There was that which lay between us that made us afraid, afraid with great fear, that drew us together because of our hate and our fear, that pushed us apart because we so feared both our hate and our love. We were like those we read of in the French Revolution who were tied together, man and woman, and thrown into the river to drown or to swim."

CHAPTER XXXV

CONCLUSION

THERE WAS A LONG silence when Miss Bellamy, Miss Bard-sell, finished speaking, and the coffee grew cold in their cups where it waited. Fielding took out another of his cigars but this time he did not even attempt to light it. He put it down carefully by the side of the other two. He said, speaking in a low voice, one barely audible, and directly to Miss Bardsell:

"If we made up our minds to it, you and I, we could for-get all this. Why not?" But neither of the other two answered him and his own voice was flat and without hope, as of one who pleaded for mercy but knew it could not be. He said: "It was Myerson did it. Myerson killed him. Myerson."

"That would still leave us asking who shot Myerson and why," Bobby said. "No reason why Myerson should want to murder anyone and he didn't go about armed. It's plain how he came in. He was a hanger-on of the Burden gang, a kind of odd job man. No good in a crisis. Apt to lose his head, so he was never let in on the actual job. Or wanted to be. But useful as a go-between and could be trusted because he would never dare be anything else. He could see of course some plan was being carried out and he wondered what. He knew Fred Biggs, Frank Bardsell, that is, was in touch with the Burden gang. He helped in the details. He was told to help in laying a false trail. He knew valuable help was being given the gang and that all Frank Bardsell asked in return was for a show to be made of faked stuff in the village, and for one genuine ring to be dropped in a certain spot. He could see there must be something behind all that and he wanted to know what."

"Trying to frame me, that was what," Fielding said, and now in a very injured tone.

"Poetic justice," Bobby said. "You framed the elder Frank Bardsell, and the younger one meant to frame you. He may have thought that even if he couldn't manage to get you into the dock he could at any rate bring you so much under suspicion as to ruin you socially and perhaps even in business."

"Vindictive," Fielding complained. "What's the sense? No one's ever the better for that sort of thing. I told him. It's all over and done with, I said, and he laughed and said it wasn't done with, not by a long way, and wouldn't be till I was done with, too."

"Was that when you shot him?" Bobby asked.

"That was Myerson," Fielding repeated.

But Bobby ignored this and continued:

"Probably Myerson thought there might be pickings to be had if he could find out what it was all about. That's why he hung around in a way that puzzled and worried us a lot. But certainly with no idea of murdering anyone and no reason why he should want to. What happened must have been something like this. He had made up his mind to do a bit of snooping. What the Burden gang used him for generally. Possibly he had spotted the air raid shelter as a kind of handy headquarters. He may have heard about tramps using it for sleeping in. Or he may have heard a shot and come to see what was happening. He may have merely been watching, or following someone he had seen moving. What everything does go to show is that he was there in time to see the dead body and the half-dug grave. Then there was nothing else to do. Was there?" he asked Fielding abruptly.

"I got him to help," Fielding said, and it was as though he saw again, and once more again lived through, that tragic and dreadful night. "I promised to pay him well if he kept quiet. He said he would, he swore he would. But I could see there was no trusting him. He·would have sucked me dry and then betrayed me at the end. Besides, I couldn't help seeing what a help it would be. Everything would go to show Biggs had killed him. Well, that was true, morally. It had all happened through Biggs. He was to blame and only fair he should take the blame." Fielding paused and looked angrily at Bobby. "Only for you snooping and meddling," he said, "that's how it would have been." Then he turned and looked at Miss Bardsell, listening intently, in deep silence. He said: "That way you would never have known and there wouldn't have been anything to come between us any more."

"Nothing," Miss Bardsell said. She said very slowly: "I think perhaps it might have been like that if I had never known."

"But for him," Fielding said, and again looked angrily at Bobby. "Rooting out what's best forgotten."

"Only in time, as time passed," Miss Bardsell went on in the same slow and now almost dreamy tone, as if she were slipping back into one of her earlier moods of deep, far-off abstraction, "I think I should have known and then I think I should have killed both you and me." She indicated Bobby with a slight, almost imperceptible gesture. "Only for him," she said.

"Yes, I know," Fielding said unexpectedly. "I thought of that. I thought perhaps in time you would know. Things can't be kept quiet for always. They pop up somehow. I thought if that was the way it had to be, it had to be and O.K. by me."

"Did you think that?" she asked, turning her gaze full upon him. She put out her hand and he laid his upon it; and as she and her brother had looked at each other across the dead body of their mother, so it was now that these two looked at each other across as it were the dead body of her brother. And Bobby, looking on, wondered.

Fielding turned to him and now with defiance. "I'm not done yet," he said. "All this stuff you're trying to put across—no proof, no evidence, no witnesses. Nothing. Just guesswork. Take it into court and you'll be laughed out again. Guesswork," he repeated, and he wiped his forehead on which now stood cold drops of perspiration.

"I'll guess some more," Bobby said. "You soon recognized Miss Bardsell and it didn't take you long to recognize her brother. There had to be some reason why Biggs wanted to wangle a job with you. And once you knew who he was, it again didn't take you long to understand that his visits to Miss Bellamy—Miss Bardsell, that is—were to lay plans and to push her on to help in what he meant to do. You must have realized very soon that your idea of getting me here as a kind of warning to scare him off what he intended, wasn't going to work. Indeed I expect you began to see that it was going to be the other way, that he was intending to use my presence to make things even worse for you. So I think you made up your mind you had to do something and you tried to come to some arrangement with him."

"I offered to go fifty-fifty," Fielding said gloomily. "I put it to him to let bygones be bygones. Fair enough. It was what I cleaned up when old Mr. Bardsell wouldn't go on— everything would have been all right but for him turning pig-headed at the last and I did warn him—well, that was what put me first into the big money. I said then his sister and I could settle down comfortably and forget what was all over and done with and couldn't be helped any more. Wasn't that fair enough?"

"Fair enough," Bobby said, but his voice was grim and hard. "What did he say?"

"He lost his head completely. Raved. Shouted. Threats. I reminded him how I had gone out of my way to give him an alibi over that smash-and-grab raid when you thought you saw him. I said: Didn't one good turn deserve another? No good. He wouldn't listen. He got his pistol and began to wave it about. He said he would put a bullet through me and her, too, if I ever dared so much as mention her name again. Well, I had a pistol, too."

"So you shot him?" Bobby said.

"That was Myerson," Fielding repeated.

"Why should he?" Bobby asked. "No motive—and no pistol. He wasn't the man to go armed. Why had you taken a pistol with you?"

"It was only common sense. I made up my mind I had to have it out with him and I knew he could be violent. I knew his temper. I had a right to defend myself, hadn't I? Self-defence, that's all." He was speaking not so much to Bobby as to Miss Bardsell, to her in self-justification. "Self-defence," he said again, watching her anxiously. "That's what it was. He said he would never rest till he had me where I put his father. He said there wasn't ever going be a·smash-and-grab raid but something would be found to bring me in. Or if there was a big burglary, then my car, or a car with my car's number, would have been seen, or something of mine would be found near. It was going to be like that every time."

"He hadn't a very high opinion of us," Bobby remarked. "We aren't so easily taken in as all that. I daresay he could have made it awkward for you, though—especially with a record like yours to work on."

"There's been nothing against me for years," Fielding said indignantly. "But I could see I was up against it. He didn't sound sane. He started waving his pistol about again. He said it would save trouble and he had a good mind to use it right away. I thought he meant it. I saw it had to be him or me and I got in first. Self-defence. Nothing else. You see that?"

"No," said Bobby.

"I didn't mean it was," Fielding said with a sudden change of manner. "I mean it would have been if it had been like you're trying to make out. But it wasn't. You've no proof," he said.

Miss Bellamy, Miss Bardsell, raised her head from her cupped hands on which she had been resting it. She looked at Bobby. "Have you?" she asked. "You talked about a handkerchief. What handkerchief?"

"There isn't any," Fielding said. "Not to count, I mean. How could it?"

"You gave me one of yours that night," Bobby reminded him, "and it was sent for examination and analysis by our experts."

"Why? What for?" demanded Fielding angrily, scornfully, and yet with unease as well. "Wanted to find blood on it, I suppose? There wasn't. There couldn't be. You can't bluff me. If there had been, is it likely I would have given it you or let you have it?"

"There's no question of bloodstains," Bobby told him. "The analysis doesn't mention blood. No reason to. It was brick dust that I was thinking about."

"Brick dust?" repeated Fielding, puzzled, uneasy, still defiant.

"You told me that night," Bobby explained, "as you may remember, that you had a painful blister on your hand which had kept you awake. I could see more work, a good deal in fact, had been done in the way of pulling down the shelter walls. Yet the odd job man from the village—Sadler was his name, I think—who had been engaged on the job had himself told us just before that he hadn't done anything there for some days. So who had? Was it you, I wondered? And if so, why? and was that how you had hurt your hand? An interesting speculation. And it struck me that anyone busy throwing down the shelter walls would be working in a good deal of dust. And I thought that a lot of that dust would have got up his nose and very probably he would have had to sneeze once or twice. A homely and useful inference. If so, it seemed likely that the mucus on the handkerchief would show a high proportion of brick dust. We knew it was a clean handkerchief, fresh from the laundry, for the laundry delivery had been made that same evening, and your housekeeper had happened to mention that it had been so late you hadn't had a handkerchief left and she had been obliged to borrow some for you. This one, however, was your own, with your initials on it. So I asked myself two questions. Had the blister on your hand any connection with the work done on the air raid shelter walls, that work not having been done by the man on the job? Secondly, how had brick dust got on your handkerchief, clean from the laundry only a few hours previously? The blister might have been explained as a mere coincidence. But how had the brick dust, if the analysis found it, got there? That seemed a question difficult to answer. And if you like to look for yourself and see what the analysis says, there's the report for you to read if you want to."

He flung it on the table as he spoke. Fielding made no effort to pick it up. He sat very still and he knew that doom was upon him.

"I thought all the time you had something up your sleeve," he said. "Natural place for a handkerchief," he said and laughed. "Well, you win and good-bye."

He sprang to his feet as he spoke and without pause or hesitation dived clean through the window, glass and frame and all, straight into the arms of one of Superintendent Bell's men, waiting there.

"This way, Mr. Fielding, please," the man said. "I'm afraid you've cut your face but we'll soon fix that," and as the two in the cottage sat there silently they heard the sound of retreating footsteps.

"Father and mother," Miss Bardsell said, "and Frank, too, and now him as well."

"There is nothing I can say or do," Bobby said and got to his feet. "If you think there is, or if my wife? I may ask her to come to see you, may I?"

She was not listening. She picked up the analyst's report Bobby had thrown on the table, by the side of those three cigars that to him at least had told so plain a story of a slowly mounting sense of coming doom so well controlled so long, but in the end breaking down so suddenly.

"He was very clever," she said. "So are you. If it hadn't been for the handkerchief you wouldn't have been able to do anything." She paused and said in her old abstracted voice: "We could have been happy together if only things had been different."

And to Bobby it was as though he listened to humanity's eternal cry, repeated through the ages.

A little awkwardly, he said: "You have your music still."

"No," she said. "I shall never play again."

"Your opera you were working on?"

"Oh, that," she said. "He—" She did not mention any name but Bobby knew. "He had sent it to people—big people. He paid any fee they asked. They all said the same—stiff and imitative. I expect they are right."

Bobby said nothing. But he was surprised. He remembered that wild and passionate playing of hers, like nothing he had ever heard before, like nothing, he believed, that anyone anywhere had ever heard before. Stiff and imitative were the last epithets he would have anticipated. But perhaps it was only the doubt and anguish she had known that had released powers that otherwise would never have reached the level of expression. She was looking idly at the analyst's report and her expression changed. In bewilderment she looked at Bobby. "But it says," she exclaimed, "that the traces of mucus are entirely normal with no trace of any unusual substance."

"I know," Bobby agreed. "I suppose my idea that the brick dust he was working in must have made him sneeze, was all wrong. I told him if he didn't believe it, if he didn't think it possible, as he knew bloodstains weren't possible, as he would have known it wasn't possible if it all hadn't happened much as I suggested, then I said he could look for himself. He didn't. He knew it might be as I said and he daren't put it to the test. He thought he had better try to escape instead and so with safety there before him on the table, he proclaimed his guilt instead."

THE END

AFTERWORD

NIETZSCHE IN MUSIC

Melody and Malady in *Music Tells All*

"Without music, life would be a mistake."

— Friedrich Nietzsche, *Twilight of the Idols*

"A disturbing element. Not, I fear, a good influence. Ever since she came, there has been — what shall I say? Unrest. Definitely. A kind of pagan element. I shall never forget the Sunday she played for us in church. It seemed as though what she played was a denial of the whole body of the Christian faith, as if she were telling us that hate is stronger than love, and that pity and mercy were no more than foolish weakness." He paused and then as his two listeners watched him in wonder and surprise at this outburst, he said loudly: "Nietzsche in Music."

Music has always held a unique, magical influence over people. It is a phenomenon—a force that can be minutely subtle or aggressively overpowering, has the power to play with our emotions, and our minds, and has the potential to change the way we are. Perceived to a large extent through our ears, music can also reverberate within our bodies and move our hearts physically as well as metaphysically.

It is ironic that, when the local Vicar in *Music Tells All*, at a loss to describe in words the music played on the piano by Miss Bellamy, summarizes it as "Nietzsche in Music," he is invoking the author who famously praised music as one of the most important elements in human existence.

Mrs. Bellamy's piano music is described intermittently throughout the novel, and each time her music has an unsettling effect on the listeners. Furthermore, when various characters attempt to describe the music, they are at a loss to capture in words its nature—except that it seems to hold a decidedly ominous note.

The author's description perhaps comes closest to conveying Mrs. Bellamy's music:

> Then her hands flew along the keyboard and the room was filled with a roaring torrent of sound, threatening, ominous, and angry as thunder crashing overhead. Then it softened, it nearly died away and rose again in a long lament, so that one heard in it the wailing of all women sorrowing for those who would return no more. It grew louder again and muttered and growled, full of menace and distant, helpless rage. A crash of discords that violated every known law of harmony and yet made a kind of angry harmony of their own, succeeded and ended.

Bobby Owen suspects that Mrs. Bellamy's music refers to the mystery surrounding the crimes in the story, and that Mrs. Bellamy is either deliberately or unconsciously referring to what is at the heart of the matter.

For the reader, it is an intriguing clue that remains elusive, because we can't hear the piano playing of Mrs. Bellamy! Instead, we must try to *imagine* what the music sounds like, and all we have to go on are the descriptions of the music in the text.

Having reached the end of the story, and the mystery, we can perhaps imagine better what Mrs. Bellamy's music *might* sound like, having had the events in her and Mr. Fielding's earlier lives related. Still, the reader is ultimately left in a curious position where they have been given the opportunity to imagine their own version of Mrs. Bellamy's music—to imagine music that captured all the intricacies of the human mystery in the story.

The final irony is in the title of the book: *Music Tells All*. During the course of his investigation, Bobby Owen feels that Mrs. Bellamy's music holds the answers to the mystery, but, even for those in the story who hear the music, those answers remained out of reach—only the effects of the music make a deeply-affecting emotional impression on the listener. So, though in a sense the music does "tell all" on the emotional level, on the purely prosaic level (who did what to whom and why and where?) the music refuses to tell Bobby Owen, or the reader, anything.

~ ~ ~ ~ ~

Music Tells All, the twenty-fourth novel featuring Bobby Owen, shows Owen well-settled in his progressing career in the police force,[1] and in his married life with Olive. This novel also has the distinction of featuring the involvement in the case of Superintendent Bell, head of the county C.I.D.— previously Sergeant Bell from Punshon's other series of Carter & Bell novels. Bell had outlived his partner Carter, and his appearance in *Music Tells All* is his final appearance in Punshon's stories.

In previous Ramble House reprints of Punshon's Bobby Owen novels[2] I have tried to fill in the details of the author's life and work. The English crime fiction journal CADS (Crime and Detective Story) has issued two excellent supplementary publications which shed much light on the details of Punshon's life and work.

---

[1] At the beginning of the novel Bobby Owen describes his position at Scotland Yard as "temporary-acting-junior-under-deputy-assistant-commissioner—unattached."

[2] *Triple Quest* and *Dictator's Way* (Ramble House, 2013).

Punshon's Policemen: The Two Detective Series of E. R. Punshon [3] by William A. S. Sarjeant, is a highly detailed and comprehensive exploration of Punshon's two detective series featuring Bobby Owen and Inspector Carter & Sergeant Bell. Sarjeant gives detailed separate accounts of each series and bibliographies of the series novels and, in the case of Bobby Owen, short stories.

Was Corinne's Murder Clued? The Detection Club and Fair Play 1930-1953 [4] by Curtis Evans, is a detailed history of The Detection Club during the years 1930 to 1953, with a particular emphasis on the Club's fundamental criteria for acceptance for membership. Punshon joined The Detection Club in 1933, and was a reliable member, both in terms of his crime fiction meeting the approval of fellow Club members (especially Dorothy L. Sayers) and with payment of his membership dues. There are many passing references in Evans' history to E.R. Punshon and his association with the Club; when the Club was revived following World War Two, Punshon, then 74, became Treasurer of the Detection Club, and dutifully worked to fulfill his role.

Gavin L. O'Keefe
South Berwick ME
September 2013

~ ~ ~ ~ ~

---

[3] CADS Supplement No.4, 1995.
[4] CADS Supplement No.14, 2011.

Front of dustjacket from the first edition (Gollancz, London, 1948)

~ ~ ~ ~ ~

Among contemporary reviews of *Music Tells All* were the following positive notices from English and Australian newspapers.

Western Morning News (England), 8 May 1948

A detective story written with unusual care about characterization and dialogue.

Hull Daily Mail (England), 3 April 1948

For a change there really is an unusual idea in the detective story *Music Tells All* ... and E.R. Punshon, the author, is to be congratulated on exploiting it to help in sustaining the mystery and suspicion surrounding two murders. Briefly, an accomplished musician plays as she feels, gives a weird stormy music that the detectives feel is somehow linked with the double crime. But the solution is not to be found in any variant of the old hot or cold parlour game. Suspicion moves from character to character and the interest never flags.

The Advertiser (Adelaide), 26 June 1948

In leisurely fashion, Mr. E.R. Punshon in *Music Tells All* links up a smash and grab raid on a London jeweller's shop with two murders that take place soon afterwards in a village where Detective Inspector Bobby Owen—temporarily at Scotland Yard—and his wife Olive have just moved into a charming house.

The house itself is important to the story. How did it happen that Bobby Owen was chosen, out of hundreds of applicants, as the tenant of this desirable cottage?

Readers of this pleasantly discursive mystery will find out: they'll also learn just why Miss Bellamy's strange, haunting music "tells all."

This is one of the better Punshons.

The Argus (Melbourne), 12 June 1948

Music Tells All is a most entertaining crime detection tale based on unbelievable premises—that a woman tells the tale through her playing of her piano. Never before have all the characters in any story been so allergic to music. Apart from this, it is reasonable enough, though the finding of all the essential evidence in police files becomes monotonous and seems to indicate flagging zeal on the part of the writer. (G.A.H.)

~ ~ ~ ~ ~

RAMBLE HOUSE's

HARRY STEPHEN KEELER WEBWORK MYSTERIES
(RH) indicates the title is available ONLY in the RAMBLE HOUSE edition

The Ace of Spades Murder
The Affair of the Bottled Deuce (RH)
The Amazing Web
The Barking Clock
Behind That Mask
The Book with the Orange Leaves
The Bottle with the Green Wax Seal
The Box from Japan
The Case of the Canny Killer
The Case of the Crazy Corpse (RH)
The Case of the Flying Hands (RH)
The Case of the Ivory Arrow
The Case of the Jeweled Ragpicker
The Case of the Lavender Gripsack
The Case of the Mysterious Moll
The Case of the 16 Beans
The Case of the Transparent Nude (RH)
The Case of the Transposed Legs
The Case of the Two-Headed Idiot (RH)
The Case of the Two Strange Ladies
The Circus Stealers (RH)
Cleopatra's Tears
A Copy of Beowulf (RH)
The Crimson Cube (RH)
The Face of the Man From Saturn
Find the Clock
The Five Silver Buddhas
The 4th King
The Gallows Waits, My Lord! (RH)
The Green Jade Hand
Finger! Finger!
Hangman's Nights (RH)
I, Chameleon (RH)
I Killed Lincoln at 10:13! (RH)
The Iron Ring
The Man Who Changed His Skin (RH)
The Man with the Crimson Box
The Man with the Magic Eardrums
The Man with the Wooden Spectacles
The Marceau Case
The Matilda Hunter Murder

The Monocled Monster
The Murder of London Lew
The Murdered Mathematician
The Mysterious Card (RH)
The Mysterious Ivory Ball of Wong Shing Li (RH)
The Mystery of the Fiddling Cracksman
The Peacock Fan
The Photo of Lady X (RH)
The Portrait of Jirjohn Cobb
Report on Vanessa Hewstone (RH)
Riddle of the Travelling Skull
Riddle of the Wooden Parrakeet (RH)
The Scarlet Mummy (RH)
The Search for X-Y-Z
The Sharkskin Book
Sing Sing Nights
The Six From Nowhere (RH)
The Skull of the Waltzing Clown
The Spectacles of Mr. Cagliostro
Stand By—London Calling!
The Steeltown Strangler
The Stolen Gravestone (RH)
Strange Journey (RH)
The Strange Will
The Straw Hat Murders (RH)
The Street of 1000 Eyes (RH)
Thieves' Nights
Three Novellos (RH)
The Tiger Snake
The Trap (RH)
Vagabond Nights (Defrauded Yeggman)
Vagabond Nights 2 (10 Hours)
The Vanishing Gold Truck
The Voice of the Seven Sparrows
The Washington Square Enigma
When Thief Meets Thief
The White Circle (RH)
The Wonderful Scheme of Mr. Christopher Thorne
X. Jones—of Scotland Yard
Y. Cheung, Business Detective

Keeler Related Works

A To Izzard: A Harry Stephen Keeler Companion by Fender Tucker — Articles and stories about Harry, by Harry, and in his style. Included is a compleat bibliography.

Wild About Harry: Reviews of Keeler Novels — Edited by Richard Polt & Fender Tucker — 22 reviews of works by Harry Stephen Keeler from *Keeler News*. A perfect introduction to the author.

The Keeler Keyhole Collection: Annotated newsletter rants from Harry Stephen Keeler, edited by Francis M. Nevins. Over 400 pages of incredibly personal Keeleriana.

Fakealoo — Pastiches of the style of Harry Stephen Keeler by selected demented members of the HSK Society. Updated every year with the new winner.

Strands of the Web: Short Stories of Harry Stephen Keeler — 29 stories, just about all that Keeler wrote, are edited and introduced by Fred Cleaver.

RAMBLE HOUSE's LOON SANCTUARY

A Clear Path to Cross — Sharon Knowles short mystery stories by Ed Lynskey.
A Jimmy Starr Omnibus — Three 40s novels by Jimmy Starr.
A Niche in Time and Other Stories — Classic SF by William F. Temple
A Roland Daniel Double: The Signal and The Return of Wu Fang — Classic thrillers from the 30s.

A Shot Rang Out — Three decades of reviews and articles by today's Anthony Boucher, Jon Breen. An essential book for any mystery lover's library.

A Smell of Smoke — A 1951 English countryside thriller by Miles Burton.

A Snark Selection — Lewis Carroll's *The Hunting of the Snark* with two Snarkian chapters by Harry Stephen Keeler — Illustrated by Gavin L. O'Keefe.

A Young Man's Heart — A forgotten early classic by Cornell Woolrich.

Alexander Laing Novels — *The Motives of Nicholas Holtz* and *Dr. Scarlett*, stories of medical mayhem and intrigue from the 30s.

An Angel in the Street — Modern hardboiled noir by Peter Genovese.

Automaton — Brilliant treatise on robotics: 1928-style! By H. Stafford Hatfield.

Away From the Here and Now — Clare Winger Harris stories, collected by Richard A. Lupoff

Beast or Man? — A 1930 novel of racism and horror by Sean M'Guire. Introduced by John Pelan.

Black Hogan Strikes Again — Australia's Peter Renwick pens a tale of the 30s outback.

Black River Falls — Suspense from the master, Ed Gorman.

Blondy's Boy Friend — A snappy 1930 story by Philip Wylie, writing as Leatrice Homesley.

Blood in a Snap — The *Finnegan's Wake* of the 21st century, by Jim Weiler.

Blood Moon — The first of the Robert Payne series by Ed Gorman.

Bogart '48 — Hollywood action with Bogie by John Stanley and Kenn Davis

Calling Lou Largo! — Two Lou Largo novels by William Ard.

Cornucopia of Crime — Francis M. Nevins assembled this huge collection of his writings about crime literature and the people who write it. Essential for any serious mystery library.

Corpse Without Flesh — Strange novel of forensics by George Bruce

Crimson Clown Novels — By Johnston McCulley, author of the Zorro novels, *The Crimson Clown* and *The Crimson Clown Again.*

Dago Red — 22 tales of dark suspense by Bill Pronzini.

Dark Sanctuary — Weird Menace story by H. B. Gregory

David Hume Novels — *Corpses Never Argue, Cemetery First Stop, Make Way for the Mourners, Eternity Here I Come.* 1930s British hardboiled fiction with an attitude.

Dead Man Talks Too Much — Hollywood boozer by Weed Dickenson.

Death Leaves No Card — One of the most unusual murdered-in-the-tub mysteries you'll ever read. By Miles Burton.

Death March of the Dancing Dolls and Other Stories — Volume Three in the Day Keene in the Detective Pulps series. Introduced by Bill Crider.

Deep Space and other Stories — A collection of SF gems by Richard A. Lupoff.

Detective Duff Unravels It — Episodic mysteries by Harvey O'Higgins.

Diabolic Candelabra — Classic 30s mystery by E.R. Punshon.

Dime Novels: Ramble House's 10-Cent Books — *Knife in the Dark* by Robert Leslie Bellem, *Hot Lead* and *Song of Death* by Ed Earl Repp, *A Hashish House in New York* by H.H. Kane, and five more.

Don Diablo: Book of a Lost Film — Two-volume treatment of a western by Paul Landres, with diagrams. Intro by Francis M. Nevins.

Dope and Swastikas — Two strange novels from 1922 by Edmund Snell

Dope Tales #1 — Two dope-riddled classics; *Dope Runners* by Gerald Grantham and *Death Takes the Joystick* by Phillip Condé.

Dope Tales #2 — Two more narco-classics; *The Invisible Hand* by Rex Dark and *The Smokers of Hashish* by Norman Berrow.

Dope Tales #3 — Two enchanting novels of opium by the master, Sax Rohmer. *Dope* and *The Yellow Claw.*

Double Hot — Two 60s softcore sex novels by Morris Hershman.

Dr. Odin — Douglas Newton's 1933 racial potboiler comes back to life.

Evangelical Cockroach — Jack Woodford writes about writing.

Evidence in Blue — 1938 mystery by E. Charles Vivian.

Fatal Accident — Murder by automobile, a 1936 mystery by Cecil M. Wills.

Fighting Mad — Todd Robbins' 1922 novel about boxing and life

Finger-prints Never Lie — A 1939 classic detective novel by John G. Brandon.

Freaks and Fantasies — Eerie tales by Tod Robbins, collaborator of Tod Browning on the film FREAKS.

Gadsby — A lipogram (a novel without the letter E). Ernest Vincent Wright's last work, published in 1939 right before his death.

Gelett Burgess Novels — *The Master of Mysteries, The White Cat, Two O'Clock Courage, Ladies in Boxes, Find the Woman, The Heart Line, The Picaroons* and *Lady Mechante*. Recently added is A Gelett Burgess Sampler, edited by Alfred Jan. All are introduced by Richard A. Lupoff.

Geronimo — S. M. Barrett's 1905 autobiography of a noble American.

Hake Talbot Novels — *Rim of the Pit, The Hangman's Handyman*. Classic locked room mysteries, with mapback covers by Gavin O'Keefe.

Hands Out of Hell and Other Stories — John H. Knox's eerie hallucinations

Hell is a City — William Ard's masterpiece.

Hollywood Dreams — A novel of Tinsel Town and the Depression by Richard O'Brien.

Hostesses in Hell and Other Stories — Russell Gray's most graphic stories

House of the Restless Dead — Strange and ominous tales by Hugh B. Cave

I Stole $16,000,000 — A true story by cracksman Herbert E. Wilson.

Inclination to Murder — 1966 thriller by New Zealand's Harriet Hunter.

Invaders from the Dark — Classic werewolf tale from Greye La Spina.

J. Poindexter, Colored — Classic satirical black novel by Irvin S. Cobb.

Jack Mann Novels — Strange murder in the English countryside. *Gees' First Case, Nightmare Farm, Grey Shapes, The Ninth Life, The Glass Too Many, Her Ways Are Death, The Kleinert Case* and *Maker of Shadows*.

Jake Hardy — A lusty western tale from Wesley Tallant.

Jim Harmon Double Novels — *Vixen Hollow/Celluloid Scandal, The Man Who Made Maniacs/Silent Siren, Ape Rape/Wanton Witch, Sex Burns Like Fire/Twist Session, Sudden Lust/Passion Strip, Sin Unlimited/Harlot Master, Twilight Girls/Sex Institution*. Written in the early 60s and never reprinted until now.

Joel Townsley Rogers Novels and Short Stories — By the author of *The Red Right Hand: Once In a Red Moon, Lady With the Dice, The Stopped Clock, Never Leave My Bed*. Also two short story collections: *Night of Horror* and *Killing Time*.

John Carstairs, Space Detective — Arboreal Sci-fi by Frank Belknap Long

Joseph Shallit Novels — *The Case of the Billion Dollar Body, Lady Don't Die on My Doorstep, Kiss the Killer, Yell Bloody Murder, Take Your Last Look*. One of America's best 50's authors and a favorite of author Bill Pronzini.

Keller Memento — 45 short stories of the amazing and weird by Dr. David Keller.

Killer's Caress — Cary Moran's 1936 hardboiled thriller.

Lady of the Yellow Death and Other Stories — More stories by Wyatt Blassingame.

League of the Grateful Dead and Other Stories — Volume One In the Day Keene in the Detective Pulps series.

Library of Death — Ghastly tale by Ronald S. L. Harding, introduced by John Pelan

Malcolm Jameson Novels and Short Stories — *Astonishing! Astounding!, Tarnished Bomb, The Alien Envoy and Other Stories* and *The Chariots of San Fernando and Other Stories*. All introduced and edited by John Pelan or Richard A. Lupoff.

Man Out of Hell and Other Stories — Volume II of the John H. Knox weird pulps collection.

Marblehead: A Novel of H.P. Lovecraft — A long-lost masterpiece from Richard A. Lupoff. This is the "director's cut", the long version that has never been published before.

Master of Souls — Mark Hansom's 1937 shocker is introduced by weirdologist John Pelan.

Max Afford Novels — *Owl of Darkness, Death's Mannikins, Blood on His Hands, The Dead Are Blind, The Sheep and the Wolves, Sinners in Paradise* and *Two Locked Room Mysteries and a Ripping Yarn* by one of Australia's finest mystery novelists.

Money Brawl — Two books about the writing business by Jack Woodford and H. Bedford-Jones. Introduced by Richard A. Lupoff.

More Secret Adventures of Sherlock Holmes — Gary Lovisi's second collection of tales about the unknown sides of the great detective.

Muddled Mind: Complete Works of Ed Wood, Jr. — David Hayes and Hayden Davis deconstruct the life and works of the mad, but canny, genius.

Murder among the Nudists — A mystery from 1934 by Peter Hunt, featuring a naked Detective-Inspector going undercover in a nudist colony.

Murder in Black and White — 1931 classic tennis whodunit by Evelyn Elder.

Murder in Shawnee — Two novels of the Alleghenies by John Douglas: *Shawnee Alley Fire* and *Haunts*.

Murder in Silk — A 1937 Yellow Peril novel of the silk trade by Ralph Trevor.

My Deadly Angel — 1955 Cold War drama by John Chelton.

My First Time: The One Experience You Never Forget — Michael Birchwood — 64 true first-person narratives of how they lost it.

Mysterious Martin, the Master of Murder — Two versions of a strange 1912 novel by Tod Robbins about a man who writes books that can kill.

Norman Berrow Novels — *The Bishop's Sword, Ghost House, Don't Go Out After Dark, Claws of the Cougar, The Smokers of Hashish, The Secret Dancer, Don't Jump Mr. Boland!, The Footprints of Satan, Fingers for Ransom, The Three Tiers of Fantasy, The Spaniard's Thumb, The Eleventh Plague, Words Have Wings, One Thrilling Night, The Lady's in Danger, It Howls at Night, The Terror in the Fog, Oil Under the Window, Murder in the Melody, The Singing Room.* This is the complete Norman Berrow library of locked-room mysteries, several of which are masterpieces.

Old Faithful and Other Stories — SF classic tales by Raymond Z. Gallun

Old Times' Sake — Short stories by James Reasoner from Mike Shayne Magazine.

One Dreadful Night — A classic mystery by Ronald S. L. Harding

Pair O' Jacks — A mystery novel and a diatribe about publishing by Jack Woodford

Perfect .38 — Two early Timothy Dane novels by William Ard. More to come.

Prince Pax — Devilish intrigue by George Sylvester Viereck and Philip Eldridge

Prose Bowl — Futuristic satire of a world where hack writing has replaced football as our national obsession, by Bill Pronzini and Barry N. Malzberg.

Red Light — The history of legal prostitution in Shreveport Louisiana by Eric Brock. Includes wonderful photos of the houses and the ladies.

Researching American-Made Toy Soldiers — A 276-page collection of a lifetime of articles by toy soldier expert Richard O'Brien.

Reunion in Hell — Volume One of the John H. Knox series of weird stories from the pulps. Introduced by horror expert John Pelan.

Ripped from the Headlines! — The Jack the Ripper story as told in the newspaper articles in the *New York* and *London Times*.

Robert Randisi Novels — *No Exit to Brooklyn* and *The Dead of Brooklyn*. The first two Nick Delvecchio novels.

Rough Cut & New, Improved Murder — Ed Gorman's first two novels.

R.R. Ryan Novels — Freak Museum and The Subjugated Beast, two horror classics.

Ruled By Radio — 1925 futuristic novel by Robert L. Hadfield & Frank E. Farncombe.

Rupert Penny Novels — *Policeman's Holiday, Policeman's Evidence, Lucky Policeman, Policeman in Armour, Sealed Room Murder, Sweet Poison, The Talkative Policeman, She had to Have Gas* and *Cut and Run* (by Martin Tanner.) Rupert Penny is the pseudonym of Australian Charles Thornett, a master of the locked room, impossible crime plot.

Sacred Locomotive Flies — Richard A. Lupoff's psychedelic SF story.

Sam — Early gay novel by Lonnie Coleman.

Sand's Game — Spectacular hard-boiled noir from Ennis Willie, edited by Lynn Myers and Stephen Mertz, with contributions from Max Allan Collins, Bill Crider, Wayne Dundee, Bill Pronzini, Gary Lovisi and James Reasoner.

Sand's War — More violent fiction from the typewriter of Ennis Willie

Satan's Den Exposed — True crime in Truth or Consequences New Mexico — Award-winning journalism by the *Desert Journal*.

Satans of Saturn — Novellas from the pulps by Otis Adelbert Kline and E. H. Price

Satan's Sin House and Other Stories — Horrific gore by Wayne Rogers

Secrets of a Teenage Superhero — Graphic lit by Jonathan Sweet

Sex Slave — Potboiler of lust in the days of Cleopatra by Dion Leclerq, 1966.

Shadows' Edge — Two early novels by Wade Wright: *Shadows Don't Bleed* and *The Sharp Edge.*

Sideslip — 1968 SF masterpiece by Ted White and Dave Van Arnam.

Slammer Days — Two full-length prison memoirs: *Men into Beasts* (1952) by George Sylvester Viereck and *Home Away From Home* (1962) by Jack Woodford.

Slippery Staircase — 1930s whodunit from E.C.R. Lorac

Sorcerer's Chessmen — John Pelan introduces this 1939 classic by Mark Hansom.

Star Griffin — Michael Kurland's 1987 masterpiece of SF drollery is back.

Stakeout on Millennium Drive — Award-winning Indianapolis Noir by Ian Woollen.

Strands of the Web: Short Stories of Harry Stephen Keeler — Edited and Introduced by Fred Cleaver.

Summer Camp for Corpses and Other Stories — Weird Menace tales from Arthur Leo Zagat; introduced by John Pelan.

Suzy — A collection of comic strips by Richard O'Brien and Bob Vojtko from 1970.

Tales of the Macabre and Ordinary — Modern twisted horror by Chris Mikul, author of the *Bizarrism* series.

Tenebrae — Ernest G. Henham's 1898 horror tale brought back.

The Amorous Intrigues & Adventures of Aaron Burr — by Anonymous. Hot historical action about the man who almost became Emperor of Mexico.

The Anthony Boucher Chronicles — edited by Francis M. Nevins. Book reviews by Anthony Boucher written for the *San Francisco Chronicle, 1942 – 1947*. Essential and fascinating reading by the best book reviewer there ever was.

The Barclay Catalogs — Two essential books about toy soldier collecting by Richard O'Brien

The Basil Wells Omnibus — A collection of Wells' stories by Richard A. Lupoff.

The Beautiful Dead and Other Stories — Dreadful tales from Donald Dale

The Best of 10-Story Book — edited by Chris Mikul, over 35 stories from the literary magazine Harry Stephen Keeler edited.

The Black Dark Murders — Vintage 50s college murder yarn by Milt Ozaki, writing as Robert O. Saber.

The Book of Time — The classic novel by H.G. Wells is joined by sequels by Wells himself and three stories by Richard A. Lupoff. Illustrated by Gavin L. O'Keefe.

The Case in the Clinic — One of E.C.R. Lorac's finest.

The Case of the Bearded Bride — #4 in the Day Keene in the Detective Pulps series

The Case of the Little Green Men — Mack Reynolds wrote this love song to sci-fi fans back in 1951 and it's now back in print.

The Case of the Withered Hand — 1936 potboiler by John G. Brandon.

The Charlie Chaplin Murder Mystery — A 2004 tribute by noted film scholar, Wes D. Gehring.

The Chinese Jar Mystery — Murder in the manor by John Stephen Strange, 1934.

The Compleat Calhoon — All of Fender Tucker's works: Includes *Totah Six-Pack, Weed, Women and Song* and *Tales from the Tower*, plus a CD of all of his songs.

The Compleat Ova Hamlet — Parodies of SF authors by Richard A. Lupoff. This is a brand new edition with more stories and more illustrations by Trina Robbins.

The Contested Earth and Other SF Stories — A never-before published space opera and seven short stories by Jim Harmon.

The Crimson Query — A 1929 thriller from Arlton Eadie. A perfect way to get introduced.

The Curse of Cantire — Classic 1939 novel of a family curse by Walter S. Masterman.

The Devil and the C.I.D. — Odd diabolic mystery by E.C.R. Lorac

The Devil Drives — An odd prison and lost treasure novel from 1932 by Virgil Markham.

The Devil's Mistress — A 1915 Scottish gothic tale by J. W. Brodie-Innes, a member of Aleister Crowley's Golden Dawn.

The Devil's Nightclub and Other Stories — John Pelan introduces some gruesome tales by Nat Schachner.

The Disentanglers — Episodic intrigue at the turn of last century by Andrew Lang

The Dumpling — Political murder from 1907 by Coulson Kernahan.

The End of It All and Other Stories — Ed Gorman selected his favorite short stories for this huge collection.

The Fangs of Suet Pudding — A 1944 novel of the German invasion by Adams Farr

The Ghost of Gaston Revere — From 1935, a novel of life and beyond by Mark Hansom, introduced by John Pelan.

The Girl in the Dark — A thriller from Roland Daniel

The Gold Star Line — Seaboard adventure from L.T. Reade and Robert Eustace.

The Golden Dagger — 1951 Scotland Yard yarn by E. R. Punshon.

The Great Orme Terror — Horror stories by Garnett Radcliffe from the pulps

The Hairbreadth Escapes of Major Mendax — Francis Blake Crofton's 1889 boys' book.

The House That Time Forgot and Other Stories — Insane pulpitude by Robert F. Young

The House of the Vampire — 1907 poetic thriller by George S. Viereck.

The Illustrous Corpse — Murder hijinx from Tiffany Thayer

The Incredible Adventures of Rowland Hern — Intriguing 1928 impossible crimes by Nicholas Olde.

The Julius Caesar Murder Case — A classic 1935 re-telling of the assassination by Wallace Irwin that's much more fun than the Shakespeare version.

The Koky Comics — A collection of all of the 1978-1981 Sunday and daily comic strips by Richard O'Brien and Mort Gerberg, in two volumes.

The Lady of the Terraces — 1925 missing race adventure by E. Charles Vivian.

The Lord of Terror — 1925 mystery with master-criminal, Fantômas.

The Melamare Mystery — A classic 1929 Arsene Lupin mystery by Maurice Leblanc

The Man Who Was Secrett — Epic SF stories from John Brunner

The Man Without a Planet — Science fiction tales by Richard Wilson

The N. R. De Mexico Novels — Robert Bragg, the real N.R. de Mexico, presents *Marijuana Girl, Madman on a Drum, Private Chauffeur* in one volume.

The Night Remembers — A 1991 Jack Walsh mystery from Ed Gorman.

The One After Snelling — Kickass modern noir from Richard O'Brien.

The Organ Reader — A huge compilation of just about everything published in the 1971-1972 radical bay-area newspaper, *THE ORGAN.* A coffee table book that points out the shallowness of the coffee table mindset.

The Poker Club — Three in one! Ed Gorman's ground-breaking novel, the short story it was based upon, and the screenplay of the film made from it.

The Private Journal & Diary of John H. Surratt — The memoirs of the man who conspired to assassinate President Lincoln.

The Secret Adventures of Sherlock Holmes — Three Sherlockian pastiches by the Brooklyn author/publisher, Gary Lovisi.

The Shadow on the House — Mark Hansom's 1934 masterpiece of horror is introduced by John Pelan.

The Sign of the Scorpion — A 1935 Edmund Snell tale of oriental evil.

The Singular Problem of the Stygian House-Boat — Two classic tales by John Kendrick Bangs about the denizens of Hades.

The Smiling Corpse — Philip Wylie and Bernard Bergman's odd 1935 novel.

The Spider: Satan's Murder Machines — A thesis about Iron Man

The Stench of Death: An Odoriferous Omnibus by Jack Moskovitz — Two complete novels and two novellas from 60's sleaze author, Jack Moskovitz.

The Story Writer and Other Stories — Classic SF from Richard Wilson

The Strange Case of the Antlered Man — 1935 dementia from Edwy Searles Brooks

The Strange Thirteen — Richard B. Gamon's odd stories about Raj India.

The Technique of the Mystery Story — Carolyn Wells' tips about writing.

The Threat of Nostalgia — A collection of his most obscure stories by Jon Breen

The Time Armada — Fox B. Holden's 1953 SF gem.

The Tongueless Horror and Other Stories — Volume One of the series of short stories from the weird pulps by Wyatt Blassingame.

The Tracer of Lost Persons — From 1906, an episodic novel that became a hit radio series in the 30s. Introduced by Richard A. Lupoff.

The Trail of the Cloven Hoof — Diabolical horror from 1935 by Arlton Eadie. Introduced by John Pelan.

The Triune Man — Mindscrambling science fiction from Richard A. Lupoff**.**

The Unholy Goddess and Other Stories — Wyatt Blassingame's first DTP compilation

The Universal Holmes — Richard A. Lupoff's 2007 collection of five Holmesian pastiches and a recipe for giant rat stew.

The Werewolf vs the Vampire Woman — Hard to believe ultraviolence by either Arthur M. Scarm or Arthur M. Scram.

The Whistling Ancestors — A 1936 classic of weirdness by Richard E. Goddard and introduced by John Pelan.

The White Owl — A vintage thriller from Edmund Snell

The White Peril in the Far East — Sidney Lewis Gulick's 1905 indictment of the West and assurance that Japan would never attack the U.S.

The Wizard of Berner's Abbey — A 1935 horror gem written by Mark Hansom and introduced by John Pelan.

The Wonderful Wizard of Oz — by L. Frank Baum and illustrated by Gavin L. O'Keefe

Through the Looking Glass — Lewis Carroll wrote it; Gavin L. O'Keefe illustrated it.

Time Line — Ramble House artist Gavin O'Keefe selects his most evocative art inspired by the twisted literature he reads and designs.

Tiresias — Psychotic modern horror novel by Jonathan M. Sweet.

Totah Six-Pack — Fender Tucker's six tales about Farmington in one sleek volume.

Trail of the Spirit Warrior — Roger Haley's historical saga of life in the Indian Territories.

Two Kinds of Bad — Two 50s novels by William Ard about Danny Fontaine

Two Suns of Morcali and Other Stories — Evelyn E. Smith's SF tour-de-force

Ultra-Boiled — 23 gut-wrenching tales by our Man in Brooklyn, Gary Lovisi.

Up Front From Behind — A 2011 satire of Wall Street by James B. Kobak.

Victims & Villains — Intriguing Sherlockiana from Derham Groves.

Wade Wright Novels — *Echo of Fear, Death At Nostalgia Street, It Leads to Murder* and *Shadows' Edge*, a double book featuring *Shadows Don't Bleed* and *The Sharp Edge.*

Walter S. Masterman Novels — *The Green Toad, The Flying Beast, The Yellow Mistletoe, The Wrong Verdict, The Perjured Alibi, The Border Line, The Bloodhounds Bay* and *The Curse of Cantire.* Masterman wrote horror and mystery, some introduced by John Pelan.

We Are the Dead and Other Stories — Volume Two in the Day Keene in the Detective Pulps series, introduced by Ed Gorman. When done, there may be as many as 11 in the series.

Welsh Rarebit Tales — Charming stories from 1902 by Harle Oren Cummins

West Texas War and Other Western Stories — by Gary Lovisi.

Whip Dodge: Man Hunter — Wesley Tallant's saga of a bounty hunter of the old West.

Win, Place and Die! — The first new mystery by Milt Ozaki in decades. The ultimate novel of 70s Reno.

You'll Die Laughing — Bruce Elliott's 1945 novel of murder at a practical joker's English countryside manor.

RAMBLE HOUSE

Fender Tucker, Prop.   Gavin L. O'Keefe, Graphics
www.ramblehouse.com   tender@ramblehouse.com
228-826-1783   10329 Sheephead Drive, Vancleave MS 39565

CPSIA information can be obtained
at www.ICGtesting.com
Printed in the USA
LVOW12s0252210716

497109LV00001B/84/P